An UNFINISHED STORM

San Juan Islands Murder Mystery #4

by

BETHANY MAINES

 Blue Zephyr Press
2661 N. Pearl, #360
Tacoma WA 98407

Cover art by **LILT**.

ISBN-13: 979-8-9867745-2-7

DEDICATION

To my readers who have been so, so, so patient.

TABLE OF CONTENTS

PROLOGUE

TISH YEARLY

I'm dead. I'm dead. I am so, so, so dead.

Tish Yearly had her head between her knees and was trying to figure out if she should kiss her ass goodbye. The front door slammed, and she heard her grandfather, Tobias Yearly, meander through the kitchen and into the dining room, his cane making a little squeak on the freshly mopped kitchen floor. She knew she ought to move but could only concentrate on breathing. She heard his footsteps stop as they arrived on the plush carpet of the living room.

"Tish?"

Tish willed herself upright and flipped her hair out of her face.

"Well, don't you look pretty," said her grandfather, gesturing to her Hollywood-level makeup and flirty fun blouse. "I mean, except for the part where you look like you're going to puke. Did you eat some bad tuna?"

Tish shook her head.

"Took too many trips around in the spin-y recliner?"

Tish glared at him.

"Well, I don't know. You did that once when you were five. What's got you looking so peaked?"

Tish opened her mouth to confess, but all that came out was a squeak.

"You're speechless?" Tobias rocked back, his eyebrows going up in shock. "Well, damn. I'll call the lawyers. How long do you think we got until the cops get here?"

"The cops?" Tish was outraged. "What exactly do you think I did?"

"Well, Tishkins, I've watched you face down murderers, lawyers, and that one very intimidating lady at the DMV and still have something to say. I figured you must have decided to go on a feminist rampage in one of those pink kitty hats and started mowing down skinheads with your Toyota or something."

"That is…"

Kind of flattering, actually.

"Not what I did."

"Well, what did you do?"

A very, very stupid thing.

When Tish had been fired, robbed, and evicted all in the same day, she'd landed on her grandfather's doorstep on Orcas Island in the San Juan Islands of Washington State, intending to only stay long enough to get a new job. But instead, she'd found a dead body and a new career. Or rather, two new careers. The first was running a brand new, premier event and wedding venue, and the second was solving mysteries with her grandfather, Tobias Yearly. Tobias was a former test pilot and CIA agent, current troublemaker, and now a licensed private investigator. The oldest in the state, as he would proudly tell anyone who cared to listen.

"I," began Tish, and swallowed hard, "lied to Nash." Her voice dropped to a whisper.

Tobias frowned.

"About what?" he asked, looking severe.

"I told him that I was spending the afternoon with you, but instead, I took a Zoom meeting with my old agent, a director, a studio rep, and a casting director about taking the lead actress role in a studio movie."

Tobias ran his tongue around his gums and sucked at his teeth.

"Soooo… What you're saying is that you failed to tell Sheriff's Deputy Emmett Nash, the fella you've been making googly eyes at for over a year, the man whose daughter worships the ground you walk on, the man that took a hell of a lot convincing to believe that you weren't going to run off to Hollywood to be an actress again—that guy—you didn't tell him about a meeting that could make you a big time actress again?"

"Yes," said Tish. "That's what I did. I love Nash, but being an A-list actress was my first dream. It was the only fairy tale I ever really believed in."

Once Upon a Time in Hollywood, 2019, Quentin Tarantino directing and trying to prove he's cool by shitting on Bruce Lee.

"It was what I trained for from the time I was twelve. Someone showed up and offered it to me on a silver platter. So yeah, I took the damn meeting."

"You didn't have to lie about it," said Tobias, in the perfectly calm tone that said she'd screwed up more than any amount of yelling.

"You don't understand Hollywood," said Tish. "Everyone talks like everything is so awesome. But honestly, half the time nothing ever comes from these meetings. I didn't want to upset Nash over nothing."

"Uh-huh. So, the meeting must have gone well because otherwise, you wouldn't be having a moment over there about lying to Nash. I take it the movie is a real thing?"

Tish nodded.

"They offered you the part?"

Tish nodded again.

"And you said yes?" Tobias looked as sour as his tone.

"I said no," gasped Tish and clapped her hands over her mouth. "Uh..."

She peeled her hands away and swallowed hard.

"They just kept talking about shoot schedules and promotion, and all I could think was how inconvenient that was going to be for the business. And then they started talking about what festivals they could submit to. And then I realized how much Nash would hate all the red carpet stuff. And then I realized that he would never do the red carpet stuff—he would probably just break up with me. And I can't have that. And then..." Tish paused to take in air. "They started talking about sending contracts to my agent, and I opened my mouth and..."

"And what?" demanded Tobias.

"You know how sometimes when you're questioning a suspect, you realize exactly what you need to say to make them say or do something?"

Tobias scratched his eyebrow. "Yes. But people don't like it when you say stuff like that out loud. It makes people uncomfortable."

"No one is as unpredictable as they like to think they are. Part of acting is making a character seem as natural as possible. I can only do that if I can work out what a person should *naturally* do in a given situation. It's just a skip from that to figuring out what someone else will do if I supply the right situation."

"Uh-huh. Again, that makes people uncomfortable when you say it for everyone to hear. We keep that on the inside so we don't scare our friends."

"You're not my friend. You're Granddad."

"Fair enough. So what did you predict your Hollywood people would do?"

"Granddad, it was like the words just fell out of my mouth. I couldn't stop them!"

"Well, what did you say?"

"I just kept talking until I had them convinced that Orcas was the place to shoot the movie. And then, I sent them pictures from my phone to pitch them locations. And I told them I could smooth the way with permitting and I could help secure funding. Granddad, I just kept going, and now..."

"Now what?" he asked with an expression that looked torn between horror and fascination.

"Now... I'm a *producer.*"

"Huh," said Tobias. "I was going to go with now you have to tell

Nash the truth. But I guess producer is a thing, too."

"Why do you think I was thinking about puking? What am I going to do?" moaned Tish.

"Just tell him the truth," said Tobias with a shrug. "It's not like anyone is going to die."

"Don't jinx us," said Tish.

With my luck, someone is definitely going to die.

CHAPTER 1

HOW TO RUIN EVERYTHING

Tish looked at the Key Grip and thought about throat-punching him as he stepped on a patch of snapdragons. She walked over, grabbed him by the shoulders, and physically moved him out of the flower bed. He looked down in surprise.

If I kill him, I won't make it over to Nash's for dinner. And I want my damn date night.

"I have a wedding here on Sunday," said Tish. "Unless you want to pay for flower replacements, stay out of the flower beds."

"Right," he said. "Sorry!"

He genuinely meant it. Everyone was genuinely *attempting* to not treat Tish's property as a Hollywood backlot. It was just that they weren't trying that hard. She had agreed to almost entirely close her property, a risk for her second year in business as a wedding venue, in return for a flat fee up front and a percentage on the backend. Theoretically, if the movie did well, everything would pan out. Right now, that was feeling very theoretical. There were at least six other producers on this film, but since this was her property, they were all literally phoning it in. They said there were scheduling conflicts and other films, but it felt like they had collectively decided that Tish could babysit everyone for the first two weeks of shooting.

And I'm not sure I can. It was months of prep work, and I can already feel this thing slipping out of control.

"All right, people!" yelled the director, coming out onto the porch of the bungalow, his head buried in script pages. "We're burning daylight here!"

And it's his fault.

Tish glared at the director. Skip Renfeld was a douchebag. Tish was trying to put a positive spin on it, but after several weeks of working with the director, she was having difficulty coming up with anything kinder to say. He was consistently late and dismissive of anyone else's schedule, and he had caused her to be late for every single one of her dates with Nash during the last two weeks. Nash had taken the movie planning process in stride. He'd been interested in the logistics of organizing a group, but she sensed that his interest in movies was quickly waning the longer that Hollywood was in his backyard.

Skip looked up from the pages and around at the waiting crew.

"Where's Taylor? I've got the rewrites!" He waved a manila folder with Taylor's name on it.

Skip had blazingly white veneers, dead blue eyes, and a carefully crafted aura of whimsical fun. He was the male equivalent of a manic pixie dream girl – someone who brought an element of instability to every enterprise and whose entertainment value had definitely worn off after extended exposure.

Skip looked around and realized that Taylor wasn't present, and his face immediately tightened into an expression of anger.

"What rewrites?" demanded Luke, looking up from where he was working on a laptop. Since Luke Green was the movie's scriptwriter, that was not a question that promised good things.

The script had been approved by the studio, and her primary studio contact had stressed that she should try to get Skip to stick to it while at the same time underlining the fact that she didn't have the authority to make him do it.

"Nothing major," said Skip. "I did them myself. Don't worry, I'm not going to ask for credit." Skip pantomimed the broadest wink possible. Skip winked a lot. It was as if he'd decided that winking was his thing. Tish didn't like it. She didn't think it went with his cargo shorts. He wore cargo shorts like he thought they were still in style. But she supposed if he wore pants, no one would see the tacky yin-yang tattoo on the back of his calf.

Luke was about Tish's age—late twenties—and looked like he was auditioning for the role of writer dressed in outfits cribbed out of GQ's style section mashed up with old Hemingway photos. He also had no power to keep Skip from changing the script. The other producers were supposed to be on hand to keep things in hand, but Tish got the feeling that none of them wanted to spend that much time with Skip.

And now I know why. He's a douchebag.

"Hey, Skip," said Frank Brooking. The fifty-something Director of Photography had long, gray hair and an unflappable demeanor. "We're set up at the gazebo."

That is code for we're burning daylight and waiting on you.

"Emma's been nice enough to do some run-throughs with one of the grips, so we're blocked and ready to roll."

That is code for we've been waiting on you for a while now, and the leading lady is tired of standing around.

"Yeah, yeah, yeah, gazebo, great," said Skip, clearly not listening and reading over his new pages again.

"All right, everyone," said Tish, raising her voice. "We're moving to the gazebo. Shooting starts in five."

The crew—including Skip—through the magic of a firm voice, began to drift toward the gazebo.

Frank smiled and gave her a wink. The other item that she'd slipped into the contract was the right to use any footage of her property produced in the course of making the film. Frank had already done some gratuitous background footage and a long drone shot that was going to look dreamy on her website. Frank was fully aware that she was using him to film a Hollywood-level commercial of her venue, and he had zero qualms about it. Not that she expected him to speak up if he did. Frank didn't seem to take a stand on much, but on the other hand, his go-with-the-flow attitude meant he didn't throw any tantrums either.

"Skip," said Luke, snatching at the pages that Skip was holding out as he walked, "we didn't talk about new pages."

"Yeah, but we're a little flat in the second act," said Skip.

"Because you killed the scene with the talking rabbit."

"No one likes rabbits," said Skip. "They poop."

"Everything poops!" yelled Luke, flapping his arms. Everyone turned to look at him. Yelling about poop was an excellent way to look insane. It was part of Skip's magic that he made everyone else look like the crazy ones.

The gazebo on the far side of the lawn had seen an entire summer of weddings, and Tish was proud of her refurbishments. She'd added new cedar shingles to the pointed roof and extra-fancy wood bits to the eaves. It looked one dandelion wish away from having sprites whisk out of it.

"Oh, are we actually shooting?" asked Emma Olivier as the crowd approached. "That will be nice for a change."

Emma was a blonde model-slash-actress who was inhabiting the role that Tish had been offered. Tish had felt insulted that they'd hired a model to replace her and had to admit to more than a bit of jealousy for the first week of shooting.

"Don't tell me how to run my set, baby," said Skip. "Let the professionals do their jobs."

Considering that Emma was the only one who showed up on time and knew her lines back to front, Tish felt her teeth grit at the insult.

Skip finally lifted his head out of the script and looked around. "Where's Taylor?"

Tish checked her phone.

Come on, Kyle, don't let me down.

She let out a sigh of relief as a text popped through. Kyle Heron was a drug dealer. Well, mostly a drug dealer. The legalization of weed was forcing the entrepreneurial, if philosophically lost, twenty-one-year-old to explore new dimensions. Something his girlfriend

Amber, a waitress at a local restaurant, was ecstatic about. Tish was ambivalent about the drug dealing. She appreciated Kyle's connections, ability to drive fast, and willingness to try new things. She knew Tobias disapproved of him, but Tish found him useful. And besides, how was he supposed to get out of the drug business without non-druggy friends? Today, he was driving Taylor Blake from the ferry dock.

ETA: Two minutes.

"He'll be here in two minutes," said Tish. "We should get set up."

"These pages don't make any sense," said Luke. "Like literally none."

"We might need to do some rearranging in post," said Skip. "But I mean, the point of this thing is surrealism. It'll be fine. People love the David Lynch schtick."

"No, people like things to make sense," said Luke.

"Then you shouldn't have written in talking bunnies or whatever," said Skip.

"They're symbolic and give voice to characters' inner thoughts. This is just Emma and a bunch of half-naked women running around!"

"Yeah, people love that," said Skip.

"Nudity is not in my contract," said Emma with a frosty tone.

"It's not nudity," said Skip. "It's topless. Besides, I saw most of your tits in that Versace print spread. You can't exactly complain now."

"That is an inappropriate comment," said Tish, surprising even herself. "You're out of line."

And this is how I end up getting fired from things. I can't keep my mouth shut, can I?

Skip blinked at her in shock. "I'm just saying—"

"No," said Tish. "You were commenting about her body and her choices. That's unacceptable. Nudity is not in her contract, and you will not push her or anyone into something she does not want to do."

I will tank this movie before I let another actress feel bullied into nudity.

The crew had fallen silent. Skip was staring at her as if he'd never had anyone call him on his bullshit before.

"This is my set," he began, taking an angry step forward. He had turned to fully face her, squaring his shoulders to take the maximum amount of space.

You are trying to intimidate me, and I will not take that.

"No, it is my set," said Tish, putting her hands on her hips in her best Wonder Woman pose and projecting her voice so that as many people as possible could hear. "It is quite literally my property, and I am the producer. If you cannot play by the rules, then you can go play in someone else's sandbox."

She watched him try to decide what to do next. She wasn't backing down, and she suspected that Skip didn't know what to do. He didn't have any other moves up his sleeve. His face wrinkled up and went red like a giant baby.

"Fine!" he yelled, throwing down the pages.

He stormed off toward the house. On the porch, Tish could see Brianna Meadows watching the temper tantrum. Kyle pulled up in his green Jeep Wrangler and Taylor Blake, AKA the star of the movie, jumped out of the passenger side of the Jeep.

"Hey, Skip," he said cheerfully. "We ready to shoot?"

"Stupid bitches ruin everything!" yelled Skip, storming past him. They all watched as Skip jumped into his car and peeled off down the driveway.

"What just happened?" asked Taylor as he approached the gazebo. He took in Emma's white face and the wide-eyed crew. Taylor had been playing peacekeeper since the shoot started. She got the feeling he was already tired of the role. Skip kept calling Taylor *my best bro* and talking about the three previous movies they had worked on together. It had made Tish wary of Taylor, but so far, Taylor hadn't done anything more than show up late to everything, which was annoying, but she had just started adjusting his call time up by a half-hour.

"Did Skip lose his shit again?" Taylor added a light half-laugh and swept sun-kissed brown bangs out of his eyes with a casual flick of his hair. No one else laughed.

"Well, boss," said Frank, coming over to her, "what do you want to do?"

Tish looked at the script pages on the ground.

"You're blocked and set?" she asked, looking up at Frank.

"Yeah," he said, nodding.

"Then we shoot," said Tish.

CHAPTER 2

WHAT WE ALL THINK

Tish rolled her head around her neck and watched as the cast and crew headed for the various vehicles down in the lower lot, AKA the field she used for wedding parking.

Frank was locking up the camera in the equipment van that was parked by the house. Kyle was on the porch waiting for her.

Shooting the scene had been a collaborative effort. She had never had ambitions for being a director, so soliciting advice had seemed like her best bet. Despite his grown-up Disney star looks, Taylor Blake had come through with practical and artistic thoughts. Tish thought he'd probably been considering directing already. Emma had been surprisingly thoughtful about her character and willing to try the scene multiple times. And Frank and the crew had been kindly helpful.

"Frank," she said, approaching the cameraman, "tell me that we got something worth our time."

"Yeah, boss," he said, flashing a grin. "It looked good. I'll shoot you a link to the dailies when I have them."

Tish nodded. "Thanks. Then we can move on to the tower tomorrow? Our closure permit is only good for three days. It will be a thing if we don't get out there tomorrow."

"Yeah, I've got the second crew up there today getting background and B-roll. I'll check in with them tonight, but they said their stuff went fine. They're set up and ready for the morning."

Tish breathed out a sigh of relief. An amateur video from Quincy, the college-student-slash-mystery-blogger featuring Tish, Nash, and the medieval-style tower with the magnificent view of the sound had been responsible for convincing the studio to bring the movie to Orcas. It was the must-have scene of the entire damn film, and Tish wasn't about to blow it.

Frank paused and then looked around. He tugged on his long ponytail and eyed Kyle but apparently decided Kyle was too far away. "When I send the link to the studio, I'll have to send the dailies to Skip, too." Tish tried not to wrinkle her nose. "This isn't any of my business," he added, "but someone should have told you that Skip is notoriously hard to work for."

"I'm trying to figure out why he even got hired," said Tish bitterly.

"He's got a lot of juice around town," said Frank. "I heard one exec say Skip has been around long enough to know where all the bodies are buried. I don't know what his deal is—I just show up and shoot movies. I get paid one way or another, but I know you've got a lot riding on this film. If you're squaring up to go against Skip, I think someone should warn you that he plays dirty."

Tish appreciated the warning, but what Frank was really saying was that he was not about to put himself in the middle of her fight with the director. Which was fair but also annoying. She wanted him to pick a side.

"Thanks, Frank," said Tish. "On the other hand, if nothing gets shot, then I'm definitely screwed. So…"

"Yeah, I hear you, but my advice is to call the studio and start circling the wagons. Skip is probably already trying to get you booted. Although, honestly, I do think we got good stuff today. Anyway, see you tomorrow."

Tish smiled and then headed toward the porch, where Kyle was trying to pretend he was smoking a cigarette. Kyle kept his hair clipped short to combat his unruly curls. She thought his girlfriend usually did it because getting out to a barber was a pain, but Amber's skills had improved, and Tish thought his fade was looking sharp today, and the curls had been left a little longer on top.

"Kyle, you know if Grandad comes by and sees you, I'm going to get in trouble."

"He's already inside, and I lit up after he came over, so all I have to do is put it out before he comes out, and he's never going to know."

"He's totally going to know. He's a bit deaf in one ear, not smell deficient, and blind. What's he doing over here?"

"Talking to the actress lady," he said with a shrug. "The one that played Granny Smith in that Technotronic Legend movie. How come she looked like a grandma in that movie but totally like a MILF in real life?"

Tish ran that through the matrix of Kyle-speak in her head. He was referring to Brianna Meadows, the sixty-something actress playing the heroine's grandmother and the fairy queen.

"Because makeup exists," said Tish. "Also, she was, like, forty in that movie, and she's been playing grannies ever since."

"Huh. Well, she came in to do some costume or makeup thing, and then your gramps came in. I think they're still in the kitchen drinking coffee or whatever. The makeup people left, though."

Tish sighed. Kyle wasn't the only one who thought Brianna Meadows was a MILF. Not that her grandfather would have described her that way in a million, trillion years. Tobias would, and had, described Brianna as a very attractive and talented woman. And while, in general, his respect for women was gratifying, in specific, his crush on Brianna was one more headache she didn't need.

"Hey Tish," said Luke Green, coming up from the gazebo, "thanks so much for today. It feels like you're saving my movie." His voice throbbed, and Tish saw Kyle blink at the amount of emotion on display. "I went into this with such high hopes. It's my first studio feature, you know. I poured everything I had into this script, and I couldn't believe how lucky I got with casting, but Skip is turning this into a nightmare."

"Yeah, Taylor hates his ass, too," said Kyle.

"Really?" asked Luke, looking surprised. "It was Taylor who recommended Skip. I thought they were like best pals."

"Dunno," said Kyle, taking a drag. "All I know is that Skip gives him serious anxiety."

"Is that why he keeps being late?" demanded Tish, suddenly wondering about the wisdom of pairing up a pot dealer with someone who had anxiety.

"Yeah, he's on full-on avoid, avoid, avoid maneuvers. Fortunately, I stash edibles in the glove box, and I've got the *I'm One With the Universe* audiobook on my phone. It always helps when people go on a paranoia joyride."

Or maybe it was my best decision ever.

"Edibles?" asked Luke, perking up.

"Twenty percent under retail, no tax, and made with Canadian product. Brownies, gummies, and chocolate-covered salmonberries."

"Salmonberries?" asked Luke.

"Unique to the Northwest, sustainably grown, handcrafted by a local candy maker."

"Bev's taking side orders?" guessed Tish.

"I didn't mention any names," said Kyle, looking offended.

"Her chocolate really is the best," said Tish.

"I pay her up front, and she costs a mint, but it's so worth it," said Kyle.

"And now I'm sold," said Luke. "Cash only?"

"I can do Venmo and Paypal," said Kyle, standing up. "Right this way."

"Sweet," said Luke. "I swear, if this movie doesn't fold, we're all going to be on edibles because of him."

"I'll stock up," said Kyle.

"No, no stocking up, Kyle," barked Tish, but he only grinned.

"To tell the truth," said Luke as they walked toward Kyle's car, "I wish the movie would fold rather than let Skip make it his way. That way, I could keep the option money, and I wouldn't have to bear the crushing disappointment of seeing him ruin my vision."

Kyle led the writer toward his car, and Tish shook her head. She sympathized with the writer, but his *crushing disappointment* was making a lot of money for the island.

Taylor and Emma were drifting toward her from the gazebo. They looked deep in conversation, and Tish tried to decide whether to interrupt. Tish could see why the casting director had pushed for the pairing. They looked natural together. Emma, with her willowy frame and doe-eyes, looked like a fairy book princess. She'd had Taylor pegged as boy-band level tough, but on film this afternoon, he'd managed to project an unexpected grit that Tish found appealing and surprising.

Taylor looked up and smiled at her, and it was blindingly clear why he had over a million followers on social media.

"Tish," said Taylor, "did you talk to Frank? When can we see the dailies?"

"Skip won't let me see the dailies," said Emma bitterly.

"Frank said he'd send them to me," said Tish. "We can probably look at them tomorrow morning, if nothing else. He said he felt good about what we shot, and so do I. I'm going to send them to the studio first. I want them to know that we're working, even if Skip isn't."

Taylor's smile became strained.

"Tish, I really felt good about today," said Emma earnestly. "Thanks for standing up for me. I know you kind of put yourself on the line, and I appreciate it. Although, for the future, you should know that Skip can want whatever the hell he wants, but my contract is pretty iron-clad. I don't do any nudity that I'm not one hundred percent comfortable with. My agent used to work for Disney, so you know…"

"They don't mess around," said Taylor with the knowing laugh of someone who had spent his childhood working for the mouse.

You still looked pissed and scared shitless at the time. Maybe you're not now that you've had time to think about it, but pushing buttons and demanding everything now is what Skip does.

"It's not that I think he can force you to do it," said Tish. "It's that he's harassing you repeatedly, and I won't support that."

Emma looked thoughtful. "I guess I just sort of expect that," she said, and Taylor looked at her in surprise. "It happens so much. I have to pick my battles. But Skip hates me. He thinks I slept with someone to get the job. A lot of people think that, but I auditioned like everyone else. I thought it would die down once he saw me work."

Except that your agent called directly and got you an audition instead of sending in a headshot and hoping for the best like everyone else.

"Only he's just gotten worse," said Tish. "And I'm tired of it."

Emma unexpectedly leaned in and hugged her. "Thanks! OK, Taylor, are you coming with me to get something delicious? I swear I'm going to get so fat here!"

"I should probably tell Kyle…" said Taylor, looking around.

"Don't worry about it," said Tish. "He's selling Luke some edibles. I'll tell him where you went."

"Ooh! Edibles!" chirped Emma.

"They're really good," said Taylor as he followed Emma toward her car. "The chocolate is amazing."

Tish sighed again as Taylor and Emma took off down the driveway.

At least I'm finishing in time to get dinner with Nash.

Tish wanted desperately to climb in her Toyota and head straight for Nash's house, but there was still the matter of Tobias. Reluctantly, Tish went around to the back of the house, intending to go in through the back door. Instead, she found herself stopped dead at the edge of the brickwork patio. Tobias and Brianna Meadows were sitting at the outdoor table and enjoying a glass of wine.

There was nothing scandalous about that.

Brianna laughed at something Tobias said, flipped her auburn hair over her shoulder, and made a quick flick of one hand that barely brushed Tobias's fingers.

She is flirting with Granddad! Not allowed! Not allowed!

Tish was aware that Tobias had a flirtatious situation-ship with Eleanor, the local thrift shop owner. It couldn't be called a relation-ship because nothing had ever been said. But there was a general understanding—by most of the other people on the island, if noth-ing else.

"Oh, Tobias," said Brianna, laughing. "You crack me up! And my goodness, can you pick a wine!"

"Yes, my wine," said Tish sourly.

"That I picked out for you," said Tobias, with a smile that said he had no regrets.

"Oh, Tish," said Brianna, looking up and grimacing. "Sorry about your run-in with Skip. Was it just awful?"

"Uh, it was annoying," said Tish, who wasn't prepared to have her feelings explored by a stranger.

"That's Skip all over. Too bad he's the reason this entire project got green-lit." Brianna sighed heavily.

Was he, though? I mean, Skip said that, and Taylor sort of nodded, but really?

"I mean, I'm sure we're all happy to have his expertise on board, but he can be temperamental from what I hear," continued Brianna.

"He's a sexist pig," said Tish bluntly. And Brianna made a face that said she agreed but didn't want to say it out loud. Tish remem-bered when all of her conversations had been wrapped up in pars-ing expressions like that. No one in the business had wanted to say anything about anyone—at least not anyone who could affect their career.

Brianna took a measured sip of her wine. "Do be careful," she said. "Skip can be a handful. Just ask Taylor. It's not like Taylor want-ed to make that dreadful *King of the Road* movie. But Skip is very good at getting his way."

"Did you get everything set up with the makeup crew for tomorrow?" asked Tish, changing the topic to something they wouldn't have to dance around.

"Yes. I love them, of course. They're darling."

"They were excited to meet you," said Tish. "I think one of them said she worked with your daughter."

Brianna shrugged and smiled as if to say she had no idea. "Like I said, they're darling. They've just never had a wrinkle in their life. But fortunately, I was able to point them at some products that won't make me look like a hag."

"I don't think that's possible," said Tobias.

"That is a charming thing to say," said Brianna. "But in high-definition, I assure you that it is. And not all products that work for younger skin look good on those of us who have been around the race track a few times."

For once, Brianna delivered the statement in a drily practical voice instead of her usual polished and gracious beauty queen tone. Tish liked her better for it.

"Well, as long as there is the explosion of glitter required in the script, then I think we'll be OK," said Tish.

"Oh, yes, I will have more glitter than a stripper," Brianna said with a laugh. "Even before the glitter bomb. I talked to the special effects guys, by the way, and they assured me that it's edible glitter."

"Oh good," said Tish. "I was meaning to get around to that. I was not looking forward to having to vacuum the grass."

"I'm sorry," said Tobias, trying not to choke on his wine. "You were going to do what?"

"It's bad for wildlife, Granddad, and it isn't biodegradable. It sticks around forever. I allowed one—*one*—wedding to have it last summer, and there's still traces of glitter in the azaleas."

"I…" Tobias opened his mouth a few times and then shook his head. "I never really thought about the environmental aspects of glitter."

"It's a practical consideration," said Tish with a shrug. "I don't want to rush anyone, but I'd like to get everything locked up. I promised Nash I'd try to make it over for dinner tonight."

More like he promised me that if I got there before ten, we could eat real food and make out.

"No problem," said Tobias, picking up the bottle and shaking it. "We killed this one anyway."

And Eleanor's going to kill you if she catches wind of this little business.

CHAPTER 3

NORA HARLOW AND CLAIRE NASH

Tish pulled into Nash's bungalow with a sigh of relief. As was common with many island properties, the garage was larger than the house. Orcas Island had a homestead mentality. Stuff required space. A house was for sleeping and all the irrelevant bits of life. Also, barns and garages were cheaper to build and might be able to skate by without permitting.

Nash's motorcycle was parked in front of the garage, a pail and sponge next to it. He'd clearly been catching up on his manly chore of vehicle washing. Tish had come to acknowledge that one of her turn-ons was watching someone do traditionally manly activities. She couldn't tell if it was ingrained patriarchy or if she just liked watching Nash bend over and scrub and-or chop things. Either way, she wasn't planning on mentioning it to anyone anytime soon.

Tish felt relieved that this wasn't one of Nash's parental weeks. She loved Nash's daughter Claire—the ten-year-old was smart, darling, and funny. She was also a complete nookie blocker. It was tough to get some adult alone time with a ten-year-old cheerfully popping up at the most inconvenient times.

Tish pulled in behind the bike and got out of the car. She looked around and saw Nash on the far side of the yard, splitting firewood. A very traditionally manly job that she also enjoyed watching. He saw her and waved before leaving the ax in the log he was working on and ambling back toward her. Tish stood and watched her six-foot-four hunk of Sheriff's deputy boyfriend walk toward her with a sigh of happiness.

Needs slo-mo, but the golden hour light is not hurting.

Tousled brown hair, broad shoulders, and blue eyes could make any girl sigh, but it was Nash's library sciences degree and ability to quote Shakespeare that had Tish head over heels for Emmet Charles Nash, and at this point, she didn't even pretend it was otherwise.

Nash got closer, and Tish began to get a bad feeling. Nash was not smiling, and he had the awkward set to his shoulders he got when he was telling her that she couldn't mess around in a police investigation.

But I'm not interrupting police business even a little bit today. I'm too busy.

"OK," said Nash, holding out his hands as if she was the one who owned a gun, "I don't want you to be mad."

"Then you should stop now," said Tish.

"What?"

"Literally, never in the history of humanity has anything followed that statement that didn't make the other person mad. I mean, I understand not *wanting* me to be mad, but historically speaking, the odds are not in your favor."

"Historically, like in the history of all mankind?" asked Nash, raising his eyebrows, his hands dropping to his side. "Or just the Yearly family?"

"Either," said Tish. "I don't make the odds, baby. I just report them."

"Oh, God," he said, facepalming himself. "I'm in so much trouble."

"You're just realizing this now? You're the one who started out with not wanting me to be mad."

"You just called me *baby*. Next up is some sort of film noir jargon. It's the equivalent of Tobias calling me *son*. I just took a swan dive into being in deep shit with the Yearlys."

"Once again, I do not make the rules here," said Tish. "No one made you get out on the diving board. As far as I can tell, you do this for fun."

"I am starting to wonder about that," he said thoughtfully, but sliding an arm around her waist. "You really might be right. It's like I have a death wish. It's like you're the roller coaster of my life." He pulled her close.

"And you like to throw your arms up at the top and go wheeeeeeee all the way down?" Tish asked with a giggle.

"Apparently," he said, grinning and leaning in for a kiss.

"Hey, Tish!" yelled a voice from the house. Tish looked over Nash's significant shoulders and saw Nora Harlow waving from the front door.

"No," said Tish and then flailed like she was four, letting Nash hold her up. "No, no, no, no, no! Nooooooo. I cannot!"

"She's working tomorrow!"

"I'm aware of that," hissed Tish. "I got her the job."

Because I'm an idiot.

"Yes, and I have to say that has gone a long damn way to making co-parenting easier this summer. But her babysitter got sick, and they canceled the early morning ferry run because the *Chetzmoka* had engine trouble. So it made more sense to come out tonight."

"The ferry? You're blaming ferry repairs for the fact that your ex-wife is at your house?"

"With our daughter," he protested.

Like that makes it better. Why would having Claire here make it better?

"Oh, my God, she's staying the night, isn't she?"

He grimaced. "All of her friends are off-island now."

"What you mean is nobody on the island likes her enough to let her spend the night."

"Well, Claire is staying here, so it would be kind of weird."

"No, it would not be weird," said Tish. "Claire is staying in her room because she belongs at this house. Where is Nora staying?"

"Also in Claire's room," Nash said firmly.

"Tish!" Nora yelled from the doorway. "Stop making out with my husband and come inside."

Tish felt Nash physically wince like he'd been sucker punched in the kidneys.

"She's joking. It's just a joke," he said.

"I'm laughing so hard," said Tish through gritted teeth.

"I'm making dinner!" yelled Nora. "I want to hear all about everything."

"She's not making dinner," said Nash. "Claire is making tacos. Nora's drinking wine and making sure Claire doesn't burn anything."

Drinking wine and burn patrol are my jobs. If I cry, I'm going to be that girl. I can't be that girl, but I really want to cry right now.

Tish shoved her emotions down and shook off Nash's hug.

"You are never going to believe the day I've had," she said brightly, turning to focus on Nora.

"Tish," growled Nash, but she ignored him and walked toward the house.

"I have wine!" exclaimed Nora. "Come in and tell me all about it!"

Tish went up to the porch and looked down at the red-headed Nora Harlow, who always looked like a rock-a-billy pixie.

I always forget how tiny she is.

"Well, the director re-wrote the script without asking with a scene for the leading lady that contained nudity, and when I said he couldn't do that, he threw a fit and stormed off."

"Oh, my God!" gasped Nora. "But, I mean, we're still shooting tomorrow, right?"

Nora's acting ambitions pre-dated Claire's unplanned arrival and had revived post-divorce. It had been one of the stumbling blocks between Tish and Nash. He had assumed that Tish's past acting career made her too much like Nora for her to be an actual human being with feelings.

"Of course," said Tish, with a smile. "But FYI for you, if Skip randomly starts asking if you do nudity tomorrow, that's why."

"Hm," said Nora, looking thoughtful.

"What? No," said Nash, stepping up to the porch. "No *hm*. The answer is no."

"I don't think you get an opinion," said Nora tartly.

"Tish!" he barked, looking to Tish.

"What?"

"We're not making nude-y movies on Orcas!"

"Nude-y movies? And people say I've been hanging out with Granddad too much," said Tish.

"Hey, Mom," said Claire, coming to the door, "I need you to get the cheese grater down."

"I looked, baby. I don't know where your father moved it to."

"I'll get it down, Claire," said Tish.

"No, Mom can do it."

"Maybe," said Nora. "If he moved it to one of the tall cabinets, then we'll need one of the beanpoles to get it."

"You're helping me," snapped Claire. "You have to get it."

"Claire," said Nash, sounding surprised.

Don't know why. She's been acting like that since filming started, and Nora started spending time on the island.

"Mom is helping me!" yelled Claire and went back inside.

"Apparently, I'm helping," said Nora, with a smirk, and followed Claire inside.

"Sorry," said Nash, still sounding confused. "I'm not sure what's up with her. But seriously, what's going on with this director?" he demanded, switching topics.

"He's a narcissistic, sexist jerk. Who also apparently tipped the scales for getting the movie greenlit. So I'm going to eat dinner, then head home to check the dailies and call the studio to see if I can avoid getting fired off of this movie."

"You can't get fired. Can you? You're a producer."

"And I'm providing investors and local facilitation. I can't get fired, but I can get side-lined. It depends on how much the studio thinks Skip is worth. On the other hand, if we don't start producing actual footage soon, they'll cancel the whole thing."

"That won't happen," said Nash, soothingly.

"Happens all the time," said Tish. "Loads of movies don't make it across the finish line. That's why the studios take out insurance."

"Oh," said Nash.

"This is a multi-billion-dollar business," said Tish. "The numbers have to pencil out, or they move on to the next one. They don't care who gets steamrolled in the process."

"Oh," said Nash again.

"And no offense, but I'm on the clock. So I may just eat your food and head out."

"I was making a fire pit."

"Yeah, a romantic fire pit with your ex—my favorite thing ever," said Tish, and then instantly regretted her tone. "Sorry. It's just been kind of a day."

"And it's not over," he said.

"Not really," she said, forcing a smile.

He sighed. "I'm sorry." He reached out and grabbed her hand. "I didn't know she was coming, and I didn't know how to say *no* with Claire staring at me. Believe me, this was not how I was picturing our evening."

Tish laughed tiredly and leaned against Nash.

"You know what the worst part is? I have to get up tomorrow morning, go up to Mount Constitution, and watch other people re-enact our date. Although, for the record, they're totally going to wire Taylor in so he barely has to climb up the tower."

"Pssh. Weenie. Not climbing? Is he even quoting Shakespeare?"

"No," she said, giggling. "Not even. So, you are way cooler."

"Well, yeah," said Nash. "That goes without saying."

Tish leaned in to kiss Nash.

"Dad, come on," said Claire. "It's dinner time."

"We'll be right there," said Nash.

"Is Tish staying? I only put out three plates."

"Then we'll get out another one," said Nash.

Tish felt like someone had dumped ice water down her back.

"You know what?" she said, smiling brightly. "It's fine. I'll go eat with Granddad. I have to talk to him anyway."

"No," said Nash. "We're eating dinner."

"If there's enough," said Claire.

"There's enough," said Nash, glaring at his daughter.

"It's fine," said Tish, stepping off the porch. "I'll see you both later."

"Tish!" Nash turned to come after her.

"Dad, it's going to get cold."

"It's fine," said Tish.

"It's not fine," said Nash.

"Nash, I'm tired. I'm not up to this," she said. "I can't manage all of…" she waved in Claire's direction. "I just want to turn off my brain for a bit. Go have dinner. I trust you. It's not a thing. I'll call you tomorrow."

"Dad!"

Nash pivoted to look at Claire, and that was all the time Tish needed to get back to her car and escape.

CHAPTER 4

THE ORCAS HOTEL

Instead of going home, Tish drove straight into Eastsound and pulled in at the Orcas Hotel. The restaurant was packed, but she skipped that and went to the bar. Flinging herself into an empty bar stool, she slumped down as far as she could.

"Hollywood life is going that well?"

Tish turned to look down the bar to where Matthew Jones was accepting an Old Fashioned. Matt was a dark-haired thirty-something who was on the verge of opening a pot delivery business. He usually wore jeans and a t-shirt and looked like any other island resident, except that he drove a yellow Ferrari and wore a watch that retailed for more than a used car. The pot delivery business was a start-up, but he wasn't new to the industry. She was about to reply when another voice hailed her.

"Tish!" She turned and saw Elayne Doerty waving at her from a table. "Tish!"

Elayne was wearing her usual hippy skirt and Birkenstocks, with her long gray hair in two braids. She stood up from her table and leaned in with her eyes amazingly wide.

"I heard from multiple sources that Tobias is cheating on Eleanor with Brianna Meadows!"

"Uh…" said Tish.

"Oh my God, it's true!"

She felt Matt gently press his cocktail into her hand.

"It is not true," said Tish, knowing she'd already blown it. "I have introduced him around to the cast and crew. Brianna is the only one in the same age bracket, so, yes, they have spoken."

"She is a beautiful woman who is casting her wiles at our Tobias," announced Elayne.

"Uh…" said Tish.

"And do we really think our Tobias would do that?" asked Matt, perching himself on the stool beside Tish. "We all know he was in the CIA. You know he's trained against the wiles."

Elayne looked like this ridiculous theory actually held weight.

"Well, still!"

"Granddad and Eleanor are fine," said Tish. "Everything's fine."

"I will be stopping in to see Eleanor," said Elyane.

"And as her friend, you will not be repeating such nonsense," said Tish. "Or helping others spread it around. That would be very hurtful, and if I hear more of it, I will know who to blame."

Tish returned Elyane's glare with one of her own. Elyane made a hmph noise and swished back to her table.

"We're all fine here?" asked Matt quietly when Elayne was gone. *Star Wars, 1977. Harrison Ford ad-libbed that line.*

Tish took a gulp of the Old Fashioned, feeling the pleasant burn of the whiskey as she swallowed.

"That's the line you want to go with?" Matt continued. "You realize that's, like, twenty seconds before they jump into a garbage chute with a monster and a squish-o-matic."

"That never made any sense to me," said Tish. "Why have a monster in there if you're just going to squish it?"

"I assumed that the monster was an escapee who lived on garbage, and it had a way out under the water," said Matt.

That's actually a viable theory.

"Well, we really are fine here," said Tish.

"Liar."

Tish sagged. "My director is a narcissist. My cast hate him. We're so far behind schedule I'm freaking out. My grandfather is flirting with an actress. And—"

"Here's another Old Fashioned, Matt," said Delbert, the bar tender. "Tish, when you're done with Matt's drink, do you want one of your own?"

"Yes. A Tobias special, please."

"Bloody Mary, extra tabasco, etc. Got it. We're so excited about this movie. It's been bringing in a lot of tourists and cash for this early in the season. Keep up the great work!"

Delbert bustled away, and Tish groaned.

"And everyone keeps telling me how great it is that I'm bringing all this work to the island."

"So, we're all fine here," said Matt, taking a sip, his eyes twinkling.

"Nora is spending the night at Nash's with Claire because I got her a job in a speaking role."

"Oooh. That is… not good."

"It's fine," said Tish.

"That's not fine."

"I'm an idiot."

"Maybe," agreed Matt. "You know, I don't have an ex-wife. You could always break up with him and go out with me."

"Yeah, that's what I'm going to do," said Tish, rolling her eyes and taking another drink. Matt chuckled.

"Excuse me," said a woman, brushing by them. Tish recognized Elayne's best friend, Indigo, as she went to Elayne's table.

"Do you think Indigo heard that?" asked Tish.

"Probably," said Matt, and Tish groaned again. "Relax. It will serve Nash right if he hears through the grapevine that you're leaving him for the devilishly handsome me."

"I don't think he'll believe it, but I don't think he'll be happy about it," said Tish.

"Then maybe he shouldn't have let his ex-wife sleep over."

He's not wrong.

Matt waited for her to argue and then laughed when she didn't.

"So what are the odds of me getting my investment back?" he

asked when she took another drink.

"I will make this movie happen," growled Tish. "It's happening. Everyone who invested is getting their money."

"I'm not worried about it, Tish," he said, putting a hand on her arm. "I don't invest what I can't afford. Don't kill yourself over this."

"I'm not going to kill myself," said Tish. "I might kill Skip Renfeld and every other man in my life right now, but... I'm sticking with justifiable homicide."

"Come eat dinner with me," said Matt. "You can complain about Nash, Skip, or whatever his name is, and your grandfather."

"Do you mean that?" asked Tish woefully. "Because I will. I try not to, but right now, all the people I complain to are the people I'm complaining about."

"Yeah," he said, putting an arm over her shoulder and giving her a little side squeeze. "I mean it." He waved at Delbert, who pointed them at one of the bar tables on the far side of the room from Elayne and Indigo. Matt pulled out her chair for her, and as she was sitting, Taylor and Emma came in.

"Oh, hey, Tish," said Emma, smiling. Tish watched her assess Matt and come up with the wrong answer.

"Taylor, Emma, this is Matt. He invested in the film."

"Oh, nice to meet you," said Taylor, extending a hand. They shook, and Tish saw Taylor take in Matt's watch and get the right answer. "Did Tish offer you a tour of the set? I love giving investors a chance to feel the movie magic."

It was such a polished answer that Tish was surprised. Taylor had a more worldly grasp of the movie business than she had expected.

Matt chuckled. "You're just out at Reginald's, aren't you?"

"Yeah, we're going up to Mt. Constitution tomorrow," said Tish.

"Reginald's?" repeated Emma with a frown. "You're the third person who has said that. Isn't it Tish's property?"

"Reginald was the previous owner," said Tish.

"We sure do miss him," said Delbert, setting down her drink. "But it's been great having you here, Tish, and at least you and Tobias caught the guy. Specials for dinner?"

"Yes, please, Delbert," said Matt.

"Whatever table is open," said Delbert to Taylor and Emma and bustled away.

"Did we just get told to seat ourselves?" asked Taylor with a frown.

"We did!" exclaimed Emma happily. "I love it here."

"Sorry," said Tish, not feeling the need to cater to Taylor's ego but deciding to make the minimum effort.

"No, it's great. I just... Haven't had that happen in a while. What did he mean, you caught the guy?"

Matt chuckled. "Yes, Tish, do explain your other job."

"We're not discussing my other job," said Tish firmly. "Are you guys ready for the tower tomorrow?"

"I took some rock-climbing lessons," said Taylor nodding. "But I think I might go out a little early and do a practice run-through to get a feel for it."

"Wait until someone is there," said Tish. "Do not go falling off the damn tower."

"I won't!" promised Taylor, looking offended. "I just want to practice before Skip comes in and starts telling me I'm climbing wrong."

The kitchen door opened, and the chef poked his head out and then smiled and waved.

"Tish! Matt!" he exclaimed, taking off his apron as he approached the table.

"Quest!" she said, standing to get a hug. Quest was a twenty-something kid who was attempting to make the Orcas Hotel a fine-dining destination. Matt shook his hand.

"Delbert said you two were in. Do you have a little extra time tonight?"

"I'm not going anywhere," said Matt.

"Great. Then forget the specials. I'm going to try out a few of my new dishes on you. You're both in for the long table dinner, right? I'm toying with some ideas."

"I swear, Quest, I have to run a marathon after those dinners," complained Tish.

"I take no responsibility for calories," said Quest. "I just make good food."

"Too good!"

"Not my problem!" said Quest cheerfully. "Just let Delbert know if you need anything."

Quest returned to the kitchen, leaving Emma and Taylor gaping after him.

"Why do I feel like I'm looking at the King and Queen of Orcas?" demanded Emma.

"It's a very small community," said Tish. "We just all know each other."

"OK, but how do I get in on this long table dinner action?" asked Taylor. "I *will* run a marathon if the food is good enough."

"It *is* that good," said Matt with a laugh. "I keep being afraid that someone will scoop Quest up."

"Or…" said Tish and then stopped.

"Or what?" Matt asked suspiciously.

"Or someone could help him establish his own restaurant."

"I love how you always have fresh ways to spend my money."

"It would be good for the island."

"Mm-hmm. I will consider it if it ever comes up."

"Just a thought," said Tish with a shrug.

"You and Tobias," said Matt, shaking his head. "And your thoughts."

Tish's phone chimed, and she jumped. "Dailies!" she squeaked, seeing the email from Frank.

Emma and Taylor were immediately around on her side of the

table and peering over her shoulder as she tapped the link. They were only thirty seconds in when Tish breathed a sigh of relief.

"Oh, they're good," said Emma.

"Knew it," said Taylor confidently. "It felt solid. We just need to get this to the studio. We can show them that the production is moving."

"Yeah," said Tish. "Yeah. We're fine. We're going to be fine."

CHAPTER 5

THE TOWER

Tish blinked blearily at her phone, which was loudly declaring that her grandfather was calling. That was an insane notion. It wasn't even seven o'clock yet. It wasn't that her grandfather couldn't get up early. He was fully capable of it. But if he was going to rise with the dawn, then there damn sure better be a boat and a fishing rod in the immediate future. Otherwise, he preferred to stay home and enjoy the morning with a newspaper and a cup of coffee that contained enough half-and-half to make the beverage qualify as a dairy product.

But her phone continued to say—loudly—that Granddad was calling.

The call better not be coming from inside the house.

"Hello?" asked Tish, picking up cautiously.

Black Christmas, 1974. The origination of the slasher trope of the killer calling from inside the house.

"Uh…" said Tobias, "Tishkins, you didn't really like that director fellow, did you?"

Tish pushed back the covers and sat up. Last night, she had been so happy. Matt was always an excellent date. The dailies had been outstanding. Her email to the studio had been a masterwork of throwing Skip under the bus without sounding like it.

"You mean Skip, the terminally undermining, toxic narcissistic asshat? No, I don't like him. Also, and not for nothing, but what kind of grown man calls himself Skip? If you're over twenty and naming yourself after a children's activity, you should probably rethink your life choices."

"Good one," said Tobias. "You should put that on the bird site. I'll endorse that statement."

"Uh…"

Shit. Shit. Shit. He's not supposed to know about #GranddadSays.

"Meanwhile, I… well… I called Nash already, but I don't want you to be surprised."

"Granddad, where are you?"

"I thought I'd take Brianna up to Mt. Constitution to watch the sunrise. She said everyone was shooting up here today, and I didn't think she'd be able to appreciate the view properly with everyone messing around with cameras and everything. It's a real pretty view."

"I'm aware of the view," said Tish sourly. How was her grandfather getting more romantic vista viewing than she was? She got to her feet and began to stagger down the stairs toward the coffee pot.

"Yeah, well… Thing is…"

Tish took stock of the conversation thus far. She'd gotten distracted by her hatred of Skip.

I didn't listen to what he actually said. Always listen to what he actually says.

Tish paused, hand reaching for the coffee pot. Outside, birds were arguing about whose turn it was to chirp annoyingly loud.

"Granddad, why did you put Skip in the past tense?"

"Well," he cleared his throat. "That's because Skip has now… passed."

"What?" bellowed Tish, startling Coats, who glared up at her from his dog bed in the dining room.

"Yeah," said Tobias. "Dead as a doornail. It *looks* like he fell off the tower."

"No, no, no, no," said Tish. "You heard Brianna. He's why we got greenlit. We need him!"

"Well, unless you've got some sort of *Blythe Spirit* capabilities, I think you're out of luck."

"I don't think we want a ghostly apparition of Skip wandering around," said Tish. "That would be horrible. I think *Weekend at Bernie's* would be more applicable."

"And I don't think you should mention an eighties dead body comedy in the same breath as a Noel Coward play, but mostly, I think you may not be taking this as seriously as it deserves."

"I'm taking it very seriously!" snapped Tish, tossing a baggy cardigan over her shorts and tank top, wedging her feet into the closest pair of rubber boots, and grabbing her car keys. "Now hang up with me and take pictures with your phone. You know Detective Spring and Nash are going to try to keep us out of this."

"Took 'em before I called you," he said smugly. "Now hurry so you can beat Nash."

"On my way!"

We're so screwed. Without Skip, the studio is going to pull funding. I've got jobs and investors on the line here. I cannot lose this deal.

It was only when she was rounding the curve to the parking lot below the tower that she realized that she was probably a horrible person who was thinking about her own problems first and not being concerned that Skip was dead.

She sat in the car for a long moment once she parked, trying to thread through the cloudy soup of emotions churning through her chest.

She got out and saw Tobias walking swiftly toward her, his cane making quick clomping noises.

"Granddad, I'm not sorry he's dead!"

"Yeah, that happens. Don't worry about it."

"No! He's a human being and, and…"

That is literally the best thing I can say about Skip. That is horrible.

"Yeah, and unfortunately, he didn't live the kind of life that made people miss him."

"People try and kill me all the time. Am I living the kind of life that would make people miss me?"

"Don't be ridiculous," said Tobias. "I'd miss you. If nothing else,

I need you to change the tall light bulbs."

Tish glared at her grandfather. "My life worth is equivalent to my ability to climb a ladder?"

"That was a joke," he said soothingly. "Everyone would miss you. Nash and Claire and everybody."

"Not sure about Claire right now," grumbled Tish.

"Although, in some ways," mused her grandfather, "trying to kill you actually proves that your presence would be missed. If you weren't mucking things up for someone, they wouldn't want you gone. Your presence changes the world! Kind of a compliment when you think about it."

"Not the kind of compliment I want!"

"Well, I tried. Let's go see Skip before everyone shows up."

Mt. Constitution was the highest point in the San Juan Islands and in 1936, someone had seen fit to build a medieval tower at the peak. On a clear day, the coastline of Canada was visible. During their clandestine dating phase the previous summer, Tish and Nash had seen fit to climb it and spontaneously spout a little Romeo and Juliet. Some illicit drone footage had been taken of the moment, and Tish now found herself staring at the facedown body of Skip Renfeld on the hard rock at the foot of the tower and wondering if she were to blame somehow. The peak of the mountain was hard, barren rock, surrounded by a low wall and some scrubby underbrush that dropped into trees. Usually, there were picnic tables, but they had been cleared away for the shoot.

"Brianna thought it was Skip," said Tobias. "Being face down and all, we can't really be sure."

"The tattoo on the back of his calf is pretty distinct," said Tish, trying to ignore the fact that the leg was bent at an unnatural angle.

"I didn't think it was worth turning him over," said Tobias. "Whatever's left isn't going to be pretty, and he's cold. Pretty sure it's been hours. Must have happened sometime last night. We got here at six."

"Where is Brianna?" asked Tish, looking around. There were signs indicating that the summit was closed for the day, and the film crew's boom lift was already in place at the far side of the clearing. They had left it up and elevated, which Tish found vaguely unsafe, but what did she know about cranes and lifts?

"Waiting in the car," said Tobias. "She was pretty shaken up. I said I was taking care of calling the cops and things. Which I did. Then I called you. You know Peter would get squiffy if I didn't call him first."

Peter, who everyone else had to call Detective Spring, was going to be annoyed regardless of what Granddad did.

"Absolutely," agreed Tish, still staring at the remains of Skip Renfeld. It was an odd sensation, knowing that the thing in front of her had been alive and insulting people only hours before. "Something is wrong, Granddad."

"Lots of things are wrong. What's got you worried?"

"He shouldn't be here. He was lazy, and he thought this scene was dumb. I was pretty sure he was going to try and bail on it. Why would he be here early or even last night?"

"Good question," said Tobias. "That I'm sure Detective Spring will ask."

"Granddad," said Tish. "Before they get here, I would like to engage you on behalf of the studio to investigate."

"Tish, you know I'll investigate for free."

"Oh, I expect your rates to be extremely reasonable, or there will be no new lightbulbs for you. But all I'm saying is that later this morning, when I've got six studio execs on the phone, I will be telling them that I have a former CIA operative investigating the situation. So when Spring arrives, I expect you to do your nice old man bit and suck up like a damn barnacle. I want to know everything he knows before he knows it."

"He's not going to buy the nice bit," objected Tobias. "He's met me. Don't worry. I think we have arrived at some amount of reciprocity with Spring. I don't think he will try too hard to keep us out. We can just be ourselves."

"Whatever you think best," said Tish. "But I need to at least sound like I'm in control of the situation."

"Don't worry, kiddo," he said, patting her shoulder. "I've got your back."

"Thanks, Granddad," said Tish, turning away from the body and knowing it would go in the file in her brain that only came out late at night when she was alone. "We should go back down so Nash doesn't think I'm involving myself in a police investigation."

"Well, Nash is *definitely* not going to buy that," said Tobias, leading the way. "He's not only met you, he knows you and has seen you naked."

"I'm not sure what that has to do with anything," said Tish.

"Your grandma always knew when I was up to something," said Tobias.

"That's because you were always up to something," objected Tish, following Tobias down the sloping path toward the little gift shop and parking lot. Tobias laughed.

"That's true. But my point is that when you're doing the horizontal mambo with someone, you get so you can spot when they're up to mischief."

"Where is Skip's car?" asked Tish, surveying the small parking lot. She could see Brianna in her grandfather's rattletrap pick-up truck, but only one other car was in the parking lot. "I swear his rental was blue."

"The only vehicles in the parking lot when we arrived were the Lincoln Continental and that moped in the corner. The Continental has Oregon plates, which is a bit odd. And the moped is an Orcas special."

"No license plate?"

"And it looks like the key is a screwdriver. Both are as cold as the body. I didn't see anything particularly identifying in either."

"We're going to need to figure out where he went after he stormed off the set last night."

Tish frowned at the empty parking lot. In the summer, it was usually jam-packed. Today, the gift shop looked a little lonely, with only the rented equipment storage unit next to it for company. The film crew had wanted to get all the bits in place first, so they weren't trying to rig and shoot all in the same day. Last night, they had sworn that everything was set for today's shoot.

"Here comes the fuzz," Tobias said, jerking his head toward the road where they could see the flashing lights of a police vehicle. "Once Spring is done questioning me, I'll peel off and make some calls. I'll see what I can dig out of the island grapevine."

"Great," agreed Tish, pulling her sweater across her chest and wishing she'd stopped to put on all her clothes, including a bra.

Nash's Sheriff's Department SUV pulled to a stop in front of the gift shop, and the passenger side door opened, and a stocky woman in a baseball hat got out. She had close-cropped gray hair and a detective badge dangling from a chain around her neck.

"Well," she said, her gaze finally coming to rest on Tish and Tobias, "you must be the Yearlys."

"I reckon so," said Tobias. "Who're you?"

"Detective Pamela Warshaw. I have notes about you."

Tish glanced at Tobias.

There goes that plan.

CHAPTER 6

THE DETECTIVE

There was an official police van following the SUV, and the woman spoke briefly to the driver and then turned back to Nash, who had climbed out and was clearly about to walk over to them. Whatever the woman said gave Nash a neutral, professional expression, and Tish grimaced.

Ooh. That is not usually a good face.

The detective marched past them without comment, followed by the crew from the morgue van. Tish turned back to Nash, who shrugged but stayed put in the driver's seat.

"I guess we're supposed to stay here?" Tish looked at Tobias to see if he had any other thoughts.

"Oh, that was definitely the subtext," said Tobias, fiddling with his hearing aid.

"Should I go talk to Nash?"

"Nah, don't want to look like we're blatantly pumping him for information. No reason to tip our hand."

"She said Spring left her notes. I'm guessing she's got our playbook."

"Can't have," said Tobias. "Pete didn't have all of it, so she's definitely still behind the curve."

"Mmm," said Tish. "But I'm probably also behind the curve. I feel like I haven't studied up on police detectives enough."

"The thing you have to remember is that when they take the test to become a detective, they're not attempting to get a specific score. They're looking to rank in the top percentile. So, really, they're only competing against who is in the room that day. That means that some are brighter than others. And you won't know what you get until you're talking to them. It's the same as interviewing anyone else—try and let them talk until you figure 'em out."

"I think she's going to be interviewing us," said Tish.

"They always think that," said Tobias cheerfully.

Tish was about to give up and go talk to Nash, but he was on the phone and seemed to be doing a lot of eye-rolling. The minutes ticked by, and eventually, Tish saw the detective walking back down the path from the tower. Pamela Warshaw looked well-tailored but practical except for the police-issue baseball cap, which was still very stiff-brimmed.

"What do you think is with the hat?" asked Tish. "It doesn't seem to go with her ensemble."

"It does look a bit… fresh," said Tobias. "Hard to tell with her kind of individual, though."

"Granddad, what did that mean?"

"Policemen are not known for their sartorial skills."

"Police officers," whispered Tish, trying to get the gender-neutral label in before the detective came into hearing range.

"All right," said the detective, stopping in front of them and scrutinizing her notebook without looking up.

Tish looked from the new detective to the Sheriff's vehicle—where Nash was leaning against the hood with his arms crossed—and back.

"Yearlys…" the detective said, flipping to a fresh page.

"Yes, Yearlys, but where is Detective Spring?" asked Tish.

"He's out on medical leave," said Pamela, giving Tish's outfit the once over.

"Ah!" exclaimed Tobias. "He must have finally committed to the knee replacement surgery. I'll have to call him."

A sour look crossed the detective's face.

Someone doesn't like that we've got Spring's number.

"He was debating ceramic versus titanium," said Tobias, turning to Tish. "I want to hear how it goes. The doc said last time that I might be able to upgrade because there have been advancements since the last plane crash."

"The last plane crash?" demanded Pamela. "How many have there been?"

"Just the six. We don't count the other three since they never got off the tarmac."

She's considering how to respond. She thinks Granddad's messing with her, and she's not wrong, but he's also not lying.

"Let's get back on topic," said the detective.

Oooh. Look who's refusing to take the bait.

"Miss Yearly, if you could wait over there with Deputy Nash," the detective pointed to the Sheriff's vehicle, "I'll talk to you after I finish taking Mr. Yearly's statement."

"Uh..." said Tish.

"Oh, I don't think I could possibly feel strong enough without Tish's support," said Tobias cheerfully. "I'm old and frail."

"Mr. Yearly, it sounds less believable when you announce it so loudly."

"We do need to work on your delivery," agreed Tish.

"Doesn't have to sound believable," said Tobias, cheerful. "Just has to be said. I want Tish to stay."

"Well, I'm the detective, and I say no."

"Oh. Too bad. Tish call Sam. Tell her the police are harassing me again and to dig up all the paperwork from last time."

"I'm not harassing you. I'm attempting to eliminate unnecessary people from this investigation. And I would like to get the two of you off my crime scene as soon as possible. And back to your lives."

The last part was said through clenched teeth.

"It's easier if you give in," said Tish. "Didn't Peter say that in his notes?"

"Detective Spring has his methods. I have mine."

So he did say that, but you're choosing to ignore it.

"Why are you here, Miss Yearly? The call report didn't mention you—just Mr. Yearly and a Ms. Meadows."

"I called her," said Tobias.

"Do you usually answer for your granddaughter?" asked Pamela drily.

"Only when I think she's going to be rude to the police," said Tobias. "She has a little bit of an authority problem."

"Must be genetic," said the detective.

"Oh, yes, yes, I agree," said Tobias, nodding. "Her grandmother was very anti-establishment."

Tish tried to smother a laugh behind her hand but only partially succeeded. She cleared her throat and pretended to cough.

"So glad the death of a human being is amusing to both of you," said Pamela.

"It isn't, actually," said Tobias, "but then, neither is a police detective who is too busy protecting their territory to talk to witnesses like human beings."

And boom. You just got Granddaded. That one is going on Twitter.

"The problem is that you two aren't witnesses or human beings. You're private investigators. That makes you professionally up in my territory, and I don't particularly feel the need to share."

"I'm not a private investigator. I'm a producer," said Tish. "Of the movie the deceased is supposed to be directing, and Granddad discovered the body. Like it or not, we're involved."

"And I would like to get you uninvolved as soon as possible. So, if you would wait over there next to your boyfriend, I'll get to you after I've taken the witness's statement."

Tish looked at Tobias. They could dig in. Being annoying AF was a Yearly specialty, but was antagonizing the detective worth it? Tobias raised an eyebrow, and Tish nodded.

Not worth it.

Tish walked past the detective, pretending to head for Nash, but after a few steps, she veered off and headed for Tobias's truck and

Brianna.

But also not going to do what I'm told.

Nash raised an eyebrow as she went past but didn't move.

It's possible that I do have an authority problem.

Brianna opened the car door as she approached.

"Hi, Tish," she said with a sad smile. Brianna's hair was up in a ponytail, and she managed to nail the vacation beach vibe with linen trousers. "I can't believe this. I just can't believe it."

"Yes, it's very upsetting," said Tish, and Brianna looked up at her with a quizzical expression.

"Tobias said the same thing."

"Well, it is upsetting?" offered Tish, not sure where to go with the comment.

"Yes, but I think what you both meant is that it's upsetting for other people."

Shit. Totally got called out.

"Um… It's not that it's not upsetting. It's just that the only help we can offer now is to help find the killer."

"Yes, but you both are not upset by the physical reality of seeing a body. I'm afraid I had to sit here and think about not throwing up for a while."

"Oh. That kind of upsetting. Yeah. That's a reality. How are you feeling? I'm sure I can find you some water."

"As long as I think about other things, then I'm all right. Mostly, I'm looking at pictures of my daughter."

"Is that her?" asked Tish, smiling at the photo on Brianna's phone. It showed a bouncy-haired teen in a cheerleader uniform.

"It's been a while since she looked like that," said Brianna, looking at the photo with a nostalgic smile.

"I think that every time I see my high school photos," said Tish with a laugh. "Sometimes I think I look like a completely different person."

"Yes," agreed Brianna, shutting her phone off. "It's hard not to miss those days."

"I think that's the parent in you," said Tish. "I don't miss the days of zits and endless ruminating on whether or not he really *liiiiiikes* me."

Brianna laughed. "Yes, it's definitely the parent in me. But what do you think happened to Skip? You don't really think he was murdered, do you?"

"Um… I mean… It's possible Skip climbed out over the parapet and fell, but it's actually pretty hard to fall off that tower. Otherwise, I would have died about eighty times over when I was nine, and Nash wouldn't have made it past twelve."

"Oh," said Brianna.

"Um, I wanted to warn you that the police detective seems a bit… brusque. So you might need to bring some press junket attitude to the situation. She's just grumpy because she doesn't like Granddad and me."

Brianna's forehead managed a wrinkle. "Why wouldn't she like you?"

"Mmm… you may not have noticed this about us, but we are somewhat lacking in our ability to follow rules and toe lines, which annoys law enforcement personnel."

"But didn't Tobias say you're dating law enforcement personnel?"

"Yes, but Nash reads a lot of books."

Brianna stared at her, and Tish tried to come up with another answer because it seemed like one was expected.

Nope, I've got nothing.

"So, anyway, if you say that you just met us, she might like you better. But mostly, just answer her questions, and we'll get you back to the hotel."

"But Tish," said Brianna, "what are we going to do about the movie?"

We're screwed. The movie is dead, along with Skip. I was delusional up there with Grandad. There's no way I can salvage this situation. Face facts.

"Well, this is why studios have insurance. I'll see what I can do about keeping us afloat. Maybe they can ship us a new director, but it might just be that this movie wasn't destined to get off the ground."

Brianna nodded. "It's really too bad. It had such promise."

At least it did until Skip got ahold of it.

"I wonder what he was even doing up there," said Brianna. "He wasn't usually a morning person."

"No, definitely not," agreed Tish.

Brianna smiled and shrugged. "He was probably reviewing the shooting plan for today."

"Or new ways to screw up the shooting plan."

"Oh, Tish," sighed Brianna.

"Yeah, sorry," said Tish, realizing the thought had been tactless, if honest. "I'm going to talk to Nash for a minute. Like I said, maybe distance yourself from us, and the detective will untwist her knickers."

"I'll keep that in mind," said Brianna, looking amused.

Tish backed away and turned back to Nash. He gave her a raised eyebrow, and Tish made a face. What she wanted right now was a hug. The detective knew she was dating Nash, so that could probably be OK.

She had almost made it to the bastion of safety that was Nash, when she heard her grandfather raise his voice.

"Well, detective, why don't you just write up my statement for me since you know so much!"

She paused in mid-stride, her eyes locked on Nash.

"So close," he said, shaking his head.

"But so far," she agreed and turned back around.

CHAPTER 7

REPERCUSSIONS

Tobias was already stumping her direction, his eyebrows set to furious.

"She said I was prejudiced!" he barked at her.

"Well, I mean… Everyone has a little—"

Tobias gaped at her. "I am not! Sam is my lawyer. I support all the alphabets!"

"Oh. That kind of prejudiced. Um… I think maybe they wouldn't like being referred to as alphabets?"

"Well, I will stop saying that when they stop adding letters."

I am not laughing. That is not appropriate. An ally would not laugh. Oh, God, this is really hard.

"Gah!" Tobias waved his cane in fury and headed for his truck. Brianna was getting out and staring at the commotion.

"Well, Ms. Yearly," said the detective, approaching in his wake, "do you have something to say about my hat?"

Tish looked at the hat in consternation. "Uh… It looks new? I don't really…"

Pamela stared at Tish, and Tish stared back. She had no idea what Tobias had said, but if he was being offensive on purpose, then the list could be extensive.

"Why are you here?" demanded Pamela.

"Skip is the director on *Wind Above the Sea*. I'm the producer. Granddad called me when they found the body. After he called the police."

"Wind Above the Sea?"

"Title of the movie. Did Granddad say something about *you*

people?"

Pamela's face went stoically blank.

"I'm not saying it's necessarily better, but he probably meant police officers. Everyone else is just people."

"There is nothing wrong with being a police officer!"

"Nothing that great about it either," said Tish. "It's just a job. Is this really what you want to talk about?"

"No, I want to know why you're here!"

"I told you. Skip is my director. We're supposed to be shooting here today. In fact, I'm going to have crew showing up here in about an hour if I don't start calling people."

Pamela tapped her pen on her notebook. "So, if you're not expected to start shooting for another hour, why was Skip here early?"

"I don't know. But he looked, you know… stiff. I was thinking he might have been here last night."

"Oh, and how many dead bodies have you seen?"

"Um…" Tish tried to count that up. "Four. I guess. Sort of five. They wouldn't let me look at Mars's body. Probably just as well. I don't really want to think about it."

There was more tapping. Tish had no response for tapping, so she went back to her original topic.

"Anyway, Skip wasn't very bendy, and the blood looked dry. When will Mitch come back with a TOD?"

"Dr. Haverson," said Pamela, enunciating the Island County Coroner's title clearly, "will tell *me* the time of death when he sees fit."

Well, excuse the crap out of me. If Mitch doesn't have a problem with me using his name, I don't know why you do.

"When was the last time you saw the deceased?"

"Yesterday about four-thirty. He stormed off set because I told him he couldn't sexually harass people."

"Did he usually do that?"

"As far as I can tell, yes. I've never worked with him before, but the implication seems to be that he's a walking MeToo violation and a general asshole while also being a talented director. Can't say I saw much of his talent."

"I meant storm off the set."

"Oh. No? He usually just took an early dinner or lunch or whatever. Didn't bother with storming."

"I'll need to talk to anyone who could have seen him after he left."

Tish shrugged. "Knock yourself out. Pretty sure the island is used to it at this point."

"Hey, Detective Warshaw," said Mitch, jogging down the path from the summit in his white bunny suit. "Hey Tish! What did I say about getting you a punch card? Stop finding bodies for me!"

"It was Granddad this time!"

"We'll just put all the Yearlys on one card. Find a dozen bodies, and the thirteenth autopsy is on me!"

Tish laughed as Mitch jogged by.

"I'm just going to grab a few things from the van, but I'll let you know my best guess on TOD as soon as I can!"

Oh, my God, I'm trying not to laugh. I think her eye is starting to twitch. She's even more peeved off than Detective Spring on his first outing with us.

"No," snapped the detective. "They are not police personnel!"

"Yeah, of course!" said Mitch, miming a big thumbs up, and Tish suspected that even the detective could tell it was a complete lie. Pamela growled in anger.

"Anyway," said Tish, "you were going to ask people about Skip?"

"Yes, I'll need you to make a list of who talked to him."

"Oh. I don't know who talked to him. He was staying in a rental in West Sound. But I don't know where he went after he left the set."

"Well, then where did you go?"

"I went to Nash's for a few minutes and then had dinner at the Orcas Hotel. Then I went home, talked to Granddad for a little bit, and went to bed."

I want to say that her face is going to get stuck like that, but I think it's too late.

"Thanks, you can go now."

"Gee, can I, really? How nice of you. Oh, wait, just like Dorothy, I could leave at any time. It was always within my power."

Wizard of Oz, 1939. Yes, I am a friend to the friends of Dorothy, but you are being a bitch.

"What about Dorothy?"

Tish realized with startling clarity that she and the detective were not speaking the same language.

"I… Can't talk to you," said Tish. "You're not my kind of people."

"Sorry, my hat doesn't say MAGA," snapped the detective.

"What?" Tish blinked at the detective in confusion. "Oh. This is how Granddad ended up here. OK. Well…"

I feel a deep need to explain myself, and I somehow think that will not go well at all.

"I'm going to back away slowly," said Tish, matching her movements to her words. "Nash usually keeps a vegan protein bar in his glove box. You know, in case that's of interest. OK, bye."

She could feel Pamela's eyes on her all the way over to her grandfather's truck.

"How'd it go?"

"Same as you. That really got weird in a hurry. I suggested she get a granola bar out of Nash's glove box in case she was hangry."

Tobias chuckled, but Tish shrugged.

"It works on Claire. And to be honest, most of the other people I know. Hunger rage is real. Still not sure what was up with her hat."

"Who knows," said Tobias sourly. "At this point, I think we should head out and start trying to figure out how Skip got here. Whatever clues are here at the scene, we've either seen them already and don't know it, or we've missed them. But if we didn't catch something, she's not about to tell us about it. So there's no point in staying. Plus, I want to get Brianna home."

"Yeah," agreed Tish, nodding. "I need to call the rest of the crew and head them off before they start showing up here. I'll go tell Nash what the plan is. Maybe he can pick up some info while he's here."

Tobias nodded, and Tish went back to Nash, who was still waiting patiently by the Sheriff's vehicle.

"I want a hug so much right now," said Tish as she approached, "but she's still glaring at me, isn't she?"

"From a distance, but yes," he agreed, and Tish groaned.

"Why is she so weird?"

"Don't know. She barely spoke on the way up here. So, did you and Tobias work out a plan?"

"Yeah, we're going to get out of here since it's obvious that we're not welcome."

"Did you use that much sarcasm with her?"

"I may have told her there was a granola bar in your glove box, but I swear she started it."

Nash laughed. "I mean, sure, if it works on ten-year-olds, then it most definitely works on cops."

"Who knew that parenting book I bought would be so handy?"

"You bought a parenting book?" he asked, looking puzzled.

"I... Uh... Well, *When Not to Parent Your Partner's Child* seemed applicable, and it came with checklists." Tish believed in checklists.

"Tish, did you do homework for Claire and me?" His eyes twinkled.

"Psh. No. Maybe. Shut up."

"You know what I'm going to do?" He leaned in very close to her, and his voice changed to a husky whisper. "I'm going to clean your grout."

Damn it. He knows.

"You talk so dirty to me, and I love it," she said. He leaned back with a cocky grin. He knew he had her number. "Unfortunately, I will have to wait to put that promise into action. Granddad and I are going to do the thing, so…"

Nash's expression changed to puzzlement.

"The thing?"

"The one you disapprove of."

"The one where you cheat at pinochle and almost cause a riot among the old folks at the Grange?"

"We did not cheat," said Tish. "I'm just fundamentally bad a pinochle. I should not be forced to play."

"Well, I agree, but you lost that bet. And while I appreciate that you are a woman of your word, I don't really like having to convince old people that cheating at pinochle isn't a crime. Or having them insist that I arrest my girlfriend either, for that matter."

"It was really just Elayne."

"Tobias laughed so hard I thought he was going to have a heart attack."

Next to the car, Tobias tapped his watch and glared at her.

"But pinochle wasn't actually what I was talking about. I was talking about the other thing."

"Oh, the thing where you investigate a crime?"

"Uh… Well, yes?"

"Great, I'll come with. The detective said I could feel free to go. I've just been waiting to talk to you. So, let's hit the road and solve some crime."

"You can't come with us!"

"Why not?"

"You're the fuzz!"

"The fuzz?"

"The pigs! The man! The po-po!"

"Two out of the three of those are offensive, and the other is misogynistic."

"The five-O. The law. The heat. The bulls."

"I… am… I'm not sure if I'm impressed, horrified, or turned

on by your cop slang vocabulary."

"You know it's all three," said Tish, giving him a subtle wink.

"Probably. But I'm still coming with you."

"No! We talk to all kinds of people, and not all of them like you. You will ruin our rep."

"Your reputation is as a cantankerous set of busy-bodies. I swear I will not bring that down. I'm not even sure that's within my power, really. Besides…"

"Besides what?"

Is Nash getting serious face? Over this?

"Well, it's not like we've gotten to spend a lot of time together recently. And it's not like I want a murder investigation to be our quality time, but I will take what I can get."

"You think I don't want quality time?" yelped Tish. "I have been trying! I'm trying so hard! And then every time I actually make it to your place, there is your damn ex-wife!"

He grimaced. "Yeah. It's sucking."

"Sucking!"

I just flailed like some sort of drowning naked mole rat.

"Kim Possible and Ron Stoppable were the best crime-fighting duo ever. Fight me."

Kim Possible, Disney TV series, 2002 – 2007. Teenage cheerleader crime fighting at its best.

"I'm going to stop letting you watch cartoons with Claire."

"I haven't been doing a lot of that either. In fact, I haven't been doing a lot of anything. I'm tired of it, and I want my life back, but stupid people keep dying. And I want my boyfriend back, and I want my Claire back, but now she hates me."

Shit, I said that out loud.

"She doesn't hate you."

Tears are imminent. I'm freaking out.

"She didn't even get me a dinner plate!"

"I…"

He's supposed to say something reassuring, and he's not doing it. Probably because he thinks it's true. Oh, God, he thinks it's true. Claire hates me.

"OK," said Tobias, stumping into the conversation at the worst possible time. "Whatever's going on, let's move it along. I want to get Brianna out of here."

"Right, of course," said Tish. "She was really upset about seeing the body. We shouldn't make her stay. Why don't you take her back to her rental, and I'll meet you back home? I need to start making some calls anyway."

Tobias squinted, looking between her and Nash. "Yeah, OK. Nash, are you heading back to work?"

"Yeah," said Nash.

He sounds grumpy. He looks grumpy, too. How is this my fault? It's his stupid ex-wife!

"Yeah, I'll be running down these two vehicles," he said, jerking his thumb at the car and moped still in the parking lot. "I'll have to turn over whatever I find to the detective, of course. But I'll stop by later if I find out anything."

Tobias distinctly did not look at Tish. "That would be real neighborly, and I would appreciate it, but don't get yourself in trouble on our account."

"That's why it will be an in-person conversation that you will forget later."

"I'm old," said Tobias. "I forget stuff all the time. I can never remember where I hear things. Well-known fact."

"Unfortunately true," said Tish.

"Don't start with me, young lady," said Tobias. "See you at home."

"See you later," said Nash, and he left, too.

Why do I feel abandoned? I'm a strong, independent woman. I don't need menfolk! I just like my menfolk.

Grumpily, Tish went back to the car. She was most of the way back to the car when she saw her phone buzzing with a number that

she had entered into her phone as His Royal Highness of Movies –
Alan.

"Hey Alan," she said, picking up as she parked the car. "Thanks
for calling."

"Hey, 911 texts get my attention," he said cheerfully. "But I gotta say, I'm loving the dailies. I know, I know, Skip's a little difficult
to work with, but from the footage, it looks like you know how to
handle him."

"Yeah…" said Tish. "Um…"

"OK, I really do know that Skip can be hard to take, and I read
between the lines in last night's email. You're worried about harassment stuff. I hear you. And I already put in a call to him. As soon as
we connect, I'll get him to tone his act down."

"Um… actually… He's not going to be calling you back."

"Did he pull one of his *I quit* stunts? Total bluff, I promise. He
hasn't even called me and demanded more money."

And now he never will.

"Um, I got a call this morning. Skip was found up on Mt. Constitution just after sunrise."

"That's the tower place, right? You said you were shooting there
today. Wow, I can't believe he got such an early start. Skip is usually
in bed until brunch."

Hey, you actually did read my email. I did try to keep it short.

"Yeah, Skip was apparently pushed off the tower."

"Holy shit."

"The police are investigating, of course. I haven't called the rest
of the crew yet. I wanted to talk to you first. They're going to have
questions."

"Well, but I mean, how soon until Skip gets out of the hospital?"

"Um, Skip's dead. He was murdered."

"I… but… I…He can't be dead. We're making a movie."

"Well," said Tish cautiously.

OK, here we go. Let's just put the situation out there and let him react.

"Skip wasn't really meshing with the cast or vibing with the *studio-approved* script. So, I'm not sure... I mean, we could stop the movie, but I was going to talk to you about finding someone with a different vision anyway."

"But is it bad taste if we just ship you a new director?" mused Alan. "That's probably bad, right? People will think we're mercenary."

"I can talk to the cast and see how they feel, but Skip was well known for his love of movies. What if we soldier on in his memory and put a dedication card on the title sequence?"

There was a silence on the other end of the phone.

"I'm not hating that. Why don't you do a little temperature test on the cast and see how we're feeling over there. I mean, he wasn't actually there for any of the footage from last night, was he?"

"Nope."

"OK, but the studio cares about our people. We would have to really show our solidarity with... people. And if they don't catch who did it, then it just looks like we're being callous toward Skip's family. I'm assuming he has some. But it looks bad if we're making movies while his killer is still wandering around."

"You want the killer brought to justice swiftly so that we can continue in Skip's memory," supplied Tish, reframing the messaging for him.

"Exactly. Do you think the police can do that?"

No. Not really.

"I couldn't say. I've never met this detective before. But I have already been in contact with a local private investigator who is a former CIA operative. The local police are investigating, and, of course, we support them, but I thought the company would want to have someone taking it with the utmost seriousness."

"Yes. Yes, that is what we want," said Alan, and Tish could hear the smile on his face through the phone. "Utmost seriousness. I appreciate that you're acting so swiftly. This is great. Your guy will catch the guy, and then our guys will get back to business."

"Right," said Tish.

Oh, God, I just promised we could catch a murderer.

"Skip will be remembered fondly," said Alan cheerfully. "I'll talk to marketing about appropriate statements. I'll give them your number. We may need some talking points. Keep me updated on the situation."

"Yes, of course," said Tish.

"Catch you later!" The line went dead, and Tish shook her head.

CHAPTER 8

THE CREW GATHERS

Tish left her third message and then texted the next four people to call her. Cell phone reception could be crap on the island, but she didn't think she could actually text Skip's dead as a message.

I may be Generation Millennial Zed Whyyyyyy or something, but I'm still living with a Boomer. He would bean me over the head with his cane.

While she was waiting for callbacks, she went and changed into actual clothes and started making breakfast while she considered whether or not to get out the murder board. They hadn't ever moved the whiteboard back to the shed and were currently storing it in the mud room. They had used it last time they'd had people over and played Pictionary. It always caused commentary—what could they possibly do with a full-sized whiteboard in a residential home?

Keeping track of murder suspects, of course! What else do people do with their white boards?

She was about to sit down to a Tobias special of a fried egg sandwich when the doorbell rang. Puzzled, she opened the door and found Frank Brooking and the entire shooting crew in the driveway. Frank was standing on the front porch while the others rearranged some equipment in the truck. His long gray hair was down today. There was a hair tie on his wrist, so she thought it was about to be corralled back into his usual hippie ponytail. He was staring toward the dog run where Coats was barking furiously.

"Coats! Knock it off!" Tish yelled.

The chocolate lab barked a few more times and then snuffled optimistically at the fence. He usually got let out to sniff the visitors at some point.

The Yearly house was set well back from the main road. Tobias had built a long gravel drive that cut in from the road down to the house before curving back up to join the road. In the U-bend between the house and the road, there was an extensive line of pine trees to block the road, provide shade for one of the storage sheds and space for additional parking. In many ways, the Yearly House—a steeply pitched A-frame—was built backward. The front of the house overlooked the view of trees and water, while the back faced the drive. It was just that once parked, no one ever walked around to the front. The common entrance was the hall and door with the postage stamp of a deck. Which was why Tish was constantly threatening to install a doorbell camera to see who was approaching the back door.

"What did Skip do now?" Frank demanded, standing on the single stair down to the gravel drive. "I finally get everyone to show up on time and he pulls some sort of stunt. I swear, he lives to screw up my shoots. Please tell me you didn't fold to his bullshit."

"Um," said Tish. Half the crew was staying in Anacortes so getting them to get to the ferry on time had been problematical, so she appreciated Frank's complaint, but she wasn't sure how to respond.

"Does he even want to shoot this movie?"

For once Frank wasn't downplaying his feelings about Skip and his lack of professionalism.

"He's dead," said Tish.

"What?" Frank didn't look shocked. He just looked confused.

There was a yelp as the gaffer fell out of the truck bed and onto the driveway.

"What?" demanded the gaffer, whose name Tish thought was Irving, from flat on his back on the gravel.

"Sometime between last night and dawn this morning, Skip was pushed off the tower at Mt. Constitution."

"So, we can't shoot today?" asked the secondary photographer, whose name was probably Ellis.

"Shit," said Frank. "The studio's going to shut us down, aren't they?"

"But," said the gaffer, climbing to his feet, "what was he doing up there in the first place?"

"You know he was messing with our equipment," muttered someone in the van, but Tish didn't see who.

"If the studio closes us up, that's going to blow a big fricking hole in my finances. I've got child support to pay. How soon until they shut us down?" demanded Ellis.

"I already talked to Alan. He loved the dailies, by the way. My impression is that if the case gets resolved quickly and that everyone is… emotionally fine with continuing to work then the shoot will continue."

Frank looked back at his crew and seemed to do a head count before turning back to Tish. "Emotionally we're fine," he said drily.

"Tish, can I come in and wash my hands?" asked Irving, plaintively dusting off his himself off.

"Yeah, sure," said Tish. She held the door open and watched as the entire van full of crew members trooped into her house.

She was about to close the door when she heard the roar of an engine out on the road beyond the trees and the crunch of tires on gravel told her that someone would be coming down the drive at speed. Moments later, Kyle's jacked Jeep whipped into view. She could see Taylor in the passenger seat, possibly leaving finger dents in the dash. Kyle screeched to a stop and Taylor tumbled out looking white.

"Skip's dead? Kyle said the police scanner said there was a body. And then you said to call you about Skip. Never text *call me*. Call me is code for disaster!"

"Yeah," agreed Tish, "it really is. And yes, Skip's dead."

"But, but, but…" Taylor pushed his bangs out of his eyes and then looked around at Kyle as if Kyle would have some answers.

"The crew is already here," said Kyle, spotting the truck full of equipment. "Why don't you go in and talk to them?"

Tish glared at Kyle.

"Good idea," said Taylor, fumbling for his phone. "I've got to call Emma and my agent. This is terrible!" Taylor brushed past her, already dialing.

I would bet real money that he calls his agent first.

"The crew was leaving in a minute," said Tish as Kyle came up to the porch. "Now I'll have to get rid of all of them."

"If he sticks with me, he's going to eat like another twelve blueberries. I didn't think you'd want him stoned out of his gourd while there's a murder investigation going on. The cops are going to probably want to talk to him, right?"

Damn it. That's actually correct.

"Yeah, and speaking of which, you need to steer clear of the cops. It's not Spring this time. It's some new detective we've never met. And trust me, she's not going to be very excited about your business."

Kyle grimaced. "Right. Yeah, I'll keep myself on the DL, but I might need to remind Taylor to keep my name out of his mouth."

Before she could stop him, Kyle headed into the house too. Tish glared around the yard, daring someone else to pop out of the woods.

"Can I drink the coffee?" asked Ellis as she entered. She really had the hardest time telling some of the crew a part. They all seemed like thirty-five-ish white guys in t-shirts and cargo pants that usually held a roll of electrical tape in one of the pockets.

"Yeah, sure," said Tish, with a sigh. "Mugs are in the cupboard above the pot."

"Thanks! This smells like the coffee I used to make when I was in college."

"If you mean that your college coffee was black as your heart and twice as strong then you'll love it," said Tish.

Ellis laughed. "Perfect. That is exactly what I'm looking for."

Tish sat down to her breakfast at the dining table and looked out into the living room where Taylor and the crew were on their phones. Probably her work of disseminating the information was about to be done for her.

"Man," said Ellis, doctoring his mug, "I can't believe Skip is actually dead. I've never worked with him before, but Frank said he was a snake. But still, this business is full of snakes. Can't believe someone actually killed him." He had selected an owl shaped mug in brown and purple glaze that Tish thought Tobias had excavated from the Exchange, but was probably an Orcas Pottery original.

"I didn't realize Frank had worked with him before," said Tish.

"Yeah, although, apparently Skip got him booted off the last picture. Frank was set to start shooting and then—bam—Skip got the production company to replace him with some young kid. Frank was pissed."

"Yeah, I would be too," said Tish. "I'm starting to think no one liked Skip."

"Irving is convinced that Skip was messing with the equipment we had up there. We had it locked in the storage unit by the gift shop, but Skip had all the codes. Did you get a chance to look around?"

Tish scratched her head. "I don't think so. The storage unit was still closed and the boom lift was up."

"We didn't leave the lift up," said Ellis. "That's unsafe."

"OK," said Tish.

Does it mean something? He wasn't pushed off the lift. I guess it means that Skip or the killer messed with it. But what does that mean?

Tish chewed her fried egg sandwich and tried to think of what to do next. There was a knock on the door and she gestured at Irving to go answer it.

My mouth is full, and you all need to make yourselves useful.

Irving, already used to taking her orders, hurried to the door.

"Oh my God," said Emma, brushing past Irving to go directly to Tish. "Is it true? Skip's really dead?"

"Yeah," said Tish. Emma's hair was up in a messy bun, and she was wearing what Tish thought of as the model no makeup look but was actually makeup that men just didn't know existed.

"Yeah," said Tish.

"You are taking this so calmly," said Emma. "I feel like I might need a Xanex."

"You don't," said Tish. "You need to go out on the deck and meditate in the papasan chair."

"Oh! I should do that," said Emma staring out into the living room where the floor to ceiling windows showcased the view. "That's lovely. You could hold a yoga retreat."

"Granddad doesn't approve of yoga pants."

"I know. I follow Words From Granddad. His opinion on hats had me second-guessing all of my headwear. But then I realized I never wear any of my hats ironically. I'm very serious about them."

"Totally within the old person guidelines then," said Tish.

"And also, I look good."

"Totally within my guidelines, then," said Tish. "Taylor and the crew are in the living room, but if you need a minute, you can head out to the deck."

"I'm probably fine. Maybe I'll just get some coffee."

Emma dropped her overstuffed Birkin on the table and headed to the kitchen. It was an unassuming brown leather that retailed for at least ten thousand, and Emma was using it as a gym bag to tote her change of clothes. Tish sighed. Ten thousand dollars was a new roof for the bungalow or half the money she needed for the barn renovation. Emma might play at being a struggling actress, and maybe once upon a time, she had been a starving model, but since she hadn't pawned the Birkin, Tish guessed that paying the bills wasn't one of the things Emma was struggling with. Tish watched as Emma opened random cupboards until she found the mugs.

Emma perused the mugs as if the selection was of the utmost importance. She selected a factory-manufactured cup that had a swirling glitter pattern on it.

"I just cannot believe..." Emma paused to pour the coffee, "that Skip's dead. I just saw him last night!"

"When did you see him?" asked Tish, sitting up straight.

"After dinner! You two left—Matt is so cute, by the way—Taylor and I walked around, and we were heading back to the ferry dock. But Taylor forgot his jacket so he ran back to the restaurant. I stayed put because you did *not* lie. That food was delicious, and all I could manage was a slow waddle. The chef is a dream! What did you say his name was? Hunter?"

"Quest," said Tish, waiting for the story to come out.

"So talented! Anyway, I was waiting for Taylor and Skip pulled up on a moped, of all things. He demanded to know how committed I was to the movie. So rude! I took a page from your book and told him he wasn't pushing me out of the movie. I auditioned. I got it. I'm doing it. Shit. Are we doing it? If Skip's dead, are we getting canceled? No! This is my shot at a leading role."

"We're tentatively still going," said Tish. "I talked to Alan. We're hoping to get Skip's killer caught, and then we can soldier on in Skip's honor."

"Nice," said Emma, lifting her mug in a toast. "You are so smart. You know, I was really nervous about working with you when I heard you turned down the part. I didn't get that you were, like, totally onto bigger fish."

Big Fish. 2003 A Ewan McGregor surrealist fantasy from Tim Burton, as if there were another kind of Tim Burton movie.

"Well, mostly, I just hustle. What else did Skip say?"

"He just said, yeah, yeah, yeah, doing it, great. Perfect. And then asked about Taylor. It was bizarre, now that I'm thinking about it. Like either of us would just up and quit."

"Did he talk to Taylor?" asked Tish.

"No, I told him Taylor would be right back, but Skip said he'd get Taylor later. Then he roared off. Well, puttered off slowly, but you could tell he meant to be all *Fast and Furious* about it. Although, there was a lot of weaving, and I kind of thought he was going to crash for a minute."

"Was he drunk?" asked Tish, frowning.

"No? Maybe? I don't know. I was trying not to get that close to him. The moped smelled like gas."

"Huh. Weird," said Tish, picking up her phone and swiping out a message.

PRETTY SURE SKIP DROVE UP TO THE TOWER ON THE MOPED. NOT SURE WHERE HE ACQUIRED IT.

"Right? Anyway, that's the last I saw of him," said Emma, shaking her head. "Too crazy."

Nash gave her text a thumbs up. Which could mean that he couldn't talk at the moment or could just mean he'd received the message.

Why did I say we would find the killer? The movie has insurance. So what if it fizzled out?

"What time was that again? After dinner?" Tish did some math. She'd watched the dailies with Matt, Emma, and Taylor. Emailed the studio, eaten dinner, and then bailed to go home and do some prep work for the upcoming wedding. "So it must have been after eight?"

Except that I promised everyone a movie would get made here. And everyone was really excited about it, and I wanted to look cool. It's only cool if I make it across the damn finish line.

"I think?" Emma shrugged. She went up on her tiptoes and peered into the living room. "Hey, real question, do you think Taylor is dating anyone, like, seriously?"

"Not that I'm aware of. He doesn't call anyone that I've noticed. He texts some home-bros and calls his agent. That says not seeing anyone seriously."

I seriously need to reconsider my goal-setting. Why can't I ever shoot for something reasonable like a normal human?

"OK, cool," said Emma nodding.

"You thinking about changing that?" asked Tish, and Emma shrugged.

"Maybe. I mean, he's got three million followers. Who wouldn't be interested? But I thought I should check who's on the field before I start making plays."

"It's open as far as I know, but I'm not the referee. Might have to check with someone who actually knows."

"I'll have my agent call his agent," said Emma nodding, as she headed into the living room. "Good advice."

"I actually, I meant..."

Never mind. Agent to agent heart to heart will probably work.

Tish was washing her breakfast dish when the screenwriter arrived. Luke was driving a vibrant blue rental Ford that looked like someone had squashed a car into half the size of a family sedan. She hoped he'd gotten a discount on the rental fees for it being ugly. He ran up to the house and looked like he was going to make a dramatic entrance or pound on the door, so Tish opened it ahead of him.

Stealing dramatic entrances is probably mean, but it really is enjoyable.

"He's dead?" gasped Luke, stumbling into the hall.

"Yes," said Tish.

"That's terrible," he said at last, but he looked like he was trying the sentiment on for size.

"Sure," said Tish. "Everyone else is in the living room. But how about you? When was the last time you saw Skip?"

"Uh..."

That went on too long.

"At the shoot when he stormed off," said Luke.

"Huh. OK. Head on in."

Luke gave her a puzzled look but did as he was told. Tish went out on the front porch and shut the door behind her. She heard her grandfather's truck before she saw it. The rattle of the engine was distinct.

He parked in his usual spot in front of the garage and eyed the other vehicles.

"I see we got visitors," he said as he planted his feet on the ground. His usual jeans and outdoorsy button-up shirt looked fresh out of the laundry to Tish's eye. She hadn't noticed that while they were on the mountain.

"Half the movie cast and crew," said Tish. "Did you get Brianna back to her house? She seemed pretty upset."

"Yeah," said Tobias, looking thoughtful. "Not what anyone wants first thing in the morning, I suppose. She said to call her once you knew what the studio wanted to do."

"Um… I may have promised the studio exec that we would find who killed him so we could keep the movie going."

"Then that's what we'll do. Don't worry. We'll figure it out," he said, settling his cane and climbing out of the truck.

"You are way more confident than I am," said Tish, and Tobias chuckled.

"Yeah. I know. It's one of the benefits of having done this professionally. This isn't my first time promising someone that I'll solve the problem without a single idea about how."

Tish shook her head. "I was just thinking that I needed to stop doing that."

"Nah, that's how you get experience. Don't worry. We got this."

Granddad level confidence is what I aspire to.

CHAPTER 9

TALKING TO PEOPLE

"OK," said Tobias as they paused at the end of the hall, looking at everyone in the living room. "Break it down for me. What have you found out?"

"Emma saw Skip on a moped last night, probably after eight. I'll have to check the ferry schedule for a more exact time. Someone messed with the boom lift on Mt. Constitution. Possibly Skip, but could be the killer. Don't know why either of them would, though. Pretty sure Luke Green," she tried to subtly point, "the writer, is lying about not seeing Skip after he left the set. That's all I've got so far."

Kyle sidled over. "I think that Irving guy might have talked to Skip last night," he whispered. "And I'm pretty sure Taylor's hiding something, but I don't know what."

Tobias gave him an approving nod. "Good job. You can go get a chocolate out of the elephant."

Kyle looked confused. "The elephant?"

"Cookie jar on the mantle. Children who are good get chocolates," said Tish. The elephant had been in use as long as Tish could remember. She was pretty sure it had existed when her father had been little. Kyle beamed and headed for the elephant.

Kyle is an adult. Adult-ish, anyway. And he's really excited about the chocolate and the approval and that pretty much says it all about his parent's lack of interest in his life. I'm like five years older than he is? Granddad is rubbing off on me. I don't need to parent Kyle.

"OK," said Tobias, "I'm going to go be old at some people." Which was what Tobias called looking thoughtful and supportive while asking leading questions.

"I feel like I should check in on Taylor," said Tish, eyeing the movie star who was sitting on the Chesterfield and talking to Emma. Tish took a step toward the Chesterfield, but she was still trying to formulate what she was going to say to break up the duo on the couch when Ellis stepped in front of her.

"Um… Tish," he said, his voice dropping as he looked around.

That automatically makes you look suspicious. Why do people do that?

"Can I talk to you for a minute?" The cameraman looked nervous, and twisting his owl mug around in his hand.

"Sure," said Tish. "How about outside?"

She gestured to the porch and Ellis nodded. Once the sliding door was shut, Ellis took a deep breath.

"God, I love the air here. So much oxygen."

Up in the Air, 2009, George Clooney. How does that man always look so good in a suit?

"What's up, Ellis?"

"OK, you're a producer, so I'm supposed to tell you. That's what's supposed to happen."

"OK," said Tish. "So you're doing your job."

"Yeah, OK, but see yesterday, Frank sent us out to the tower to set up for today's shoot. We did a few passes with a drone. We set up the boom lift and did some background shots and then we wired for the stunt work."

"Yeah, you're wiring Taylor in so he doesn't fall off the tower when he climbs up the side?"

"Yeah. The stunt guys looked at it and said it was a cake walk and that Taylor shouldn't have any problems." Ellis patted the many pockets of his cargo shorts and finally pulled out his phone and glanced at it. She hadn't heard an alert, so she assumed it was an anxiety phone check.

"Yeah, Nash climbed up it no problem and he doesn't do rock climbing or anything."

"What?" Ellis dropped his phone back in his pocket.

"My boyfriend… Never mind. Doesn't matter. What's the problem? It sounded like everything went OK yesterday."

"Yeah, it did. But I just talked to the guys and one of them got a call from Skip later in the evening. After he stormed off the set. And he gave Skip the pin code to the lock on both the boom lift and the storage box."

"OK," said Tish nodding.

"But is that better or not?" demanded Ellis.

"What do you mean?"

"Well, if Skip went up there and messed around with stuff and then fell off… that's an accident, right? But what if they pull our insurance? Then that shuts us down. Is that better or worse than him getting shoved off?"

"I'm not sure," said Tish. "But either way, you took appropriate steps to secure the items. If Skip messed with stuff, then it's on him and not on the rest of the crew."

"Yeah, except Thiago said that he was sitting with Frank and Frank told him to go ahead and give the numbers to Skip. So… that's… we're back to us being involved!"

Interesting. Frank didn't mention that.

"No, as the director, Skip is still the boss. You couldn't have known what Skip was going to do."

"Yeah, well, it was a safe bet that it wasn't going to be anything good," said Ellis derisively. "I would have fudged the numbers and then told him I didn't know what was wrong when he called back and that we'd look at in the morning. Or just not picked up the phone the next time around. Why don't people know when to lie? Never let people touch your equipment."

"Hard truths, man," said Tish. "But don't sweat it. Once the police check everything out, we'll get back up there and be able to see what got touched."

Ellis shook his head. "I need this movie to happen. Thanks for trying to keep it on track."

"Just doing my job," said Tish as Ellis went back in.

Tish thought about following him, but didn't see Taylor and tried to come up with the energy to talk to anyone else. Inside, she saw Tobias patted Frank on the shoulder and then came out to the deck, carefully shutting the sliding glass door.

"OK, I got the address where Skip was staying."

"How?" demanded Tish.

"They said it was a bright blue house over on Crow Valley Road."

"There could be more than one," said Tish.

"Could be, but there ain't. Kari Lee painted hers green last summer and that just leaves that summer home that gets rented out."

"OK, so we know where he was staying. What do you want to do about it?"

"I want to go search it. There are at least three people in there who spoke to Skip last night and all of them report that the conversation was... odd. I think he was up to something and I want to know what. I think the house is a good place to start."

"I also think he was up to something," said Tish. "But that means that it's actually more likely he tripped and biffed it off the tower himself."

Tobias looked thoughtful. "Maybe. But I'd still like to take a look at his house and figure out exactly what he was doing."

"OK, but what are we going to do about the house full of people?"

"You'll call that Pamela woman and tell her the crew are all here if she wants to talk to them and then we'll leave Kyle in charge. That way we know we won't run into her at Skip's place."

"We can't leave Kyle in charge," said Tish.

"You're always saying how he needs some responsibilities so he can step up. Here's his opportunity."

"I told him to lay low and avoid the cops because of you know... the drugs."

"They all seem fully capable of covering up their drug habits and Kyle can say he's doing odd jobs for you."

Mmm… strongly possible.

"They're going to eat us out of house and home," said Tish sourly, glaring through the windows at the Hollywood gathering.

"We'll add it to my bill," said Tobias with a grin.

Tish made eye-contact with Kyle and jerked her head. He nodded and then took a moment to extricate himself and move out to the porch.

"What's up?" he asked.

"Granddad and I are going to go search Skip's place."

"Awesome. I'll go with you."

"No, we need you to mind the madhouse while we're out. Plus, we're calling the cops and telling them to come talk the yahoos in there."

"What? No! That's not… That's just babysitting!"

"Yeah, and we're counting on you to do it," said Tobias. "And also, can you call up Quincy and ask her to do some googling and see what she can find out about Skip."

"Mm," said Tish. "I forgot about Quincy. She's out on summer break now or about to be." The engineering college student was their most recent acquisition. She had been undertaking the extensive project of digitizing all of Tobias's files about the Orcas residents.

"I think she's using they-them now," said Kyle. "They changed it up on socials, but yeah, I can call them."

Tish grimaced. She had also seen the pronoun switch, but had promptly forgotten about it.

"What?" demanded Tobias.

"Quincy wants to use non-gender specific pronouns," said Tish. She had found that this kind of thing went better if she just said it bluntly. Tobias didn't grasp the metaphors of modern soft-peddling.

"That's weird."

"It's what they want."

"But Quincy is a girl."

"Yeah, well sometimes being a girl sucks and sometimes someone doesn't feel like all the things that everyone else thinks a girl is or maybe they don't feel like a girl at all."

"Well, but that's someone else's bullshit," said Tobias, scratching his head. "Why can't she just be herself?"

"They're trying to be," said Tish.

"Can't I just call her Quincy?"

"Yes, absolutely, you can call them Quincy," said Tish and Tobias rolled his eyes.

"OK, well, Kyle, call Quincy and tell Quincy to get digging on the computer."

"You got it, boss," said Kyle, with a firm nod.

"You're still a boy, right?"

"Last time I checked."

Tobias shook his head and rolled his eyes again. "OK, come on, granddaughter she-her girl person, let's go do this."

Tobias stumped off the porch, clearly intending to go around the outside of the house, and Kyle made a face at her. Tish shrugged.

Tish got them into her car and was on the road before Tobias spoke again.

"Rebel Without a Cause."

"1955. James Dean and Sal Mineo," said Tish automatically.

"Yeah, probably," said Tobias. "I don't remember the year. But James Dean. They asked him, 'What are you rebelling against?'"

"And he said, 'What d'ya got?'"

"It's not that great of a movie. I watched it the other week on TCM. I think it mostly got famous because Dean died a month before it was released. Watching it now, I have to say my top reaction is that the fifties were weird."

Tish chuckled.

"But the idea that all these kids are desperate for something and adults can't even fathom what they're miserable about. That feels real. Maybe it's that way every generation. I don't know. You forget what you didn't know when you were young. When you're old, you feel like you've always known the things you know now. Anyway, that's probably the long way of saying I don't get the pronoun thing. I really don't. But I guess I don't have to. Quincy can be whatever."

"You support all the alphabets," said Tish.

"I guess," said Tobias with a shrug. "Mostly, I just like people and dislike assholes."

"Fair enough."

The trip from the Yearly house to Crow Valley took them up through Eastsound and then down the other leg of the horseshoe that was Orcas Island. It wasn't long as the crow flew, but by Orcas Island speed limits, it was a bit of a journey, and Tish found herself contemplating her own growing sense of unease. She'd been uncomfortable since the start of shooting, and instead of getting better, it was quickly growing.

I'm good at being uncomfortable. I dive off the deep end. It's what I do. And investigating isn't even new. Granddad and I can do this. Why is this getting to me?

Tish pulled up to the blue house on Crow Valley Road and looked around. Skip's rental car was in front with the hood up.

"I guess we're in the right place," said Tish.

"I guess we know why he was on a moped," said Tobias.

They climbed out of Tish's Toyota and approached Skip's car. There was a fresh dent in the bumper.

"I wonder what's wrong with it?" Tish peered under the hood, but it just looked like car bits.

"Heh," said Tobias, pointing. "Someone removed the engine relay."

Tish looked where he was pointing and saw nothing in particular.

"What does that do?"

"It lets your car start. When I was in Venezuela, I used to take mine out every night so the car wouldn't get stolen. I tried just dis-connecting the battery, but the car thieves had the hood popped and wires back on in no time flat."

"When were you in Venezuela?" asked Tish.

"Uh… you know… that one time. I wasn't there very long."

Someday, I would really like to have his service record.

"Uh-huh. Meanwhile, that sounds like something you would have to know about cars to do," said Tish. "Who would want to disable Skip's car?"

"Don't know," said Tobias with a shrug. "But it's nothing but a hunk of metal without it."

"Hm. OK, well, let's check the house."

They both turned, and Tobias automatically headed for the side path that would take them to the backyard. Tish didn't argue. The blue cottage looked like it had been renovated sometime in the early part of the decade, but the flush of improvements had given over to the island malaise, and now the backyard looked like it was clinging to the garden design through strength of will and lawn mowing. Tish and Tobias both surveyed the area, and Tish homed in on the fountain area while Tobias went directly to the door.

"Found it," said Tish, holding up the fake rock with the spare key.

"Not locked," said Tobias.

"Granddad, are you wearing gloves?" asked Tish, putting the rock down.

"That Pamela woman seemed like the kind who will want to do all things on the check list," he said, holding out a pair of rubber gloves for her.

"Well, now I really do feel like I'm breaking and entering," she said, taking the gloves.

"We're just trespassing," said Tobias dismissively as he opened the door.

Tish and Tobias stepped into the living room, and Tish pushed her sunglasses up on her head, trying to adjust to the dim interior.

"Uh…" said Tish, looking around in dismay.

"I don't think he's getting his rental deposit back," said Tobias.

CHAPTER 10

SKIP'S HOUSE

The sliding door on Skip's rental house opened directly into a dining room area. The kitchen was to the right and the living room was on the other side of the open dining room. The house felt oppressive, like someone should have left a window open to keep the air moving. But nothing moved, including the heavy dusting of feathers and colorful paper that covered every surface. Skip's computer sat on the dining room table. She could see one of the manila folders that Skip usually carried around with him under a dusting of feathers.

"Did he sacrifice a duck or something?" asked Tobias picking up a white feather.

His voice sounded too loud in the hot silence of the house.

"Maybe?"

Tish tapped the space bar on the computer, and it gently whirred to life. A password screen popped up over a wallpaper image.

"Do you think Quincy could crack that?" asked Tobias.

"Even if she can, I don't think we have the time to call her, and I don't think we should steal the computer."

"Ha! You said *she.*"

"Yes, fine," snapped Tish. "I never said changing pronouns was easy. It's a work in progress."

Tobias shrugged, but looked smug.

Oh, my God, you are so competitive. Possibly, that might be the pot calling the kettle black.

"About the pronoun thing though…"

Tobias looked up.

"You know how the adults didn't understand in the movie, but the kids still end up dying for that thing they couldn't name?"

"It's pronouns not drag racing," said Tobias.

Tish wasn't sure how to explain without sounding like a PSA or a drama queen.

"Yeah, well, some of the stats sure make it look like it's drag racing." She avoided eye contact and her eye fell on the papers beneath the feathers. Tish picked up one of the loose sheets of blue paper.

"These are the special effects pages."

"What does that mean?" asked Tobias.

"Blue pages are for the special effects team. Purple," she pointed to the dining room table that was covered in purple sheets, "are for the props crew. Red would be speaking roles. Yellow is non-speaking."

Tobias moved closer to the table and peered at the pages without disturbing them. "He's been drawing on lots of them. Not sure what though. Something with cables." He took out his phone and snapped a few photos. "And... Um. Hm."

Tish took a few hesitant steps into the room but turned back to look at her grandfather, caught by something in his tone.

"What is it?"

"He's printed out your IMDB page," said Tobias.

Tish frowned. "Is that still up? I mean, I'm sure it's still up. But I stopped paying for all the extras. Does it say anything beyond my credits?"

The Internet Movie Data Base allowed for a paid version that gave industry users expanded options. Letting her membership lapse had been the final death knell in her career as an actor and had hurt more than she'd ever admitted to anyone.

"A bio, credited rolls, doesn't look like much to me. I think there's more about you on your wedding website. Which I keep meaning to talk to you about."

"Sarah says I have to be personable. She says people are buying me as much as the venue. I'm high-production value with big city aesthetic in a rural area and that means I can charge top dollar to Microsoft millionaires."

Sarah was Tish's best friend and the marketing professional behind Tish's wedding endeavors. She had also written most of the copy on businesses website.

"I'm sure Sarah's right, but that sounds like a load of utter hogwash. Do those words actually mean anything, or do they just sound good strung together?"

"Possibly both," said Tish. "Sometimes I'm not really sure."

"Mm," said Tobias, snapping another picture of the pages on the table.

Did I just get misdirected?

"Why do you think he has my page printed out? Why bother printing at all?"

"Nothing wrong with printing and I couldn't say. Can you see where all the feathers are coming from?"

Now that was a definite shove off topic.

"I don't know," said Tish, taking another few steps into the living room. If anything, it was even more of a blizzard. There was a wood stove at one end of the room, and on the brick surround, a feather-covered lump attracted attention. Drawing closer, she saw that it was a pillow with a singed round hole in the center.

"Is this a bullet hole?" she asked, frowning down at the wilted object on the floor. She sniffed the air and detected the faint scent of gunpowder like a lingering firework.

"It kind of looks like it," said Tobias. "I don't see a dead body."

"Should there be a dead body?" asked Tish in alarm, looking around as if one might pop out at them.

Weekend at Bernie's. 1989 comedy that gave rise to the classic Roger Ebert line that movies about dead bodies are seldom funny.

All Tish saw were more feathers, pages, and long bit of wire on the floor near the couch.

And yet, it's the second time I've thought about Weekend at Bernie's today. Is the fact that it remains in my consciousness a sign of its quality or its atrocity—like Showgirls?

Showgirls, 1995, an NC-17 box office bomb that saw kids show actress Elizabeth Berkley making the jump to the big screen with a very adult role that was mocked, but has since become a camp standard.

"Why would anyone shoot a pillow?" asked Tish, when no bodies seemed forthcoming.

"Well, if you need to shoot somebody but you don't have a silencer, sometimes people will try to use a pillow." Tobias poked at the pillow with his cane, lifting it up to inspect the other side. "But this looks a little odd." He snapped a picture of the underside.

"Odd, how?" asked Tish as he lowered it back down and snapped a picture of the top.

"Not sure."

"OK, well—"

There was an audible clunk from somewhere in the house. Tish turned to look at Tobias, who raised his eyebrows.

"What do we do?" whispered Tish.

"Investigate," Tobias whispered back. "It's in the job description."

"Ha. Ha. What if it's the someone who shot the pillow?"

"Good point," said Tobias. "And I'm not packing heat today."

Heat, 1995. Dinero and Pacino in the first time they were ever on screen together, despite both having starred in the Godfather Part II.

Tobias tip-toed over to the front door, unlocked it, and opened it. There was another clunk, and this time, Tish could hear that it was from upstairs.

Tobias gestured for Tish to move to the kitchen area and then went over and banged on the stair railing with his cane.

"Hey! Whoever is upstairs, you've got thirty seconds to come down before I call the cops!"

There was a long moment of silence and then the sound of running feet. Someone hurtled down the stairs and out the front door.

"Granddad!" yelped Tish, launching into motion. "He's getting away!"

"Yeah," he agreed as she ran past him. "Don't want to be stuck in here with him."

Tish followed the man out of the house. He was tallish and moving fast. She jogged to the end of Skip's car and stopped. Tobias was right. They didn't know what kind of threat they were dealing with. And Nash would probably throw a major fit if she got injured again.

As she watched, the burglar, or whatever he was, vaulted the neighbor's fence and disappeared into the woods. Tish turned to Tobias, who had made it out to the porch.

"What—" she began but was cut off by the sound of crunching tires and an aggressive motor. One of the Sheriff's vehicles jerked to a stop behind Skip's car.

"Tish," yelled Ronny, rolling down his window. "Was that someone running away?" Ronny Fullbright was about forty-five and had been raised on the island. He'd gone to the mainland for a bit after college but returned about five years ago. He was all right if all right meant a short-armed, uptight, rule follower who somehow seemed to think the world was conspiring against him.

"Yeah," Tish yelled back, peeling off her gloves behind her back and shoving them in her pocket.

"I'm going arrest you," barked Pamela, jumping out of the SUV. "What the hell are you doing?"

"Arrest us for what?" demanded Tobias. "It's not our fault if people break and enter the deceased's residence and then vamoose when we ring the doorbell."

Nice. Way to tell me what our story is.

Pamela glared at Tobias. "You are interfering in an investigation."

"I'm a licensed private investigator acting on behalf of my client. The driveway is a public space."

"Well, it's now part of my investigation! I want you out of here!"

"We thought you were talking to the crew," said Tish. "We were trying to stay out of your way."

"Yeah, that's just what you wanted me to do, wasn't it? Not a chance. Now, you've got about five seconds to vacate the premises before I have you arrested."

"Uh, don't we want to ask them about the guy who was running away?" asked Ronny and then took a step back from Pamela's fierce glare.

"We didn't see anything," said Tobias. "White guy about six feet tall, baseball cap and one of those neck scarf mask things pulled up over his face. Blue jeans and a gray hoodie. Didn't get a look at the shoes."

Ronny pulled out his notebook and took several notes before Pamela stopped him. "We don't trust anything they say."

"Uh," said Ronny. "OK, but that's what I saw too, so…"

Pamela glared some more.

"It's fine," said Ronny nervously, tucking the pen into the spine of the notebook. "I'll just write it down later."

"You know, Ronny," said Tobias, stumping past him, and Tish saw Ronny brace for impact from some scathing comment, "one of the things that I have always appreciated about you is your honesty."

Ronny blinked and then looked at Tish as if for an explanation.

"Honesty is one of his things," said Tish with a shrug.

As is emotional blackmail, because now you will feel compelled to live up to that compliment.

"Good luck," Tish added because she knew it would make Pamela grind her teeth and followed Tobias to the car.

CHAPTER 11

PA-PA-PAPARAZZI

"Well," said Tish, after the silence had gone on for some time. "I don't know about you, but I feel embarrassed."

"Yup," said Tobias.

Tish slowed behind a truck full of hay and, for once, didn't even chafe at the speed. It turned off eventually, and Tish sped up a fraction, but hardly to big city speeds.

"I know she said she knew about us," complained Tish, "but I mean... come on. I can't believe she predicted us. We don't get predicted, Granddad! We are the volatile element of surprise that those who follow law and order do not appreciate. We are the mystery toy at the bottom of a box of cereal! The jack-in-the-box that boings out when you least expect it! And I resent someone guessing what we're up to!"

"We're going to have to step up our game," agreed Tobias. "And I think I'm going to have to do some of my own digging into Pamela Warshaw."

"Yeah, digging her a hole in the ground," muttered Tish, and Tobias snorted.

Tish slowed as she entered Eastsound and then popped up a block to look for parking in Prune Alley.

"We're doing lunch, right?"

"Yeah," said Tobias flipping down the visor and looking in the mirror, "but do a lap around town."

"But there's a parking spot up there."

"But I think there's someone following us."

"Uh... What do I do?" Tish's eyes flicked to the review mirror.

She could see a silver Prius behind her.

"Do a lap around town. See if he sticks with us."

She did as instructed, creeping forward at a slightly faster pace.

"It's Orcas; we don't have that many opportunities to pass. What if it's just someone stuck behind me?"

"If he pulls into that parking spot you're passing up, or turns off once we hit Main, then we'll know."

"Oh, good point," said Tish.

She meandered slowly down the street and then turned and looped back toward the A-1. The 1960s-style building with the distinctive shark-fin rising through the front and into the sky was Tobias's favorite meal spot. The Prius stayed behind them the entire way. Tobias watched in the visor mirror while Tish tried to concentrate on driving.

"OK, I've got another parking spot coming up," said Tish. "Do I take it?"

"Yeah, pop in. Then, when we get out, I'm going to yell real loud that I'm going to talk to Benny."

Tish pulled in and then looked at Tobias, who was watching the Prius park illegally on the other side of the street.

"Who the hell is Benny?" demanded Tish.

"He's the guy you announce you're going to go talk to when you're about to circle the target. You're going to stay here and check your phone or something. I'm going to drop back and then go have a chat while he's focused on you."

"How do we know he's focused on me?"

"I'm old. I stopped being interesting to people after sixty-eight."

"That is a very specific age."

Tobias shrugged. "I calls 'em like I sees 'em. It's periodically annoying, but can also be useful."

"Huh," said Tish. "I think it happens earlier for women."

He glared at her. "Don't start with me."

"I'm not! That was a real thought."

"Yeah, one of those feminist thoughts we don't have time for right now."

"You brought it up!"

Tobias rolled his eyes and opened the car. Tish knew she could get out and go around to help with his cane.

But I'm not going to because now is always the time for feminist thoughts, so suck it.

Instead, Tish checked her reflection in the rearview mirror and reached into her purse for lip gloss. Tobias paused halfway out the door and glared at her over his shoulder.

"Don't mind me," said Tish, smiling. "I'm just over here not noticing you because you're old."

He shook his head and levered himself out of the car. Tish followed more slowly.

"I'm going to go talk to Benny," he yelled, more or less in her general direction, but probably loud enough for the entire street to hear.

Tish waved and then settled onto the hood, pretending to check her phone while taking photos of the Prius. Because of the glare on the windshield, she couldn't get a good look at the driver, but she saw him duck his head when Tobias walked by. He straightened up again after Tobias moved past him, and then Tish saw him lift something boxy closer to the window. Was he taking pictures of her?

Tish practiced patience and tried to look interesting as she saw Tobias had circled back around and was now approaching on the far side of the car. Tish stood up and stretched, hoping that literally waving her arms would keep whoever it was fixated on her. She figured she would wait until Tobias had them cornered and then go over and join in on the interrogation.

Tobias opened the door to the back seat, and quicker than she thought he could manage, he hopped into the Prius. Even across the street, she could hear the yell of surprise and chuckled. She was almost to the Prius when she heard someone calling her name.

"Tish!"

Tish looked around sharply and saw Nora and Claire Nash as they came down the sidewalk. They were carrying Girl Meets Dirt bags, but only Nora was waving. Claire looked grumpy.

"Tish," said Nora, quickening her pace. Tish looked back at the Prius. What if it was someone dangerous? Was it better to keep Claire away or go to help Tobias?

"So glad I caught you," said Nora cheerfully. Tish looked at the petite redhead. As usual, Nora was wearing a rockabilly style, and although she had her hair up in a ponytail, it was still carefully curled in a very fifties look. Tish didn't often think that Claire and Nora looked much alike. Claire was tall for her age, with brown hair like her father, and she also usually had a big grin. Today, Tish was startled by Claire's resemblance to Nora, and she realized it was because the little girl had a discontented expression that mimicked Nora's usual unhappy countenance. Except that today, Nora looked happy and bubbly.

"I really need to talk to you!" she exclaimed, leaning toward Tish conspiratorially over her shopping bag.

"Yeah?" Tish eyed the large bags doubtfully. Girl Meets Dirt was a home goods store with wines, shrubs, and other delicious yummy things, along with a selection of kitchen and pantry tools. She couldn't imagine what Nora could have needed that required two large bags.

"Nash came home and then left like… immediately," said Nora. "And then there was that group text from the makeup team. There is something serious going down. I need to know! Spill the beans! Did Taylor Blake fall off the wagon? Ooh! Ooh! Did Emma Olivier shoot another crew member?"

"Wait, what? Emma shot who?"

"Oh, yeah, with a bow and arrow! Don't you remember? She did that entire ad campaign that was shooting stars—perfume, you know—and she took it very seriously and went and got Geena Davis's archery coach and then some crew member started something and she shot him in the hand."

"Really?" demanded Claire looking surprised. "That's cool."

"No," said Nora, "it nearly cost her the contract, and then that guy sued or something. So?" demanded Nora, turning back to Tish. "What's the big kerfluffle?"

"Uh… Skip, the director…" Tish trailed off, eyeing Claire uncomfortably.

"Mr. Harassment himself. Yeah? What did he do now?"

"Um… maybe I should text you later," said Tish, edging toward the Prius.

"Ugh." Claire rolled her eyes. "She's not going to tell you, Mom. She doesn't want to talk to you. It's fine. Let's just go."

Nora looked down at Claire in surprise.

"I don't think that's what Tish said," said Nora.

"Oh, my God!" yelled an angry male voice. Tish snapped around in time to see the driver of the Prius get out and yank open the back door of his car. "Get out of my car. Get out now, you crazy old coot!"

"Fine," said Tobias, climbing out. "But that's a terrible way to treat the elderly."

Tish could tell in one look that Tobias looked infinitely pleased with himself. Whatever the conversation had been, it had gone well.

"Mom, come on. They're weird. Let's just go home." Claire tugged at Nora's arm.

"Weird?" demanded Tish, feeling hurt.

"We've got to get this stuff home to Dad," said Claire.

"That's for Nash?" asked Tish, her eyes flicking to the bags again.

"He has absolutely nothing," said Nora, with a fake laugh. "It's like he never replaced any of the stuff I took with me."

Because he didn't want to.

"Mom buys stuff for Dad because she cares about our house,"

said Claire.

"Uh," said Nora, looking embarrassed.

And I've been trying to respect his boundaries by not buying stuff.

"What is Tobias doing?" asked Nora, frowning to where Tobias was waving at the Prius driver, who was peeling out of the parking spot in a rush.

"Weird stuff," said Tish. "Because we're weird. And we like it that way. I'll see you both later."

"OK," said Nora. "Just shoot me a text."

"Yeah, whatever. I guess I'll just call Nash's place."

Real mature, Tish. Real mature.

Tish walked over to Tobias, who eyed Nora and Claire's retreating figures.

"What was that about?"

"Claire just called us weird!"

"I thought she enjoyed that about us," said Tobias, looking surprised.

"I did, too! But yesterday, she didn't even set me out a plate for dinner! Ever since Nora's been spending more time on the island, it's like it's *Tish who?*"

Tobias grunted.

"No, not even Tish who. She knows who I am. She just doesn't want to see my face."

"Sorry," he said, patting her arm. "Kids... mean little bastards."

"No! Claire is *not* mean. She's funny and smart and loves me! At least I thought she did." Tish swiped angrily at her eyes which were threatening to leak and Tobias put his arm around her shoulders and gave her a squeeze.

"I'm sorry. Nora's probably being a bad influence."

"That's actually the worst part. Nora's been practically a normal human being! I don't know what's going on." Tish rubbed her face and straightened up. "What'd you get out of Mr. Prius Driver?"

"Ha! He was taking pictures of you, which gave me plenty of

opening, but he didn't want to talk."

"You seem pretty happy for not getting anything out of him."

"Said he didn't want to talk, not that I didn't get anything. Unfortunately, for him, he put his jacket in the backseat." Tobias held up a wallet and opened it. "His wallet fell out of the pocket."

"Granddad! That is theft."

"Nonsense. As soon as I'm done looking at it, we can drive it up to the Sheriff's Department and they can call him up and return it."

"Oh, good point. Barely borrowing at that point. What do we have?"

Tobias flipped it open and scrutinized the license.

"California license. Mr. Neil McKinley. Forty-six." He held it out for Tish to snap a picture. "Credit cards. OK... Boring. Here we go. Business cards. McKinley Media."

Tish typed in the website listed on the business card and waited while it came up on her phone.

"Oh," she said, watching as the rotating carousel of images began to autoplay.

"Those aren't great photos," said Tobias. "I don't get it."

"They aren't great photos, but they are famous people. He's paparazzi. Not sure why he's stalking me though. Any of the actors on this shoot would be way more likely to sell."

"Hm," said Tobias, flipping the wallet closed. "I think we picked him up as we were leaving Skip's place. He's not a match for whoever was searching the house. This guy was too heavy set, no matter what lies his driver's license is peddling."

"So basically, now we have two unknown suspects. We're supposed to narrow down the list! Not expand it."

"Do we even have a list? I thought we were still in the gather information about the deceased phase," said Tobias.

"I just want to skip to the end where we catch the guy," complained Tish.

"One step at a time," said Tobias. "Let's go drop the wallet off.

If we see him again, we should file a complaint for harassment. I'd do it now, but even Ronny isn't going to buy us showing up with his wallet and *then* filing a complaint."

"Ronny's a putz, but he's really not that stupid," agreed Tish. "All right, fine. And then I guess we should go home and see if the hordes have left."

"After lunch," said Tobias. "Never take on hordes on an empty stomach. Twitterfy that."

"Thanks," said Tish, reaching for her phone. "I will."

CHAPTER 12
THE A-1

The next morning dawned bright and sunny, looking like a brochure for the San Juan Islands, but it did nothing to lighten Tish's grumpy mood. She had slept poorly, and despite feeling exhausted, she also felt jittery. After a brief phone call with Alan, in which she assured him repeatedly that the crew was fine and progress had been made, Tobias suggested skipping their breakfast routine and heading into town. Tish accepted based purely on her desire to get up and do something.

They had barely settled into their usual booth at the A-1 in the far corner closest to the front window where they could see the entire room and who was coming down the street, when Matt Jones walked briskly into the restaurant and plopped down next to Tish.

"I was questioned by a Detective Warshaw yesterday evening," he announced without preamble. "Why does spending time with you always end up involving the police?"

"I have never once gotten you arrested," said Tish.

"Which is why I still talk to you, but what the hell? Also, what bug crawled up that woman's..." he glanced across at Tobias as if gauging his audience. Tobias sipped his coffee and waited with a serene smile. "Downspout and died?" he finished.

"She accused Granddad and I of being one with the MAGA hat crowd," said Tish.

"What? Does she not know that the San Juans are over seventy percent blue? We have die-hard hippies, real libertarians, and over-educated goat owners. That shit does not fly around here."

"Heh," snorted Tobias. "And that's why I'm a Republican."

"What?"

"Democracy works best when dissenting viewpoints force compromise," said Tobias.

Matt looked like he was not equipped to respond to that statement.

"Granddad's a contrarian," said Tish.

"Got it," said Matt, nodding at Tish's translation. "Meanwhile, what the hell is this woman's problem?"

"I don't know," said Tish. She was about to add further opinions, but Tobias's phone began to ring in his pocket.

"Be right back," said Tobias, getting out of the booth, staring at his phone.

"Did your grandfather just actually go answer his cell phone?" asked Matt.

"He only pretends not to know how it works," said Tish, leaning tiredly back against the cushion of the booth. "If he's the one placing calls, then cell phones are useful tools. If it's idiots he doesn't want to talk to, then he has no clue how that hunk of junk works."

She closed her eyes and waited for Amber to come take their order.

"You're in my seat," said Nash and Tish's eyes flew open. Nash was looming over the table in jeans and a t-shirt.

How does he manage to loom without even being in uniform?

"It's a free seat," said Matt, taking a sip off coffee and narrowing his eyes at Nash.

"My girl, my seat. You move over."

Matt raised an eyebrow, but moved across to the other side of the table.

"Speaking of Tobias—was he really talking on his cell phone outside or is this some sort of cunning strategy to throw off the alignment of the planets?"

Matt snorted.

"What can I say? He does not allow technology to stand in the way of an investigation," said Tish. "Which is how he mastered printing out email. Because he likes to save it for files."

Both Matt and Nash chuckled.

"I have no idea who he's talking to though," she added.

"OK, we'll grill him when he comes back in. I want to know how Matt's interview with the detective went anyway," said Nash.

Matt made a displeased grunt.

"Detective Warshaw is a very unpleasant woman. And she hates Tish and Tobias."

"I got that impression," said Tish. "I just don't know why."

"What did she ask?" Nash flipped his coffee cup upright and looked around for Amber.

"She wanted to know every last detail about dinner the other night," said Matt. "Like, were we planning to meet? What time did you arrive? What time did you leave? Can anyone verify what time you left? Did you say anything about Skip? I've never had a cop be so uninterested in me. I feel like I ought to be happy about that, but mostly, it felt really weird. And I think you should be worried."

Tish shrugged. "Everyone saw me. I'm not sure what there is to be made out of dinner and watching the dailies."

"I don't know either, but she was pretty intense."

"Hey, everyone!" said Amber. The petite waitress had switched up her bleached curls to black, but her nosering and the tattoo of a fish behind her ear remained the same as always. Amber looked at the three of them and frowned. "Where did Tobias go?"

"Outside to answer his cell phone."

Amber laughed, as she filled Nash's coffee cup. "No, really."

"No, really," said Nash. "I saw him."

"Well, the pigs will be flying next," she said in surprise. "One time, he threatened to stick his phone in my coffee pot if it didn't shut up. Meanwhile, Tish, why is my boyfriend hiding out at my place and saying the cops are after him but not after, after him? Not that I mind. He was vacuuming when I left."

Amber had just turned twenty, but her relationship with Kyle was going on year three. It was practically a marriage by Orcas dating standards.

"At a guess," said Matt, "because they want to question him about his employment by the Yearly Detective Agency."

"Tish! You're supposed to be keeping him out of trouble!"

"I don't know why you would think that," said Nash.

"Well, out of *illegal* kinds of trouble anyway! I want him to move back to the island and stop dealing."

"Well, I want him to go to work for Matt," said Tish, "but Granddad disagrees because he doesn't think Kyle would live on Orcas then, and Granddad knows that's what you want."

"Why do you want him to work for me?" demanded Matt. "And shouldn't I have an opinion?"

"Well, you're doing that whole Uber of pot thing," said Tish.

"I'm not calling it that," said Matt.

"Yeah, but that's what you're doing with secure lock boxes and everything. But I think you could be doing inter-island service, and I don't think you want deliveries going over the ferry, and I'm going to guess that the State also doesn't want that since that opens them to federal liability. But Kyle has a boat and knows a lot about the islands."

"He really does," gasped Amber, looking struck by the idea.

"What's more annoying?" asked Nash. "The fact she and Tobias have a plan for your life or that it's a good plan?"

Matt gave Nash a very disgruntled look.

"We just talk about things sometimes," said Tish. "They aren't plans until one of us actually does something about them. Anyway, tell Kyle that he can talk to the cops. I don't think there's anything to hide. Except for the usual stuff."

Amber rolled her eyes. "Not a chance. He says the pigs can suck it."

"Gee, thanks," said Nash.

"Well, not you. You know, he's always been Team Nash from back when you got arrested."

"I do, actually," said Nash, smiling ruefully.

"But anyway, Kyle says this is his island, and he's not letting some off-islander in a bad hat get the better of him."

"That's the spirit," said Matt. "And hat? I thought it was just a police ball cap?"

"It did not go with the outfit," said Tish. Matt looked like he'd never thought about a police officer's outfit in his life.

"So, does everyone want breakfast?" asked Amber, flipping open her notebook.

"No, I'm out," said Matt. "I just came to talk to Tish and Tobias for a minute. I've got to make the ferry."

"OK," said Amber with a shrug. "Nash, Tish? What can I get you?"

Nothing? If I say nothing, are they going to think I'm weird? I really don't want to eat.

"Um…"

Nash is looking at me. I know I get weird when I'm stressed. Am I being weird?

"Can I just have toast or something?"

Amber gave her a look. The A-1 did not make small meals. It was antithetical to their entire philosophy of existence.

"Why don't you bring me the flapjack combo?" asked Nash. "Tish can have my biscuit and bacon."

"Sure," said Amber. "I'll put in for Tobias's usual?"

"Sounds good," said Tish.

Amber bustled away, and Tish smiled at Nash. "Thanks. I couldn't face the full omelet hashbrown gravy extravaganza."

"Uh-huh," said Matt. "And that's my cue to leave."

"What'd we do?" asked Tish, blinking at him.

"Complimentary eating habits make me uncomfortable," said Matt, cryptically, as he stood up. "Tell Tobias I said bye, since apparently my generation lacks proper farewell etiquette."

"Hashtag Granddad says," murmured Nash.

"Exactly. See you around." Tish waved as Matt headed for the exit.

"I like him, but sometimes I think he's weird," said Tish, and Nash let out an exasperated breath. "What?"

"For thinking he's weird, you sure pop off to dinner with him whenever you like."

"I ran into him at the bar."

"We were supposed to have dinner. Us. Together."

"Yeah, well, there were only three plates."

Nash took a deep, frustrated breath.

"I would have gotten another plate if you had bothered to stick around."

"I don't know why. You had plenty of company, and apparently, Granddad and I are weird."

"What?" Nash looked confused.

Tish shrugged uncomfortably.

"I saw Nora and Claire yesterday. They were picking up stuff for your house because Nora cares about your house, and Claire said Granddad and I were weird."

"Nora said she picked up some things to say thanks for letting her stay," he growled.

"You know, I don't buy you things because I don't think I should decorate your house without asking. It's not because I don't care about your house."

"No one said you didn't care about my house!"

"Claire did!"

"I don't know why she said that!" Nash barked, slapping the table angrily. The slap reverberated louder than he meant it to, and Nash flinched and then looked embarrassed.

"Sorry," he muttered. "I really don't know what's gotten into her lately. You're not the only one that's getting ten-year-old attitude lately."

"It's fine," said Tish, sipping water and looking around the restaurant. The door opened, and Tobias came back into the restaurant. He was bouncing the cell phone in his hand, and although he waved cheerfully at Amber, Tish thought he looked preoccupied.

"What does that face mean?" whispered Nash.

"Not sure," said Tish.

Are we pretending we're not having a thing?

"Amber put in your usual order," said Tish as Tobias went through the process of lowering himself into the booth.

I don't want to bottle things up, but I have no idea what to say. But then, I never know how to address the Nora in the room.

"Oh, good," said Tobias. "I was hoping that was what her wave meant."

"Important phone call?" asked Nash. She knew he was trying to sound innocent, but Tish didn't think he quite made it.

La la la la. No problems here. Pretend, pretend, pretend!

"Dying of curiosity over there?" Tobias asked, skewering Nash with a look.

"A little bit," admitted Nash, nodding as he added cream to his coffee.

What? You can't just admit it. You have to build up…

"You don't usually interrupt breakfast unless it's a matter of international importance," continued Nash, oblivious to the rules of interrogating Tobias. "Now I'm just hoping we've got time to eat before Canada invades."

Tobias snorted and accepted the cream Nash passed his way.

"I put in a call to Pete to find out about this Pamela woman."

"How's the knee rehab going?" asked Tish.

"Not bad. He's recommending the ceramic. He says his inflammation went down twice as fast as his ex-brother-in-law's. Course, he says he also followed my physical therapist's advice on icing and rest."

"Manny really is the best," agreed Tish.

"He helped me a lot after that buckshot incident," said Nash. "Now, if we could just get him to relocate to Orcas."

"He says it's too crowded," said Tish. "I'd be happy if he'd stick with one island. Shaw, Lopez, I don't care, but I can't help move any more goats. Just because a yurt can move doesn't mean it *should* move."

"Says he needs to make it align with his chakras," said Tobias.

"You don't believe in chakras," said Tish sourly.

"Nope. But I don't gotta believe in that hoo-ha for it to be impacting Manny's living situation. Although, if I had to move goats, I'd probably be a lot less live and let live on the topic. Anyway, rehab is going well for Pete, but we had a bit of an odd go-round about Pamela."

"Let me guess, we should trust the detective and let the process work itself out?" asked Nash, blatantly rolling his eyes.

Tobias glanced at Tish, and Tish tried not to grin fiendishly.

That was full sarcasm! We're getting to him. Soon, he will come to the dark side. Whuhahahaha!

"Well, that is about what I expected him to say," admitted Tobias. "But no. Not what I got. Says he's never heard of her, and after a few confusions and conversational missteps, he says that he never left notes on us for anyone. He says writing down what he knows about us is the kind of thing that could get him committed for insanity."

Nash gave a laugh that showed he was not quite on the dark side just yet.

"But she said Spring left her notes," said Tish. "And she knew Nash and I were dating. Did you tell her?" She turned to Nash, and he shook his head.

"I was nearest to Eastsound, so I got pulled in to pick her up from the ferry from San Juan. She said barely two words to me after I introduced myself. And when we pulled up, she told me to stay put.

Seemed pretty rude to me. Even Spring at his grumpiest, never told me to babysit the car."

"Now that I'm thinking on it," said Tobias, "I don't think she said Pete left notes. She said she had notes, and we assumed."

"OK, but who else would have notes? I mean, saying notes is pretty specific. That's not: *I've heard of you.* That's not: *I've checked on you.* That's: *someone has given me information.*"

"And apparently, it's someone who doesn't like us," said Nash.

"Exactly," agreed Tish.

Aw, he said us. We're having a thing, and he still said us.

"Agreed," said Tobias.

"But it's someone who can't know us that well," said Tish. "Not if they think Granddad is anti the LGBTQ plus community."

"But well enough to predict our movements?" asked Tobias thoughtfully. "That is a bit odd."

"OK, this is going to sound out there, but someone saw her ID, right? She's not just some yahoo impersonating a detective?" Tish looked around the table.

"I saw her ID," said Nash. "She flashed it at me. And she's been communicating through the official channels at work to arrange for Oliver to be her driver. Impersonating a detective is probably technically possible but highly improbable."

"But I thank you for taking the idea seriously," said Tish.

Nash shrugged. "It does not pay to dismiss the out-there ideas. This is Orcas, after all. Last time I did that, Mrs. Perella's claim that miniature horses were performing Satanic rituals in her back pasture turned out to be true, and I looked like a total idiot."

"I remember that," said Tobias nodding. "Those horses were amazingly well-trained!"

"Were they really doing Satanic rituals, though?" asked Tish in disbelief.

"Their owner was training them for a circus act and was also a Satanist, so yes."

"Huh," said Tish. "I wouldn't have thought you could get them to make the chalk marks."

"It was very impressive," said Nash. "But it doesn't answer the question of why Detective Warshaw doesn't like you."

"Well, Pete doesn't know who she is and says she must be new to the department," said Tobias.

"Agreed," said Nash. He stared off into space for a bit, his fingers drumming on the table. "I think I'll make a few phone calls after breakfast."

Tobias looked at Tish again, and this time, she did allow herself a smile. In spite of all the *things,* Nash was becoming Team Yearly whether he meant to or not.

CHAPTER 13
RETRO BETTY

"So what's the plan?" asked Nash when they were all outside on the sidewalk. "It's my day off, and Claire is with Nora, so I figured I'd assist with the investigation."

Tish glared at him. They'd already had this argument. He smiled back at her sweetly.

"Great!" exclaimed Tobias, and Tish swiveled to stare at him in disbelief. "I was going to call you because I got this idea I want to look into, and Tish needs to go talk to Skip's neighbors and find out who stole his engine relay."

"Do we think his neighbors will know?" asked Nash.

"They'll know something," said Tobias. "And at this point, I'm not sure Pamela's smart enough to do that herself."

A car slowed down on the street and the driver waved at Tobias. Tobias waved genially back. Tish couldn't tell who it was, but that didn't mean much. Tobias knew practically everyone on the island.

"And there is the question of the moped," said Tish. "Emma saw Skip riding one, and there was one parked up at the tower. Skip didn't pull that out of nowhere. One of the neighbors may recognize it from the description."

"You know, that is exactly the kind of thing that the deputies should be assisting with," said Nash, sounding annoyed. "And as far as I know, Pamela hasn't asked any of us, and certainly not me, to assist."

"Exactly my point," said Tobias.

"Sounds like a rookie mistake to me," said Tish, trying to reconstruct Pamela's character from the limited facts they had. "Like she wants to solve everything herself."

"Could be," said Tobias. "But the end result is the same as stupid."

"Ouch," said Nash, looking amused.

"It's not personal," said Tobias with a shrug.

"OK," said Tish. "I will go talk to the neighbors. You two go do… whatever cockamamie plan Granddad has dreamed up."

That I don't want to know about. I don't want to know about any of this, really. Why can't I just go back to making sure my grass is vacuumed for the next wedding?

"Sounds good," said Tobias, nodding. "Where you parked, Nash?"

"In the pharmacy parking lot," said Nash, pointing toward the tiny collection of shops down the block.

"Great. Then, come on. We need to go see what kind of guns Brixton has."

I'm not going to rise to that bait. I'm not even going to ask.

Tish looked up at Nash as Tobias headed for Nash's truck. He looked absolutely gleeful.

"I get to go look at the guns of Brixton," he said with a beaming grin.

"What?"

"It's the Clash. 1979. Guns of Brixton?" He raised an eyebrow. "You have no idea what I'm talking about."

"Yeah, I got nothing."

"A million movie lines and facts at your command, and you can't remember a seminal work of British punk."

"I feel like your parents listened to very different music than mine growing up. But if you want to put the record on the hi-fi, we can pretend you're educating me while we make out."

"The hi-fi?" Nash snorted out a laugh. "And I don't think I know how to make out to the Clash. I'm not sure it's possible." He looked like he was trying to figure it out.

"Nash, you coming?" yelled Tobias from up the street.

"Can't I go with you?" Nash complained.

"Sorry, but that would probably look like you were interfering in Pamela's investigation," said Tish.

Nash made his annoyance and agreement known in one manly grunt.

"I don't think it'll take too long. Maybe you can play me some music later this afternoon."

"You mean if one of our annoying family members doesn't interrupt?"

"Yes, that *is* what I meant," said Tish, going on tip-toe to kiss him goodbye.

It wasn't until she was back in her car that she remembered that she and Nash were still in an argument. They hadn't resolved the Nora-Claire problem, but they had successfully managed to pretend it didn't exist long enough to get onto the next issue.

I wonder if this is what happens to married people. They stack up enough never finished arguments that sooner or later, they fall over like a dirty dish pile, and then there's a divorce.

The journey out to Crow Valley Road was faster than when she had driven with Tobias. There was no one to comment on her driving or to distract her from her thoughts.

Tish finally stopped at Skip's rental house and surveyed the landscape for what Tobias considered neighbors. The problem was that Orcas was inhabited by people who didn't particularly want people peering over the fences. In fact, most of the time, they bought enough land that fences only had to be tall enough to keep the livestock in, not keep the neighbors out. Skip's rental house was past the winery and clustered near only two other homes. Near being a relative term. She could see two garages, which meant there were at least two houses and eight sheds nearby and probably a barn that might or might not still be functional.

Tish had barely opened the car door when her phone rang. Tish eyed it nervously. These days, the phone never seemed to bring good news. The urge to hide her phone under the sweatshirt in the passenger seat, slam the door, and run far away was nearly overwhelming.

"I'm an adult," she said out loud. "I answer the phone because talking on the phone is something adults do and aren't scared of."

I'm not an adult. I don't know who is buying this, but it isn't me.

Tish peeked at the phone and was relieved to see that it was Brianna. And then was instantly nervous for a whole different reason.

"Hey, Brianna," said Tish, picking up.

"Oh, hello, Tish. I was just preparing to leave a voicemail. I haven't caught you at a bad time, have I?"

"I was driving," said Tish.

Driving adjacent. Whatever.

"But I'm parked now."

"So responsible," said Brianna with a soft laugh. "You're such a good girl. I suppose I shouldn't say that. I know you're all grown-up professionals and doing wonderfully at your jobs, but I do feel a bit… Oh, I don't know… motherly toward all of you."

Tish laughed. "Well, most of us can do with some extra mothering, so feel free."

I guess. I never really got the motherly vibe from her, but I probably shouldn't mock her feelings.

"Yes, a lot of people could, I suppose," Brianna said. "Too bad I haven't always been the best at providing it." Tish was caught by the bitter undertone in Brianna's voice and wondered where the actress was going with the call. "I'm sorry. I'm getting off track. I wanted to say that I've just had a police detective over here. She was a strange woman with a terrible haircut. Although, at least I convinced her to take off the hat."

Well, that explains the hat.

"But she asked some very odd questions about you and Tobias, and I'm not sure I made things any better."

"Yeah, she's talking to everyone," said Tish, with a sigh. "Although, not the everyone I wish she would talk to."

"What do you mean?"

"She seems to be worrying about what Granddad and I were doing. When what she should be asking is what Skip was doing and who he had managed to piss off this time."

"Skip always pissed everyone off," said Brianna with a laugh. "I'm not sure there's anything to be discovered there."

"Yeah, but he had to have done something extra," said Tish. "Something that made someone act now. And what the heck was he doing up at the tower? Did the killer go with him? Or did they follow him?"

"Reasonable questions, but I'm not sure how you're going to find out any of the answers," said Brianna.

"Meh. We'll get there eventually. And if the police detective doesn't remember how to detect, we'll have to poke her into pulling Skip's phone records."

Brianna laughed. "You seem really confident."

"Well, I have to admit that I really do not know why he was up at the mountain and how he got up there."

"Does it really matter? What if someone just followed him up there and pushed him over the edge?"

"No pre-meditation? Maybe. But there still had to be a motive. But don't worry about it. Granddad and I can usually figure stuff out. And then we'll get the movie back on track and probably get someone who will actually direct."

"Doesn't seem like it should be that hard to get someone better, does it?" asked Brianna, and for once, there was a hint of sarcasm in her voice.

Ha! I knew you didn't like him.

"Not really," said Tish. "But do you have any ideas about who was really mad at Skip?"

"Oh, gosh, I wouldn't know," said Brianna. "I hadn't met Skip before this movie."

"Oh. You said he was temperamental, so I thought you knew him."

"Only by reputation," said Brianna. "Well, I think I've probably taken up enough of your time. I just wanted to tell you about the detective."

"Thanks," said Tish. "Hey, if I can get this wrapped up in a day or two, you're still in, right? On the movie, I mean."

"Of course! But I do actually have an offer for a stage production, so if things drag on for more than a week, then I'll probably have to reevaluate."

"A week," Tish repeated.

Like I didn't have enough of a time crunch.

"Yeah, don't worry about it. Granddad and I will totally wrap this up by then."

"I'm not worried at all," said Brianna. "Tobias seems very capable."

"Mm," said Tish.

Do I say something about Eleanor?

But before she could make up her mind, Brianna was saying goodbye. Tish hung up the phone and set off up the slight hill toward Skip's nearest neighbor. She approached the brown 1980s rambler cautiously and knocked on the door. After a few moments, she heard movement from inside, and the door opened. If the house was in the 1980s, the resident was a 1950s housewife in full hair curlers and house dress, but with a fully made-up face with strongly arched eyebrows and red lips. The neck tattoo made for an interesting contrast, but Tish wasn't planning on commenting.

"Hi," said Tish, realizing that as the visitor, it was her job to speak first. She also realized that she should have come up with an opening statement. "My name's Tish Yearly."

"Whatever you're selling, I don't want it, and I'm in the middle of making a video."

"Instagram makeup tutorial?" Tish guessed.

"Vintage products for historically accurate results."

"Cool. I will follow you if you answer some questions about your neighbor."

"Yeah, all right," said the woman, leaning against the door frame. "At Retro Betty on Insta."

Tish whipped out her phone and hit follow. "OK, so have you met Skip Renfeld? The guy that was renting down the road?"

"I don't know what that douche canoe's name was, but yeah, I met him," said Retro Betty. "He came over, yelled at my kid, and then tried to suggest that he could help me with my career."

"You have a hundred and fifteen thousand followers," said Tish, glancing back at her phone for confirmation. "How was he planning on helping you?"

"By having sex with me. That's always super helpful, didn't you know?"

"Ah," said Tish, nodding. "Right. Sorry. I started living on Orcas and dating a guy who respects me, and I forgot."

Betty laughed. "Funny how that happens. Anyway, I told him to drop dead, and he told me I was ugly and fat."

"That sounds like Skip. What did he yell at your kid for?"

"Cooper is in a punk band. He calls it something else, but there's eyeliner, plaid, and they sound like shit, so I'm pretty sure they're punk."

"I miss the old days when there was rock, classic rock, hip-hop, R&B, and whatever Bjork was doing," said Tish.

"Well, don't forget the old people genres," agreed Betty. "Blues and Jazz."

"I think I'm old now. I've started liking jazz."

"It happens. One day, you think you're cool, and the next thing you know, you're telling your kid to go play in the shed because his band sounds like someone is murdering cats at top volume. That's what Skip came over to complain about. Apparently, the shed they practice in is on a direct auditory path to his backyard. I told them to turn it up to eleven."

Spinal Tap, 1984. A mockumentary of England's loudest rock band.

"Nice. So... I hesitate to ask, but I don't suppose the police have been by here?"

"Why? Did he call them? He said he was going to. I didn't believe him. Pretty sure he's the one who slashed two of my tires, though."

"Vindictive and inconvenient, that also sounds like Skip. What about last night? It looks like his engine relay was stolen. I don't suppose you or your little punk know anything about that?"

"Are you with the cops?" asked Betty, raising an eyebrow even higher than it was painted on.

"No, I'm a private investigator," said Tish.

It says Yearly Investigations on the business card, and I am a Yearly.

"Oh! You must be Tobias Yearly's grandkid!"

"Uh, yes," said Tish.

"Cool! He gave me four vintage Max Factor lipsticks he found in his attic. Unopened!"

"He hates throwing things away," said Tish.

"Fine by me. Those were worth money, and I did like twelve different videos with them. He said Reginald told him I collected, so he just showed up and gave them to me one day. Such a sweet guy! We sure miss Reginald."

"Yeah, Granddad does too. Hey, I've turned his place into a wedding venue. Are you doing outside makeup? Can I add you to my vendor list for brides who want that retro look?"

"Yeah, absolutely," she said with a shrug. "Can't hurt."

"Cool. But getting back to the real reason I'm here. Skip's engine relay..."

"I didn't take it. Mostly because I didn't think of it. My dad runs a garage on the mainland, and Cooper works for him in the summers sometimes. So Cooper probably could have stolen it, but he's not going to tell me about it. How much trouble is he in if he did? Is Skip freaking out? Hiring private investigators seems a bit much."

"Skip didn't hire us. I would not work for that guy."

"Oh, good. I kind of liked you, and I was seriously questioning your judgment."

"No, we're trying to nail down Skip's movements last night. It seems like someone stole his engine relay, and then he got a moped from somewhere."

"He stole a moped? Jeez, that guy really is a jackass."

"We don't know if he stole it or not, but maybe if you talk to Cooper, you could ask him about it?" Tish held out a business card. "He won't get in trouble from us. Although, FYI, the cops may eventually come around and ask."

"Seriously, what did Skip do?" Betty asked, taking the card

"Um… you have a worldwide platform, so I would prefer not to answer that."

Betty's ruby red fingernail tapped against the card.

"Can I do a story time when whatever it is, is all over?"

The ubiquitous video phrase meant that Betty would be sharing the story, probably while doing a GRWM—Get Ready With Me—video of her putting on makeup.

"Yeah, sure," said Tish, with a shrug.

"OK, I pinkie swear I won't tell whatever it is early. What do ya got?"

"Skip's dead. Someone pushed him off the tower up at Mt. Constitution."

"Huh. Well. Yeah, that'll be a good video. Shoot me a DM when it's done, and we'll do coffee, and I'll figure out what I'm saying."

"Sounds good. Hit me up if Cooper knows anything about the moped."

"Got it. Fist bump!"

Tish looked at the extended fist and then tentatively bumped it.

"Sorry. A teenage boy lives here."

Tish grinned. "See you!"

CHAPTER 14

STORY TIME

Tish was buckling her seat belt and wondering if she should try the other neighbor when her phone rang again. Tish looked at the number and groaned. It had a California area code, and her phone didn't recognize it. The odds were high that it was someone from the production company wanting a report.

Which I don't have.

Tish's finger hovered for a moment and then hit decline.

I already adulted once today with Brianna. I'm not doing it again.

Taking a deep breath, she started the car but jumped in her seat as the phone began to ring again.

Oh, don't think I won't decline you twice.

Tish snatched the phone out of her back pocket, preparing to block, decline, or just plain throw it out the window.

"Oh."

She hit accept and put the phone to her ear.

"Hey, Mom."

"Tish, have you been pissing people off again?"

"What kind of question is that?"

"Well, you do that a lot, so it's reasonable. I swear you've gotten worse since moving in with Tobias. You know, your father used to say he was a natural-born troublemaker."

"Sounds accurate," said Tish with a shrug.

"Yes, but you're not supposed to start taking after him now," complained her mother.

Pretty sure I started taking after him at birth, but you just now noticed.

"I think it shows personal growth," said a male voice from her mother's side of the phone call.

"You think Tish becoming more of a troublemaker shows personal growth? What is wrong with you?"

"Well, I aspire to be a troublemaker when I'm old," said Doug sounding like he'd moved closer. "So I appreciate that Tish isn't waiting."

Doug was in banking and had all the stability that her mother liked on paper and a goof-ball sense of humor that Gail enjoyed in person. Tish had been less than enthralled with Doug when she'd first heard of his existence, but he was growing on her. Particularly since he helped her mother enforce boundaries with her annoying sisters, who always seemed to think Gail would continue to clean up their messes for the entirety of their lives.

Tish chuckled. "Thanks, Doug!" she bellowed into the phone and heard her mother make an exasperated noise. "And personally," Tish added, "I feel that if there's something worth doing, then there is no time like the present."

"You can't just mash fortune cookies together and have it come out right," said Gail.

"I'll write that one down," said Tish.

"Do not Twitter that. Don't think I don't know about Words from Granddad."

"Everyone knows about it, Mom. It's a public platform."

"Tish, what I called to ask is if you'd been bothering your Aunt Dorothy again?"

"Again? I haven't bothered her for the first time, yet."

"Yes, you did. The thing with your cousin."

"Sean stole from me, got me evicted, tried to assault Granddad, and then dropped his coke on the ground in front of the cops. If that's me bothering Aunt Dorothy, then you should probably call Sean and ask what *he's* been up to lately."

Gail let out a gusty sigh. "Still into drugs. I know it's hurting Dorothy. She signed up for some support group, but she's been so weird lately. She cut her hair short. It looks really cute, but you know she was always soooo…" Gail trailed off as if looking for words. "I don't know… into appearances, I guess. She always had to have her hair and dress just right. But I saw her the other day, and I almost didn't recognize her. She was wearing jeans. On a Sunday."

Aunt Dorothy had always gone to church a lot. Tish tried to forgive her for it, but in general, Tish thought it was one of Dorothy's problems. It made her judgmental.

"Jeans on a Sunday? The world may end."

"Well, to tell the truth, I'm a little worried about the apocalypse being nigh because she was with some sort of volunteer group that was painting over graffiti."

"No way!" exclaimed Tish. "You are making that up."

"I'm not! Anyway, I tried to say hi, and she sniped at me and said this bizarre thing about how she hoped you and Tobias *didn't* get what you deserved? Or something? It was muddled and didn't make much sense. And then she went all red and ditched out just like she did in middle school when I caught her making out with her friends."

Tish burst out laughing. "Mom!"

"What?"

"You can't just wrap up a story with a second story, particularly not one that involves Aunt Dorothy making out because you know that woman never made out with anyone."

"No, she's made out with lots of people. She really did use to practice kissing with all her girlfriends in Middle School. And I know for a fact that she made out with at least four people at a dorm party in college one night."

"She went to Biola."

"Yeah?"

"The Bible College."

"Yeah, I've never understood that one. She seemed really stuck on it and kept saying it was the best place for her. I always thought it was unfortunate that she didn't break up with Todd after college."

"I always thought it was unfortunate she didn't break up with her church after the divorce," said Tish. "Those people were mean."

"They really were, weren't they? I kept trying to take her to my church, but she said we were lax."

"You mean, you actually enjoy each other's company and like to spread joy with toy drives and volunteering with Habitat for Humanity?"

"I think it was because we had a female pastor and singing, but it might have been those other things, too. That, and she said that because we had a Mahjong night on Tuesdays, we were endorsing gambling and leading people down the path to sin. Honestly though, that's one of our best community outreach activities. Everyone loves Mahjong night. But anyway, are you sure you haven't been bothering Sean or Dorothy?"

"Mom, I haven't talked to Dorothy in months. Not since your birthday party, and all I did was say hello. And I haven't seen Sean since he got arrested here on the island. So... I don't know what she's talking about."

"Hmm. Weird. Well... OK. Maybe I'll try to call her and say I liked her hair."

"Text her and say you liked her hair," said Tish. "That way, she can't read into it."

"Oh, no," said Gail, laughing. "If I text, she will *definitely* read into it. But anyway, what are you up to?"

"Oh," said Tish, hesitating. "You know…"

"Murder investigation and trying to figure out dinner?"

"Uh… yeah."

"Just go with chicken thighs," said Gail. "Slather them in some honey mustard dressing and some spices, and cook for thirty-five minutes at three-fifty. Then, put some rice in the rice cooker and get one of those ready-made salads from the grocery store. Done."

"Thanks, Mom," said Tish, without any intention of doing any of that.

"OK, Doug is making wrap-it-up motions. We've got tickets to the Fifth Ave – we're going to see Clue!"

"Flames… Flames on the side of my face," quoted Tish.

"I'm sure I will find that hilarious when I see it on the stage."

"Just remember it was one that got the chandelier," said Tish.

"Uh-huh," said Gail, who was clearly refusing to rise to Tish's movie quote nonsequiturs. "Anyway, love you, baby."

"Love you too, Mom," said Tish as the line went dead.

Tish stared at the phone, shaking her head. Tish was never quite sure if she felt supported by her mother or just confused. Moments later, she saw that her phone was transcribing a voicemail. After a moment, the message popped up as text.

SKIPPER INFIELD WAS BLACK. MALE HEIR. HE HAD DIRECT ON EVERY ONE. THAT'S HOW HE GOT ALL HIS JOBS. YOU WANT SNOW KILLED, HIM FIND OUT WHO. HE WAS BLACKMAILING THIS TIME.

Tish stared in consternation at the nonsensical words.

Damn it, I'm going to have to actually listen to the message.

Reluctantly, Tish put the phone back to her ear and listened.

And now I'm going to have to go find Granddad.

Tish pulled up at Nash's house and got out, cautiously looking around for Nora and Claire, but didn't see anyone. She was about to go up to the house when she heard the distinct sound of gunfire from the back of the house.

If he's killed my boyfriend, I'm going to be really annoyed.

Tish headed around the outside of the house and picked up the muted sound of Nash and Tobias talking.

"One more, I guess," said Nash. "I'm set."

There was a loud bang, and despite halfway expecting it, Tish still jumped. Then she shook her head and went to find out what trouble they were up to.

"Well," said Tobias, "that's that."

"That is what, Granddad?" demanded Tish, coming around the corner. "What *are* you two doing?"

"Shooting pillows," said Nash, bending over to photograph Tobias's latest victim. An array of previously discarded cushions littered the ground, cloth and stuffing exploding everywhere.

"What is this? The antimacassar massacre?"

Tobias let out a bellow of laughter.

"What's an antimacassar?" asked Nash, looking up, perplexed.

"It's that little doily people put on the back of chairs," said Tobias.

"I thought they were just doilies. They have a name?"

"Yes," said Tobias. "Antimacassar. They were used to protect the furniture from when men used to put Macassar Oil in their hair."

"I was in a play where I had to use it in some dialogue," said Tish. "But first, I had to look it up. I know it's not really a cushion. But it was the only furniture joke I could come up with in a hurry."

"I laughed," said Tobias, with a shrug.

"Why are we shooting pillows?" asked Tish.

"We're trying to figure out what was wrong with the pillow in Skip's house," said Nash. "And where Skip's gun went."

"It hasn't gone anywhere," said Tobias. "There was no gun."

"But there was the pillow with the hole," said Tish. "It smelled like gunpowder."

"Yeah, but other things use gunpowder to make explosions, and that's what Skip was testing."

"Look at all the pillows," said Nash, gesturing to their graveyard. "If we use the theory that he was trying to muffle the sound of the gun, then we get this." He gestured to a segmented group of multi-hued pads. "Burn marks on one side with a more explosive exit wound on the back."

Tish frowned. "OK," she said, scratching his head. "But the pillow at the house didn't have that. It was like it had exit wounds on both sides."

"Exactly," said Nash, grinning.

I love it when he gets excited about stuff.

"But what does that mean? Was it shot from further away? Why would you shoot a pillow? And wouldn't there be a hole in the wall?"

"Yes," said Tobias. "There would be a hole in the wall. We tested with a variety of small-caliber firearms, and there is no way there isn't a hole in the wall. Also, no matter what we do, there is a distinct entry and exit wound. Which is why I'm saying there was no gun."

"Which, to be honest," said Nash, "was his theory all along, but now we've confirmed it."

"So, what was it?" demanded Tish. "What makes a bullet hole with no bullet?"

"Special effects," said Tobias. "He was looking at all the prop pages, and he was testing a squib to see how much explosion he'd get. My guess is that he got more than he planned on and then had feathers everywhere."

"OK, but I guess that would make the question why? Why was he doing any of that?"

"I'm not quite sure yet," said Tobias.

"Meaning that you have a theory, but you don't want to tell what it is yet?" asked Tish, raising an eyebrow.

"Exactly," said Tobias, cheerfully. "What did you get at the neighbors?"

"Stuff, but I only talked to one neighbor because I got a voice-mail on my phone that I think you need to hear."

She put dialed up voicemail and put it on speaker. After she bopped through the menu, she hit the most recent saved message. The voice, when it crackled across the line, was clearly being intentionally distorted.

"Skip Renfeld was a blackmailer. He had dirt on everyone. That's how he got all his jobs. You want to know who killed him, find out who he was blackmailing this time."

CHAPTER 15

THE RIGGING

"OK," said Nash. "Well, we're going to have to call Detective Warshaw."

"Not a chance," said Tobias. "What we need to do is call someone on the blue page team."

"This is a vital piece of information," said Nash.

"Yes!" agreed Tobias cheerfully.

"It speaks to motive."

"It really does!" agreed Tobias again.

"So we need to tell the Detective."

"Hard nope," said Tobias.

Nash opened his mouth and closed it again and then looked at Tish. "How am I winning and yet also losing?"

Tish chuckled. "You agree on facts but are drawing different conclusions about what they mean. And for the record, I also think we should tell the detective."

"What?" gasped Tobias. "How can my own flesh and blood betray me like this?"

"Well, because sooner or later, we're going to want her to arrest someone, and if we don't bring her along, at least a little bit, she won't believe us when we tell her who did it."

"Exactly," said Nash, looking happy about her support.

"Although, I'm not sure I'm advocating for telling her right this second," said Tish. "We could wait."

Tobias grinned, while Nash glared at her.

"Meanwhile, why the special effects crew?"

"I have a theory about what the pillows mean," said Tobias.

"And that voicemail only makes me more certain of it, but I want to talk to one of them that was supposed to be working on the tower to know for sure."

"OK," said Tish, taking out her phone and dashing off a few texts. While she was typing, Nash's phone beeped, momentarily preventing further argument.

"I feel like I should be typing something," said Tobias.

"Your thumbs aren't up to it," said Tish.

"She is a rookie," said Nash.

"What?"

"Detective Warshaw. Just got promoted. She's normally with SPD, but she's covering for Spring while he's recovering. So your theory that she was a rookie is correct."

"Look at me, being right," said Tish proudly.

"Never doubted it," said Tobias. "But we're still not telling her."

"Yes," said Nash.

"No," said Tish.

"Tish!" exclaimed Nash.

"What? It's going to be a lot more compelling for the detective if we can give her something besides a voicemail. And I don't care if she is new. She's been kind of a wench."

"Well, yes, but now I'm aware of material evidence," said Nash.

"And that's why I didn't want you to help investigate," said Tish. "I know you don't like being in moral quandaries. I'm trying to keep you quandary-free."

"I'm dating you. You're a walking quandary."

"We've said quandary too many times," said Tish. "Now it feels weird."

"It was weird to start out with," said Tobias. "Q words always are. Look, Nash, it's not hiding material evidence. It's delaying delivery. You can tell her when you go back to work. She said she didn't want you on the case. Well, there you go. Just follow instructions and keep out of it."

"Malicious compliance," said Nash, appearing to think it over. "Yeah, I can do that, but you have to swear that you're telling her."

"Swear it," said Tobias. And Tish nodded just as her phone beeped.

"OK," she said, looking at the message. "Looks like Thiago, the effects guy, is drinking out at Olga. You want to maliciously comply with us, or are Granddad and I on our own?"

Nash was about to reply when his phone beeped again from his shirt pocket. He took it out and sighed at the message.

"Nora has some sort of... I don't know. Yeah, I guess you'd better go on your own."

"OK," said Tish, keeping her face and voice carefully neutral. "I'll talk to you later."

"Yeah, love you."

"Love you," said Tish, kissing him on the cheek and heading for the car.

They were on the way to Olga when Tobias spoke.

"Not trying to tell you your business, but why are you letting Nora waltz around Nash's place like she's queen of the castle?"

"I'm not."

There was strong side-eye.

"Nash and Nora have been working on better co-parenting, so I thought it would help if I got her a job as an extra on the movie. She was supposed to be in the tower scene, and now it's like she's everywhere."

"Uh-huh."

"Kind of seems like she's at Nash's a lot."

"And he doesn't tell her to leave!"

"So tell him to give her the boot."

"How am I supposed to do that when Claire is obviously super pissed at me! If I get mad at Nora, I'm afraid it will get worse."

"Mm," said Tobias. Which could have meant that he had opinions but was keeping them inside, or it could just mean mm.

The Olga bar, like a lot of island locales, was an older building converted to a new purpose. The interior glowed with an amber hue as sunlight bounced off the wooden planks of the walls and booths. Thiago, the dark-haired Latino special effects master with a lot of tattoos, was in a back corner with a line of beer bottles in front of him. He hadn't talked a lot on set, but Tish had read through his resume. He'd seemed competent.

"Hey, Tish," he said, looking up.

"Hey," she said, sliding into the booth opposite him. "This is my grandfather, Tobias."

"Nice to meet you," Thiago said, although Tish thought he didn't sound particularly pleased.

"Granddad is a private investigator," said Tish, aiming for honesty. "He's been retained by the company to look into Skip's death."

"Why?" asked Thiago sourly. "Everyone's better off without him."

"Yes," agreed Tobias. "I think the concern is marketing and insurance at this point."

"All hail the mighty insurance," said Thiago, raising his bottle. He nearly knocked down the line of empties, and Tish reached out and caught the teetering bottle before it took out the others, bowling pin-style.

"So it appears that Skip was attempting to manipulate some of the special effects," said Tobias, taking out his phone. "I was hoping you could clarify what he was attempting to do."

He held out his phone, and Tish saw it was showing the photos of the drawings from Skip's house.

"Son of a bitch," swore Thiago. "I told him not to pull that stunt again!"

"What stunt?" asked Tobias. "Because it looks like he's trying to cause a rigging failure to me."

"I told him I wasn't helping him again," barked Thiago. "Someone was going to get seriously hurt if that climbing rig failed. I said

I was out, but he said he would tell…"

"He would tell someone about what you did?" asked Tobias, and even though she knew he was guessing, Tish was still impressed.

"I didn't do anything," said Thiago, his finger stabbing into the table emphatically. "It was a mechanical failure. But he said if I didn't help him with all his little projects, he'd tell everyone it was my fault. He said he had evidence. Kept waving some folder around with my name on it. Never actually saw what he had, though."

"OK, but who was he trying to tie up with this little stunt?" asked Tobias.

Thiago glanced at Tish, took a final swallow of his beer, and thumped it back down on the table.

"I wouldn't know. I don't know anything. All I know is that Taylor and Tish have been real pains in the ass lately. Skip wasn't happy with either of you. After that… I don't have anything to do with anything. And frankly," he glared at Tish, "if you were smart, you wouldn't bother looking any closer than that. Brianna said the studio doesn't want whatever Skip knew to come out, and she's absolutely right. You should remember that if you want to have a career."

Without warning, he stood up and stalked off.

"Well," said Tobias, and Tish sighed.

"Mom's right. I do make people mad."

"You're not really worried about ticking off that guy, are you?" asked Tobias with a frown. "And since you're a producer, shouldn't he have been more worried about annoying you?"

"From what I hear," said a stern voice, "everyone should be worried about upsetting Tish."

Tish looked up to see Detective Warshaw coming toward them down the row of booths.

Didn't sit on the wall side, and this is what we get — ambushed by the police.

Her hat was gone, and now Tish could see that she was rocking a really awkward set of short bangs. Too short to be real bangs and too long to be the super-clipped alternative fringe. She had attempted to style them up and spiky, but the heat was causing them to wilt downward.

Don't make eye contact with it. She'll know you're looking. No one wants bad hair pointed out.

"Sorry, what?" asked Tish, looking determinedly into the detective's face.

"Bad things happen when people piss you off, don't they?"

"Um…" Tish found she had no response for that.

The detective sat down opposite them and glared with an intense ferocity.

"What?" asked Tobias, summing up Tish's feelings on the question.

"Well, Steve Winslow… he pissed you off, and now he's dead."

"He killed Reginald and tried to kill me. After kidnapping me!"

"So you say!"

"So everyone says," said Tobias.

"Then there's Craig Larson."

"Who?"

"Mars," supplied Tobias.

"Oh, right." Tish tried *not* to picture his face and almost succeeded. "Um… what about Mars?"

"He's dead."

"Yeah, I'm aware. He killed Tyler and Sunshine. I'm not really sure what you're getting at."

"Seems like everywhere I go, I hear about how Tobias and Tish take care of problems, but it's not really taking care of a problem if you just go around killing people."

"I haven't killed anyone!"

"You're responsible for their deaths."

"OK, we're done here," said Tobias, deliberately knocking over the line of beer bottles, and sending a small wave of backwash toward the detective. She jumped up with a gasp as Tish and Tobias exited the booth.

"Where were you after you left the Orcas Hotel with Matt Jones?" the detective demanded.

"I… I went home," stuttered Tish.

"Don't answer her questions, Tish," said Tobias, putting his hand on her back and pushing her toward the door. "She ain't dealing with a full deck."

"Skip Renfeld was ruining your movie," said the detective, following them. "Luke Green, the writer, said you brought the production here, so there was a lot riding on getting this right, financially and personally."

"And he said he wished the movie would fold so his story would get ruined, but he'd get to keep the option money," snapped Tish, glaring over her shoulder, even though Tobias kept pushing her.

"Your movements are unaccounted for after dinner. That matches the estimated time of death. How do you explain that?"

"Explain what? I went home and went to bed!"

"You know this island. You knew where you were shooting the next day. You could have called Skip and asked him to meet you at the tower."

"She's not talking to you," said Tobias, overriding what Tish had been about to say. "You got something to ask us, talk to our lawyer. Her name's Sam Arlen. You can find her in Eastsound. Other than that, drop dead."

Tish made it all the way to the car before she had a complete thought.

"That was… She… What the hell?"

"Yeah, you summed it up real nicely there."

"I feel like I can't get two seconds to think straight! And who the hell does she think she is? She wasn't there. Those… That wasn't my fault. Steve and Mars… They weren't my fault."

Were they?

"And, God, poor Sunshine. Maybe I should have been faster. I tried to get to her. I went to get her when she called. Why didn't I drive faster? If I could have just… Maybe Mars wouldn't have…"

"Tishkins, look at me." Tobias sounded serious, and she looked into his blue eyes, which reminded her of her father's. "None of those deaths are on you. They made the choices they made. Steve and Mars were both murderers. There is nothing to be sorry about with them. Mars killed Sunshine and Tyler, and there was nothing you could have done about that."

"Sunshine called me for help."

"And Mars killed her before she was barely off the phone. We know that from the other commune residents. You could have driven like the Indy 500, and it wouldn't have done any good. Sometimes, the best we can do for the dead is justice. Mars got what he deserved. And Steve Winslow was crazier than a soup sandwich."

Tish shuddered as the memory of the wild-eyed, pasty Steve Winslow flashed in front of her. At the end, he really had not been dwelling in the same reality as the rest of the population. She took a deep breath and then another.

"That detective is not following the facts," grumbled Tish.

"Agreed," said Tobias. "Which means that we'll have to do it. I think we've got enough pieces. Let's go back to the house and see if we can't put everything in some kind of order."

"Murder board time?" asked Tish.

"Murder board time," he agreed.

CHAPTER 16

MURDER BOARD

"OK," said Tobias, wheeling out the whiteboard from the mud room. He paused and glared at Tish's bra that was hanging off the corner. "Do you have to dry your unmentionables on the murder board?"

"It looked like it was going to rain," said Tish. "I didn't want to hang it on the clothesline."

"We have a dryer!"

"You can't put bras in the dryer," said Tish, collecting the offending item and taking it out to the hall. She hung it on the end of the banister, where she would probably forget it and offend Tobias all over again later.

"Anyway," he said firmly as she came back in.

She watched as he paused to take out his phone and take a photo of the drawing that sprawled the entire length of the board. Claire had made the most of the minimal color palette of whiteboard markers and created a fairy tale scene with a unicorn, a fairy, and a princess with a sword. The princess was labeled Claire, and the unicorn was Tish. The fairy didn't have a name, but the bright red dragon was labeled Doris in big bubble letters. She remembered Claire doubling over in laughter when Tobias had suggested that be the dragon's name. Then Tish had made hot chocolate and snuggled with Claire in the recliner, and Tobias had put in Mary Poppins on VHS.

Tish watched gloomily as Tobias scrubbed off the drawing and began to hang up pictures. She felt proud that he'd figured out how to print them out himself. He'd barely been able to turn on the computer before she'd come to live with him. Now, he could figure out emailing, searching, downloading, and printing all on his own.

"What we have here is the murder of one Skip Renfeld." He tapped the photo of Skip's spray-tanned face. "And the more we find out about him, the more the mystery becomes why no one killed him before now."

"Kinda, yeah," agreed Tish, sitting down in Tobias's recliner. Coats gave her strong side-eye from his dog bed, and she stuck out her tongue at him. Coats flopped his head back down and went back to sleep.

"What I can now tell you from his background check is that he's been arrested several times on drug charges, and the name on his birth certificate is Adolf."

Adolf. Her brain was stuck on it. How could anyone seriously still be naming their child Adolf?

"Well," said Tish, trying to wrap her head around that. "I mean, I get changing it, but if I was changing my name and there were choices, I don't think I would have gone with Skip."

"It's a name that practically screams *I have a punchable face,*" said Tobias, nodding.

"I was going to say Racist Dad at the Country Club."

"It's like the male equivalent of a stripper name," added Tobias.

"Trust fund baby who blew it all on coke," said Tish, determined not to let her grandfather one-up her.

"Mommy didn't love me."

Tish broke first and started to giggle. Tobias grinned slyly at her.

"Anyway, according to the voicemail you got, it seems like his modus operandi was to blackmail people into helping his career. Something practically confirmed by that effects guy."

"Which makes me wonder about every single person on the set," said Tish.

"Absolutely," said Tobias. "However, the only people singled out by the effects guy were you and Taylor Blake."

Tobias taped up a headshot of Taylor Blake. The young heart-throb still had the smooth polish that Disney imparted on its child stars. Tish liked the in-person version of Taylor better. He looked more human.

"What do we know about Skip and Taylor's relationship?" asked Tobias.

"Kyle said that Skip was giving Taylor major anxiety and that Taylor hated Skip. But before Kyle told me that, I would have said that the two were friendly. Skip kept calling him bro, and they worked on at least three movies together. On the other hand, despite being very nice on set, Taylor doesn't talk a lot about his own life. Emma had to ask if he was dating someone."

"OK, so we want to talk to him," said Tobias. "Who else spent the most time with him?"

"I did. And the principal cast and crew. Taylor, Emma, Brianna, Frank, and Luke."

"Ah, yes. The young writer who wanted the movie to fold. Seems like having the director die would help kill a film."

"Yes, and I'm pretty sure he lied about... something. Not sure what," said Tish. "But when he arrived here after we found Skip, there was some sort of glitch in his matrix."

The Matrix. 1999. Keanu Reeves in a nerd's wish-fulfillment fantasy that has impacted filmmaking for decades.

"OK. So he's on the interview list." Tobias hung up a headshot of Luke Green that somehow managed to look more pretentious than Taylor's. "What about the others?"

"Frank, the director of photography—that's the guy that's in charge of the actual filming—downplayed how much he disliked Skip. Apparently, there was history there, but he made it sound like he'd only *heard* things about Skip. Except that Skip got him fired off a job."

"That's some amount of motive. A bit thin for murder, but maybe we don't know the entire story."

Tobias drew an empty box next to the two photos and wrote Frank inside.

"Then we've got Emma and Brianna," said Tish. "Neither seems like they've got a motive. Emma didn't like him, but it seemed like she was rolling with the Hollywood punches and had herself pretty well protected. Brianna seemed like she was keeping whatever she felt to herself, which was probably smart. But I suppose Skip could have been blackmailing her."

"Seems unlikely. From talking to Brianna and looking at her IMDB page, I don't think that they've worked together before. Your studio guy, Alan, seems like a better target."

I appreciate that you investigated, though. Unless it was just romantic stalking? Hard to say.

"Except that he isn't here. On the other hand, even if Brianna and Emma didn't do it, they could both know something. Emma talked to Skip after dinner. There might have been more to that conversation that I missed. We should talk to them anyway."

Tobias nodded and made a separate column for Interviews, then added Brianna and Emma's pictures.

"But that does bring us back to the question of timing." Tobias went back up to the board and drew a long horizontal line from left to right. "You had an altercation with him at Reginald's, here." He made a tick-mark. "You thought that was just before five?"

"We were closing in on golden hour lighting," said Tish. "The dailies looked gorgeous because of it. But that meant that we didn't get done until nearly seven. It was probably after seven by the time I got over to Nash's and closer to eight when I got to the Orcas Hotel. So Emma would probably have seen him after nine? I was thinking it was earlier, but I don't see how it could have been."

"So it would have been starting to get dark," said Tobias, nodding and adding a tick mark to the board. He wrote in the time and then added moped underneath.

"So sometime between leaving Reginald's and seeing Emma, he

blew up a pillow and found a moped," said Tish.

"And after that, we know that he went up to the tower, but we don't know if he made any stops in between. The detective lady said your lack of alibi coincided with the estimated time of death. So we've got to figure after ten in the evening until I found him in the morning with Brianna. That's a lot of hours."

Tobias tapped the end of the dry-erase marker against his teeth.

"I'll call Mitch in a minute," said Tobias. "He'll tell me what he thought the time of death was."

"I still don't understand what he was doing at the tower in the first place," complained Tish.

"Oh, I'm pretty sure he was trying to kill Taylor—or maybe just hurt him—and then blame you for the accident."

"What?!" Tish gaped at Tobias in shock.

"He was looking at your IMDB webpage. Probably looking for blackmail material."

"Good luck," said Tish with a shrug. "I'm not saying I don't have stuff I'm embarrassed about, but I don't have a damn thing that would keep me from telling him where to stick it."

"Yeah, I think he realized it wasn't going to work and came up with a plan B. I think he tested that squib on the pillow because he was planning on making Taylor fall off the tower and then somehow blame you for it."

"I don't think that would have worked," said Tish slowly. "Taylor said he'd been taking climbing lessons and probably didn't need the rig. So even if the rigging had blown, I think it might have been scary, but Taylor probably would have been fine. And frankly, I never touch any of the equipment if I can possibly avoid it. I never want to screw anyone's stuff up."

"Sounds right. I think Skip misjudged the entire situation, but that's not surprising."

"But it's so stupid," said Tish. "It's convoluted, it's dangerous, and it has multiple fail points. It's the worst plot ever. Why he ever thought he could write is beyond me."

"I knew a writer once," said Tobias. "Friend of a friend pointed him at me because he wanted to know about guns and spycraft. He wrote thrillers. Decent books when he got the guns right. He said that since no one can see the thinking part and typing is so easy, everyone thinks they can write."

"Ah," said Tish, nodding. "Yes, the invisible labor doesn't get recognized."

"Invisible labor?" Tobias's eyes narrowed as if he was connecting the dots. "That's one of them feminist things, isn't it?"

"Not really. It's for everyone," said Tish, and his eyebrows went up suspiciously. "Let me put it this way. You know how there are two ways of grocery shopping?"

Tobias groaned. "It's not so hard to make a list! And then we don't have to go to the store more than once!"

"But then I would have to look in the fridge and pantry and think about what we're going to make for dinner this week. I like it better when you make the list, and I just do the legwork."

"Of course, you like it better! It's easier for you…" He stopped, seeming to chew on his own words. "Damn it, Tish. I'm too old to be giving new terms to being a grown-up."

Tish laughed fiendishly, and Tobias reluctantly chuckled.

"OK, I see your point. Thinking is a kind of labor, and no one can see it. But it reinforces my point about Skip. It takes a special kind of thinking to put yourself in someone else's shoes and see the world from their point of view. Skip was clever enough, but he couldn't picture a scenario where he couldn't leverage someone either through shame, intimidation, or bribery."

"OK, I'll agree to that," said Tish. "He had a plan. It was a dumb plan, but he was going to do it. Only then what? Someone pushed him off the tower. How would someone even know he was up there? Why would they do it? I mean, other than because he was a scumball."

"I think he asked someone to meet him, or brought someone with him, and then that person turned on him," said Tobias. "I think they met him up there, pushed him off the tower, and then drove away again."

"Either that or someone hiked up there and pushed him off."

"Yeah, we don't like that theory," said Tobias.

"But it's possible. You would need someone who was familiar enough with the trails."

"Yeah, it's possible, but you would have to be in shape to hike home again. Unless they knew people who could pick them up and wouldn't talk. You know, like Kyle or Matt."

Tish glared at Tobias.

"Why do you think she's pressing Matt so hard?" asked Tobias. "That's her theory. And since I know you didn't do it, I think we should look for other theories."

"I don't know why everyone assumes we could kill people," complained Tish.

"Because we could." He caught her eye. "But we don't because we're good people. Oh, what? Everyone's got a little murder in them somewhere."

"I don't!"

"You do. If someone threatened Claire, you'd plug them in a heartbeat."

Don't want to admit that he's right, but… Last time someone put a hand on her, I went Mama Bear real fast.

"That would be in defense of a child. Murder is the intentional ending of life. I don't sit around thinking about how to kill people. Except when I'm trying to figure out how someone else did it. OK," she held up a hand to forestall further argument. "We think he had an accomplice who turned on him and left. But who would he think he could trust?"

"That's where the suspects come in," said Tobias, tapping the other photos on the board.

"OK, but—" Tish began, when the doorbell chimed. Coats gave a startled woof and then staggered upright, looking confused.

Tobias and Tish looked at each other. Tobias shrugged. Tish reluctantly got up and went to the door with Coats following behind. Coats pushed his nose around her leg as she opened the door, trying to catch a sniff of who was disturbing his nap. Outside, a young person with floppy black hair, artfully applied guy-liner, and plaid pants was standing on the porch looking nervous.

CHAPTER 17

VEGAN DEATH METAL

"Hi," said Tish. "You must be Cooper."

"Oh, uh… hi. Are you Tish? My mom said you wanted to talk to me?"

"Yeah, come on in." Tish held open the door.

"Um… well, actually, my band is here."

Tish looked out the door to where a dilapidated minivan was plopped in the drive. She now had a fair amount of experience with wedding bands and saw her moment to gain their trust.

"Hey!" she yelled at the van. "You guys want a Coke and a snack?"

The engine turned off, and two more teenagers exited the van.

"Is it vegetarian snack?" asked one with lanky brown hair.

"It can be. I think we have hummus, chips, and bagels. Plus, hard boiled eggs."

"Sweet. I am trying to go full vegan, so I'll probably skip the egg."

Looking around, she tossed a sweatshirt over her bra on the end of the banister.

Granddad is going to say it serves me right for not putting my things away.

"I still don't think vegetarian is really hard-core metal," complained the third band member bringing up the rear. He was heavier and a plaid shirt over jeans that was probably meant to look grunge, but ended up just looking farmer.

"Why not?" asked Tish. "What's more metal than going against the majority population in a way that fundamentally annoys at least a third of them?"

"No cap," breathed the vegan with a reverential nod.

"Who's this?" asked Tobias as the band came trooping into the kitchen. He was already getting out the snacks and a six-pack of soda had been plunked on the counter.

"Vegan Death Metal," said Tish.

"We're not Death Metal," said Cooper. "We're more Metalcore." Tobias looked at Tish.

"This is Cooper and his band. Retro Betty's kid. You gave her lipstick."

"Oh, right!" exclaimed Tobias. "Reginald told me she collected."

"Reginald used to give me piano lessons," said Cooper hesitantly. "I really miss him."

"I do too," said Tobias, smiling at Cooper.

"I miss his sandwiches," said Cooper and then he blinked like he was going to cry. His friends looked uncomfortable.

"Thank you for telling me that," said Tobias. "He was my best friend and I miss his cooking too. It's nice to know that other people think about him."

Tish slid soda cans quietly across the kitchen counter to the boys to give Cooper a moment to recover. Cooper popped the top and cleared his throat.

"My mom said Tish came by and wanted to know about that guy down the road and a moped."

"We're not saying we know about a moped," said the vegan. "Necessarily."

"Unless we're going to get in trouble for it," suggested the meat eater. "And then we definitely don't know anything."

"Ah," said Tobias, nodding as he poured out a bag of chips and plunked the bowl in front of them, along with a plate of hardboiled eggs. "You see, we are private investigators." He pointed to the wall of the kitchen where he'd hung his license over the coffee pot.

"Cool!" exclaimed the meat-eater, looking impressed.

"And sometimes we have to tell the police things, but a lot of the time we can say that we gathered information through what are known as Confidential Informants. Also known as C.I.s. And we don't tell the police who our C.I.s are."

The band exchanged looks.

"OK, we'll be C.I.s," said Cooper. "So Mom makes us practice in a shed because she says our music has the wrong kind of funk, and she wants to be upwind."

Tish snorted in laughter, and all four of the males in her kitchen glared at her.

"Sorry, but your mom is funny. Go on."

"And we were in the shed, and we had stopped because Grover tripped over the amp wire."

The child's name is Grover? And here I thought Orcas had stopped providing me with names to be surprised by, but I see that I was wrong.

"But then Ten looks up and see some guy across the street messing with that basic cap AF jerk's car."

Tobias looked at Tish.

"Someone was messing with Skip's car."

"What does a hat have to do with it?"

"Linguists currently believe that *cap* comes from the metaphor of keeping something under your hat so that it is hidden, i.e., lying. So, *no cap* would be truthfulness. It was the *no cap* usage that rose to prominence with Young Thug and Future's hit 2017 single *No Cap* and entered wide-spread usage across the U.S."

"Ah." Tobias appeared to ruminate on that for a moment. "OK, I'm caught up. There was a guy messing with the car. What did you do?"

"Well, at first we thought he was stealing it," said the vegan, who Tish now thought was called Ten. "And we debated saying something or calling someone. But then we thought… Nah."

"Besides, before we could come to a group consensus, he kind of eased the hood down," said Grover, "and he went away again."

"And then after a bit, the guy came out, and he tried to start the car," said Cooper. "Only it didn't start. And then he came over and yelled at us, and we said someone messed with it, but it wasn't us. And then he got all pissed off and offered us a hundred bucks for Grover's moped."

"And then," said Ten, puffing up at the memory, "Cooper told him that unless it was two-hundred, he might as well go back to his house."

"And then he paid us two-hundred bucks!" exclaimed Grover. "Can you believe it? I pulled that moped out of the Exchange for fifty bucks. It barely runs! I have to turn it on with a screwdriver!"

"Grover's not supposed to drive it," said Cooper. "He doesn't have his license yet and neither does the moped, so if we tell the cops, Grover's going to get in like… massive trouble."

"It's a rusty maroon color?" asked Tish and the three boys nodded.

"OK," said Tobias and beckoned to the band. "Let's go see if you recognize the guy who messed with Skip's car."

Tish followed them across the hall to the den.

"It's a murder board!" yelled Ten, flapping his arms. "Fam! This is so awesome!"

Everyone else thinks we're weird. Who knew our demographic was teenage boys?

"Do you see the person who took the engine relay out of Skip's car?" asked Tobias.

"Is that what they did?" asked Cooper, laughing. "Good for them."

"That is a plural pronoun used as a singular," said Tobias, pointing at Cooper. "It really is used in English already."

"Yeah?" said Cooper, clearly confused.

"Pretty sure it was that guy," said Grover, peering at the pictures.

"Yeah," agreed Ten, tapping the photo of Luke Green. "That's him. He had those same dumb glasses. Absolutely no rizz."

"Thanks," said Tobias. "That's really helpful. No cap."

"She looks familiar," said Cooper, squinting at the photo of Brianna.

"She was in that one movie," said Ten, knowledgably. "She was the Grandma. I watched it like a bajillion times when I was a kid."

"Which one?" asked Cooper, looking puzzled.

"Technotronic Legend," said Ten. "You don't remember that one? I loved it."

"Huh," said Cooper, scratching his head again. "No, don't remember it. But Mom didn't let me watch PG-13 movies until like last year. I had to see Harry Potter and the Deathly Hallows over at Grover's."

Grover laughed. "I forgot about that. Did I make you watch *Edge of Tomorrow*? That's good for an old movie."

Tish felt her eye twitch.

Edge of Tomorrow. A Tom Cruise time travel movie that was absolutely stolen by Emily Blunt. And it was 2014. When did that become an old movie?

The band took their sodas and trooped out, still discussing ancient movies, and Tobias walked them out. He seemed to enjoy listening to them talk, although Tish guessed he only understood about a quarter of what they were saying.

Not that I'm doing much better. About half, maybe?

"Well," said Tobias as their van trundled away. "It's nice to know that young men have not changed at all since I was fifteen."

Tish laughed. "Really?"

"Oh, yes. Just as completely unintelligible and confused as ever. I liked them. I suspect I would hate their music, but I liked them."

They were about to go back into the house when Coats, who had wandered out into the yard, barked at a car that turned into their drive.

"Go flip the murder board to the wall," said Tobias. "That's Brianna's car."

"On it," said Tish and hurried back into the house and into the den. She quickly flipped the board over and shoved it up against the wall, only to see the remains of their last Pictionary drawing. Drawn by Claire with remarkable flare and red dry-erase marker was what looked like a bloody murder scene. Tish had to stare at it a long moment before remembering that the clue had been *electrical outlet,* and the apparent blood drops were sizzles of electricity shooting off the stick figure's hair.

It looks like a drawing of Skip's demise.

Frantically, Tish looked around for the eraser. Out on the porch, she could hear Tobias saying something about a pleasant surprise, and she wanted to yell that it really wasn't.

Brianna seemed really upset about Skip's body. She's going to think we're morbid freaks if she sees this.

The eraser was nowhere to be found. Frantically, she looked around for anything to wipe off the drawing.

Afghan... no.

Granddad's slippers... maybe?

He'll kill me.

Tissues!

Tish grabbed the tissue box and then realized that it had two tissues and a handgun in it.

Gah! When I said stop storing it in the remote caddy, this is not what I meant.

Taking one of the tissues and putting the box gingerly back on the table next to Tobias's recliner, she swiped hastily at the drawing. She was still scrubbing as Brianna and Tobias came in.

"Tish!" called Tobias, as if he didn't know where she was.

"Well, hey, Brianna," said Tish, coming out of the den and walking into the kitchen, hoping they would follow her. "What brings you out this way?"

"Oh, I just thought I should touch base and see what you thought the odds were on getting any filming done this week."

"Well, I am working on that," said Tish. "I've lodged a request to have access to the tower again, but so far, I'm being blocked by the detective. Alan put the lawyers on it though, so… fingers crossed."

Alan had also said to definitely not let Brianna wander off to do a play because they needed her serious theater credentials on the movie.

"Oh," said Brianna, with an awkward smile.

"Was there something else?" asked Tobias, ushering Brianna into the kitchen.

"Well…" Brianna hesitated, looking worried. "It might be nothing, but I know you're investigating. So, maybe I ought to tell you. I had the oddest conversation with Luke Green yesterday. I'm not saying anyone is, well, too terribly broken up about Skip's death, but Luke seemed positively elated. And he said that he felt partially responsible. It was an odd statement. I didn't know what to make of it."

Tish looked at Tobias.

"Well, it might have meant anything," said Tobias. "No accounting for some people's feelings. But we'll ask him. Can't hurt. Thanks for telling us."

"Oh, good," said Brianna, looking relieved.

"Hey," said Tish. "I've been meaning to ask about your daughter."

Brianna's face froze, and a tight smile appeared.

"If she wanted to come up and visit, I'm pretty sure we could fudge that into the budget."

"Um… we don't really see each other that much."

"Tobias!" called a voice from the living room, and Coats started to bark.

"In here, Eleanor," Tobias yelled back.

"I parked around the side," said Eleanor, tromping in from the front door, Birkenstocks in her hand to keep from tracking dirt on the living room rug. Her gray hair, held up with a complicated metal pin and deep blue skirt, gave her complete Earth Mother vibes. "I'm putting some pickles in the storm cellar. But don't worry, I'm also taking jam out."

Eleanor stopped when she saw Brianna.

"Eleanor," said Tobias, without looking in the least bothered by the situation, "this is Brianna Meadows. She's an actress in Tish's movie."

"Hello," said Brianna, smiling. "It's nice to meet you, but I must admit I was just leaving."

Tish felt like her face was stuck in a pantomime of a smile.

"Oh," said Eleanor, "well, always good to meet a friend of Tish's. Tobias, we had the first meeting of the Grange today. I've got the full list of what's accepted and the theme for this year. You have quince, don't you?"

Tobias itched his nose as if considering. "The quince don't come in until at least October. They can't possibly be ready for the Fair in September."

"Exactly!" exclaimed Eleanor triumphantly. "We'll have a leg up on everyone else! As long as you still have some in your freezer."

"I don't understand," said Tish.

"Eleanor is on the Grange committee," said Tobias. "They organize the island's display at the Puyallup Fair. And each year, the State Grange puts out the theme and what you're allowed to submit for your display. The more things you have from the list, the more points you get, and the display with the most points wins."

"Are you telling me that Granging is a competitive sport?" asked Tish. "I thought the Grange was just what we called that building."

"It is," said Tobias. "It's just also the organization dedicated to improving the lives of rural Americans. Although, when it comes to the competitions, I assure you that they are not improving mine. I have no desire to go dig through my freezer and see if I have quince."

"I'll go look," said Eleanor. "I just thought I'd ask in case Tish put a body in there or something."

"Me? He's the one that had a dead owl in there!"

"That was for Kandace's chickens."

"Oh, that makes sense," said Eleanor, nodding.

"I'm glad it makes sense to someone," said Tish, and Brianna laughed.

"I have to admit that I'm most definitely on Tish's side with that," said Brianna. "Tish, let me know if anything changes on the scheduling front. Tobias, it's always nice to see you."

Brianna showed herself out, and Tish finally managed to throw the tissue she'd kept crumpled in her hand in the garbage.

"So," said Tobias, turning back to Eleanor. "What else is on the list?"

CHAPTER 18

WRECKAGE

Tish hung up the Zoom call and flopped over on the Chesterfield.

"Went that good?" asked Tobias, coming in from the garden where he'd been doing the watering.

"That was Alan, the Prince of Movies, and the full complement of producers and major funders and possibly some random people they found in the hall to ask me how it's going and talk about Skip's death."

"How is it going?" asked Tobias, and Tish glared at him.

"We have made a great deal of progress and are working closely with the police to assist them in their investigation. We feel confident that we will have matters satisfactorily resolved within a week. However, at the moment, we cannot discuss the particulars of the case."

"That is exactly how I thought it was going," said Tobias, plopping down in the wingback chair by the fireplace.

"Granddad! We haven't made any progress!"

"What are you talking about? We have Luke and Taylor as our top suspects. Aren't you going to pick up Luke in a bit?"

"Yeah, I texted Luke last night and told him that we need to consult about the script and see if we can't identify any weird Skip edits and that he should definitely be on the island today. He's staying in Anacortes and said he'd be on the nine o'clock ferry."

They had debated trying to find Luke the night before, but after texting around, Tish realized that there wasn't any need to locate him when she could make Luke come to her. She was a producer, after all, and he was the writer. Answering to her beck and call was his job.

"How did he react?" asked Tobias.

"He texted back and then sent three excited gifs and thanked me for preserving his dream," said Tish.

"Hm, that's like won the lottery level excited for a twenty-something," said Tobias.

"Yes," said Tish.

"Speaks to motive," said Tobias.

"Yeah," said Tish with a sigh. "I just... Would you really kill someone to make a movie?"

"No," said Tobias. "But making movies isn't my dream. People will do a lot of things to make their dreams come true."

"Yeah, I guess so."

"Mind you, I'm not saying he did it," said Tobias. "But I do think it's worth finding out what he knows."

"Yeah, that's true," agreed Tish.

Her phone rang, and Tish groaned before picking up.

"Hey, Frank," she said, faking a smile.

"Hey, I know you were talking to the studio today, and I don't want to pressure you, but some of the crew are getting antsy."

"Yeah, I know. Ellis has child support to pay. You can tell everyone that we're still all a go and that paychecks are not being held up. I double-checked."

"Yeah, but these guys don't hold still well," said Frank. "If we don't get them shooting something soon, they'll wander off."

"Ah, the glories of an ADHD-driven profession," said Tish. "Look, Alan is putting the lawyers on the police. With any luck, they'll release the tower to us for shooting soon. I also need the detective to pull her head out of her ass and check Skip's phone records and stuff like that. So I'll be talking to them later today myself, and I'll reiterate the urgency."

"Oh," said Frank. "Yeah, Skip's phone records. Police do that kind of thing."

"Generally," said Tish, amused by Frank's surprised tone. "Anyway, sit on the crew. Tell them to give me another day or two to get things back on track."

"Yeah, of course," said Frank.

"You're going to be late if you don't leave for the ferry soon," said Tobias, looking at the clock on the mantle.

"Oh, crap. OK, Frank, thanks for calling, but seriously—don't let anyone take another job without talking to me first."

"No problem," said Frank.

Tish hung up the phone with another gusty sigh.

"OK," said Tish, shoving her feet into her sandals. "OK, I'm going to pick up Luke and bring him back here. I'll see you in a few."

Tobias nodded and reached for the newspaper as Tish left. She suspected that there might be some Matlock watching next. Sometimes, being old and retired looked great. The deafness and metal knees didn't hold appeal, but Matlock and a recliner seemed pretty good.

Tish puttered down the road in her Toyota, trying to marshal her thoughts. She felt like there were too many suspects. Everyone had hated Skip, and no one had said anything about it for quite literally years.

So why now? What pushed someone into killing Skip now?

Tish wanted to speed, but she checked herself and took her foot off the gas. It was Ronny's day on traffic, and he was known to have ticketed his own mother on three separate occasions. The man was heartless when it came to traffic infractions.

Her Toyota was a late 1990s model that had brought her back from California, and she was thinking about replacing it, but she had absorbed enough of the island culture that getting rid of a vehicle that still functioned seemed like a sin.

Maybe if I get movie money, I'll buy myself something new. Something with more room for Claire and Granddad.

The thought of movie money was tempting but depressing, as was the thought of Claire. Right now, nothing seemed certain. What she needed to do was focus on the task at hand. Find Luke Green and discover what he had been up to with Skip's car.

If Luke killed Skip, then the movie's dead. This was his vision. I don't see it getting made without him on the script.

Tish checked the rearview mirror and saw a beige Subaru barreling down on her. Subaru drivers were usually quite safe, but this one seemed to be cruising for a ticket. Out of annoyance, Tish slowed down to a crawl. They could go around. She had depression to wallow in. She couldn't be bothered with some mainlander who wanted to go fifty in a twenty-five zone.

Where is Ronny when I need him?

It wasn't until the Subaru was filling her entire rearview mirror that Tish began to worry. And then there was a hard jolt as the car hit her back bumper.

Her heart began to race, and she took a firmer grip on the wheel. What did she know about combat driving? Anything?

Not a damn thing.

There was a rev of a motor and a crash of metal, and Tish slammed against her seatbelt as the car jerked forward. Tish slammed hard on the brakes, but the Subaru behind her shoved her little sedan forward anyway. The steering wheel seemed to float in her hand. Nothing seemed to be working, including her brain.

There was another crash, and her Toyota jerked to the right and bounced straight toward the ditch. There was an explosion of white, and Tish felt something slam into her face. The sound of an engine raced away, and Tish felt immobilized. For a long moment, everything seemed too loud and utterly silent at the same time.

I got hit with the airbag.

She could hear the distant drone of an engine but couldn't tell if it was coming or going. Then, a car door opened and closed again.

Shit. If that's the Subaru driver, then I need to move.

She flailed out one hand and managed to get her door opened. She pushed at the white mass of airbag, trying to clear space and take a deep breath.

"Holy shit!" someone explained, and she felt the door get pulled open further.

Tish stared up into the blurry but somehow familiar face. She couldn't remember who he was. Then he raised his camera and took a picture.

Neil McKinley. The paparazzi.

"Are you OK?" he asked, putting the camera down.

"Do I look OK?" she demanded, pushing again at the billowing airbag.

"Not really," said Neil.

"Then stop standing there like a jackass and help me get out of this thing." She pushed futilely at the airbag again, trying to get her other arm across her body so she could get her seat belt undone.

"Should you be doing that? I think you're supposed to wait until paramedics arrive."

"Did you call 911?" asked Tish.

"Uh… no?"

"Then why would they show up?" asked Tish.

"Oh. Right. I guess I should do that," said Neil.

She finally managed to get a hand on the buckle of the seatbelt and fumbled around until she heard the click of it coming undone. She felt like her heart was getting set to beat out of her chest. There wasn't anything to be scared of anymore, but her body didn't seem to know that.

He pulled out his phone, and Tish took a deep breath, trying to organize her thoughts.

"Ray is probably at the phones today. Tell him to tell Nash to come and get me."

"What? Oh, hi. Uh, yeah, there's been a car accident. Tish Yearly got run off the road."

There was a brief silence from Neil as Ray yelled something that Tish couldn't hear.

"Well, she said to tell someone named Nash to come and get her, so I mean... she seems OK."

"Oh, for the love of Pete," muttered Tish.

My chance to swear up a proper storm, and I go with a Granddad favorite.

"Just give me the phone," she snapped, waving her arm in Neil's direction.

"I'm putting it on speaker," said Neil.

"Tish?" demanded a tinny voice, and Tish let her head fall back onto the headrest behind her.

"Hey, Ray," she said.

"Tish, are you OK?" demanded Ray.

"Um... mostly. I think. A tan Subaru ran me into a ditch, and the airbag popped. Pretty sure my little POS is totaled." She stretched her jaw and tried to pop her ears which were still ringing.

"You need to stay where you are," said Ray firmly. "I have the paramedics and Nash en route. Don't do something stupid like get up and walk around or, you know, try to take on a murderer like last time."

"That was not on purpose," said Tish. "I just had to pee, and I wasn't going to have that recorded on the 911 hotline."

"I'm sorry, when was this?" asked Neil, fumbling in his pocket.

"Neil, you asshat," said Tish, "stop looking for a story and help me out of the car."

"Neil, do not help her out of the car," said Ray. "Her boyfriend is a six-foot-four Sheriff's Deputy, and he's going to be really pissed off if you help her move, break her neck, and contribute to her getting paralyzed."

"Right," said Neil. "Tish, you should stay where you are."

"I do not have a broken neck! I got hit in the face with the damn airbag, but I don't think anything else is hurt. I was barely going the damn speed limit because it's Ronny's shift on traffic!"

"So what I hear you saying is that I contribute to the health and safety of this island," said a new voice from outside her field of view.

"Hey, Ronny," said Tish. "Where's Nash?"

"On his way," said Ronny, poking his head around the passenger window and looking in. "Paramedics too, but I was closer."

"Ray, Ronny's here, so I'm going to let Neil hang up," Tish bellowed toward the phone.

"OK," Ray yelled back.

"Now, Ronny," said Tish, as Neil tucked his phone away, "before we get too far down the checklist, I need you to ask Mr. McKinley over there why he was following me and if he saw the Subaru that hit me."

"I wasn't following anyone," said Neil automatically. "I did see a Subaru, but I didn't see who was at the wheel. It went around me."

"Uh-huh. Great," said Tish. "Now tell us why you were following Skip Renfeld."

"I told you! I wasn't following anyone."

"He has photos of us on his camera," said Tish.

"If you were in public, that's not an offense," said Ronny. "However, I believe Detective Warshaw is going to want to question you about that, and there will be some very serious consequences if you lie about your activities."

"I am a professional photographer."

"He's paparazzi scum," said Tish. "He takes photos of people's private lives for money."

"That is not a nice thing to do," said Ronny, coming around to Tish's side and puncturing the airbag with his pocket knife.

"And considering that the movie had barely begun filming and Skip Renfeld was not a household name, I would like to know who was paying him to keep tabs on Skip."

"I just stopped to make sure you were OK," said Neil. "I'll be going now."

"Take one more step, and I'll arrest you for fleeing the scene of a crime," said Ronny

"What? It was a Subaru that ran her off the road! You can't

arrest me."

"We just have your word for that. For all I know, you were a material contributor to this accident."

"She said she saw a Subaru!" yelped Neil.

"My memory is suddenly very fuzzy," said Tish. She could hear more tires on the road and the crunch of footsteps on gravel.

"This is blackmail!" Neil sounded outraged.

"No, that's what Skip Renfeld was doing. Now, who hired you?" she demanded.

Neil was silent, and Tish gently rotated her head until she could see him directly.

"Who hired you?" she repeated.

"Answer the question," growled Nash quietly in Neil's ear, and the photographer jumped in surprise.

"Taylor Blake," he blurted out.

CHAPTER 19

MACRO VS. MICRO

Tish walked slowly into the house, Nash following her like he wanted to be carrying her. She wasn't sure she didn't want him to be carrying her.

Coats barged past her to get to Nash, and Tobias came out of the kitchen.

"The texts said you were fine," he said, eyeing her.

"I got hit in the face with an airbag," said Tish, going down the hall into the living room. "I know I said I wanted to learn how to punch things, but if this is how it feels, I'm taking it back."

She lowered herself onto the Chesterfield and waited for the men in her life to catch up. Coats was first. Tobias and Nash came in as Coats was snuffling her all over.

"Any idea what happened to Luke Green?" asked Tobias.

"Probably still at the ferry dock," said Tish.

"Mm," said Nash. "Maybe." She looked up at him, trying to parse what he meant. "I'll go get him in a minute. If he was on the ferry, someone will know where he's at. I wanted to bring Tish home first."

"Thanks," said Tish, gently tilting her head back and closing her eyes. "The paramedics said I was OK," she said, sensing that looks were being exchanged.

"Yeah," said Nash. "They also said you should probably get checked out at the hospital."

Tish opened her eyes so that she could roll them. "Well, I'm a little bit busy at the moment, so that will have to wait."

"You're always a little bit busy lately," Nash said drily.

"Oh, sorry, is Nora not keeping you entertained?" Tish snapped and instantly regretted it.

Nash let out a snort of air, turned around, and walked out of the room. Tish looked at Tobias, who was watching her over the rim of his coffee mug. Tish flinched as the door slammed.

"Not my best moment," said Tish.

"Nope," agreed Tobias. "The two of you have been poking at each other all week. What's going on?"

"Stuff," said Tish.

He gave her a look.

"Claire keeps being mean to me. Nora keeps showing up at Nash's house. She spent the damn night! And I'm stuck doing bull-shit movie stuff. He has point blank said he wants to spend more time with me, and I want that too, but there's Nora, and then Skip, and now I got hit by a car, and he didn't even yell at me! He's stopped loving me."

"I'm not sure how we got from point A to B on that one," said Tobias, looking confused.

"Usually, when I almost die, he gets upset and yells at me about unnecessary risks." She gave a watery sniff and tried not to look like she was as upset about it as she was.

"So, he's obviously stopped loving you? That's the only option?"

"Yes!"

"We can't think of any other reasons he might not have yelled at you? Presence of other people, ongoing investigation, or possibly you didn't nearly die?"

"Whose side are you on?" demanded Tish.

"Yours."

"Really? Because it sounds like you're on his side," she grumbled.

"The two of you are on the same side," he said impatiently.

"We used to be," said Tish sadly. "Now it just feels like I'm being railroaded into some sort of breakup, and I don't want that. I want

Nash and Claire! But it's like we can't talk about it, and even when I try to talk about it or try to fix things, I get interrupted by the movie stuff."

"So go punch Nora in the face and tell her to step off."

"That is such bro advice," said Tish. "It's not helpful! And I don't even want to punch Nora. She hasn't really done anything."

"Oh, yeah, just showing up at Nash's… that's absolutely nothing. Wake up and smell the Folgers."

"It was supposed to be one night, and it's my fault because I got her a part in the movie! Only then Skip got whacked, and it's ruining my life! And I feel like a jerk for complaining about how a dead guy is impacting me, but this is where we are now!"

Tobias chuckled. "Yeah, that's where we are now. So you don't punch her, but you're going to have to deal with the Nora and Claire issue sooner or later."

"How? I can't say anything about anything. It's up to Nash, and I feel like an even bigger jerk pressuring him after I put him in this position. He has been such a saint about all the movie stuff."

"Tish." Tobias stopped and sighed, then itched his eyebrow.

Oh, God. It's even worse than I thought.

"You are doing a hard thing. And if I learned anything from the CIA and parenting, it's that sometimes there is no right answer. Sometimes, somebody just gets the shaft. And a lot of the time, it's women."

Tish opened her mouth and found that she had no response. "What?"

"In the maelstrom of geopolitics, when decisions get made, sooner or later the shit rolls down the hill, and somewhere, someone gets dead or screwed or left behind. Because what's good for the whole country ends up sucking for an individual. Most of the time, there is no perfect answer. And it's the same when it comes to parenting."

"I'm sorry, still, what?"

"Women hold a family together. Whether because of nurture, nature, or luck of the draw, who knows? You can ponder all the reasons, but it's the reality that we're dealing with. We don't have time for how we got here. And the reality is that a lot of times when decisions get made about what's best for the family, then what's best for the individual woman is not accommodated."

"Are you trying to tell me that everything you know about parenting you learned from the CIA?"

"Thankfully, no. I learned about macro and microsystems, though. Children operate on microsystems—day to day, minute to minute—and hopefully, parents operate on macrosystems because they are attempting to grow a young person into a responsible adult member of society. The problem is that operating on a macrosystem level means that sometimes, the needs of an individual get left out. I do not like Nora Harlow. I think she's selfish. And to be quite honest, I thought you were being foolish to be so nice to her."

"She has lost a lot. Losing your family and the place you live? And then having your boyfriend be murdered? That's a lot."

"Mmmm...She threw away a lot. It was her choice. Although I sympathize about Tyler getting killed for blackmailing the wrong guy, I guess."

"I'm not defending her," said Tish. "But even if she chose to break up the family, it's still a loss. Nash doesn't want to be married to her. I don't think he misses her. But I think he misses that way of life. A divorce is a death, even if you wanted it. I am not... We're never going to be best friends, but I... can't hate her either."

Tobias leaned over and kissed the top of her head.

"You are a sweet girl. And you're right not to hate her because what you have shown me in your efforts to co-exist with her is that while Nora is selfish, and I can easily argue all the *she should have knowns* and what-not, the truth is that she was making the majority of the sacrifices to be here. Your grandma and I came here after we retired, and she told me that she wasn't sure about it because she would be giving up a lot. She tried to explain it to me, and I believed her, and I listened, and I tried to adjust to make it worth it. But even then, I underestimated how much she was leaving behind. I had never invested in a community the way she had. I didn't leave the network of friends like she did. What I'm saying is that while Nash would chop off a hand for his family, he wouldn't move to L.A. He's not sacrificing much to be on this island. It suits him. It never suited Nora. She was the one who had to give up dreams and people and a way of being to be here. And I could see that if you thought it was temporary, you could feel mighty betrayed when it started to be permanent. And that makes me mad at you. Well done."

"Me? Why? What did I do?"

"You made me empathize with the villain. Nice." He nodded like she'd performed a remarkable feat. "So…" He waggled a finger in his ear. "I forgot where I was going with this. I didn't mean to talk about Nora. I meant to say… Ah. Right. You are a very macrosystems person. You make decisions based on what you think will give the optimal outcome, as we used to say. But, Tishkins," he shook his head at her, "you forget that sometimes you should be a little bit selfish. You should make decisions on what would be the optimal outcome for *you*. Not the entire unit."

"Granddad, I can't! The optimal outcome for me is if I stole Claire and dropped kicked Nora off the face of the planet."

Tobias chuckled.

"That's not funny! I can't do that!"

"Oh, that's the problem, isn't it, though? You think you could do it. Don't you? There's a little part of you that thinks if you decided to go to war on Nora, you'd end up with her husband and her kid, and Nora would be in hell."

"I'd be nice about it," said Tish. "She'd end up in L.A. with my agent, but we would have full custody."

Tobias nodded. "You're fighting with one hand behind your back because you're trying to be a good person. Good for you."

"Granddad! This is not helping."

"How about this then: he's not her husband. Claire is her kid, but Nash does not belong to her anymore. And you're right, a divorce is a loss, and that's what Claire's got right now. She's grieving and trying to get her family back, and you're the one she's lashing out at. You can cut and run, but personally, I suggest you tough it out. Kids can be abusive little twerps, but most of the time, it's because they're trying to use whatever leverage they've got to get what they need. But, of course, they're small, with underdeveloped brains and no money, so they only have emotional leverage."

For some reason that struck Tish has bizarrely funny and she burst out laughing, but stopped since it made her nose hurt, which was a weird feeling.

"And also, the fact that usually what they need is more love and reassurance makes the twerpiness easier to take. Sometimes. Not all the time. Sometimes they're just annoying little shits. But even if Claire is doing this for all the reasons we can sympathize with, it still doesn't mean she gets to treat you like that. It's OK to demand to be treated with respect. It's also OK to demand that you get time with Nash without her. Or that Nora find someplace else to sleep. And honestly, it's OK for Nash to demand those things, too, but he doesn't ask for my advice. You want an optimal outcome where you all co-parent or whatever the fancy term is these days, and that's nice. But you always have the right to demand what's right for you. They can co-parent their asses into making it good for you and not just for them."

Tish tugged on her ponytail and thought about that.

"But they're the parents. They're the experts," she said. "So I feel like my opinion doesn't count."

Tobias gave a hearty guffaw. "Oh, that's priceless. If I posted *Things Tish Says,* I would quote that, and then all the parents and grandparents would die laughing. Parents don't know what the hell they're doing at least seventy percent of the time. Except me. I figure I was shooting about fifty percent. You can twitter that."

He took a smug sip of coffee.

"I *should* twitter that," said Tish, shaking her head. "OK, fine, if I can ever get time alone with Nash, I will attempt to express my personal needs, but right now, we've got two other concerns."

"At least two," said Tobias. "What two are you talking about?"

"Well, I thought Luke was a pretty good suspect, but he couldn't have run me off the road if he was at the ferry dock. Damn it. That's what Nash meant when he said *maybe* about Luke being at the ferry."

"Yes, pretty sure he'll be investigating Luke's location. Since you told him you'd come get him, Luke would have known where you'd be more or less."

"OK, but assuming he was at the ferry, he couldn't have been driving me off the road. And then there's the fact that when I talked to that paparazzi Neil McKinley, he said that Taylor had been paying him to follow Skip around."

"So it could have been Taylor behind the wheel," said Tobias. "Or it could have been someone else."

"I just don't know why anyone would do it now," said Tish thoughtfully. "Have we made progress? We must have. We usually only get threatened if we're bothering someone. But if we've learned something, I don't know what it is."

"Hm," said Tobias. "Well, at minimum, we've learned that we have two suspects."

CHAPTER 20

LUKE GREEN

When Tish came downstairs the following day, Tobias was already up and staring at the murder board.

"Nash called," he said when she had returned from the kitchen with her mug of tea.

"He called you?"

Oh, that is so not good. We should not need an intermediary to communicate.

"He didn't want to wake you up, and he knows I don't text."

"You can text."

"But I choose not to."

He grinned at Tish's sour expression.

"What news did Nash wish to impart without waking me?" she asked, deciding to forgo her usual sparring match with her grandfather.

"Says he found Luke Green. He *was* on the ferry yesterday after all, so it looks like he couldn't have been the driver who ran you off the road. He was a walk-on at Anacortes, but then he went up to the Orcas Hotel to wait for you and got drunk. But Delbert knew he was a movie person, so they put him in an empty room and figured that if nothing else, you'd pony up for him for the room fee."

Tish sighed. "Yeah, I probably can put it somewhere in the incidentals. Is he still there?"

"Yeah. I figured I'd give you a chance to get your head on straight, and then we'd go up there."

Tish nodded gratefully and took another sip of tea.

"I forgot about Thiago," she said. "The effects guy. He was pretty pissed at us. He could have run me off the road."

"Could have been him," agreed Tobias.

You don't think it was, but you're not ready to say why not.

"Give me a couple minutes, and then we'll head over to the hotel."

Tobias nodded and went back to staring at the board.

I can see the wheels turning, and now I'm annoyed that mine aren't also turning.

They arrived at the hotel, and the front desk directed them up to the second floor. Luke answered the knock in a rumpled shirt, pants, and socks. He looked like he had just woken up.

"Hey, Luke," said Tish, putting her hand on his chest and pushing him out of the way so she could walk into his room. He blinked at her in shock.

Yeah, you thought I was nice, didn't you? Time to find out the truth.

"Tish..." he said, turning to look at her. Tobias thumped the door closed, and Luke jumped with a wince and looked at Tobias in confusion. "Mr. Yearly?"

"Come sit down, Luke," said Tish, pointing to the chair by the desk.

"I waited for you yesterday."

"Yeah, I don't blame you for what happened yesterday," said Tish. "I know you have an alibi."

"An alibi?" asked Luke, looking alarmed.

"Sit," ordered Tish, and instinctively, Luke did as he was told.

"What you don't have an alibi for is when Skip died," said Tobias, leaning on his cane and intently scrutinizing Luke, who went pale.

"I... I... I didn't do it."

"Oh, he didn't do it," said Tish, turning to Tobias.

"So convincing."

"I absolutely had nothing to do with Skip. I don't have the capacity or wherewithal to perform such a heinous crime."

"Luke, more vocabulary words only convinces me that you're

lying more," said Tish.

"Can we give that to the bluebird? Octothorpe Tish says," said Tobias, chuckling.

OK, I got bluebird for Twitter, but…

Tish paused and turned to Tobias. "Octothorpe?" she muttered.

"It's the real name of the pound sign."

"Pound sign?" asked Luke, looking confused.

"Hashtag," said Tish.

This is ruining my tough-guy act.

Tish watched as Luke's hand snaked out and pulled a notepad closer to him and scribbled out the word octothorpe without Luke making eye contact with his hand or the paper.

Octothorpe Tish says: writers are weird.

"You did something to Skip, though, didn't you?" demanded Tish.

"No," said Luke, but his voice quavered.

"Luke," said Tish firmly, "we know you took the engine relay out of Skip's car. Spill the beans. What else did you do?"

"Nothing!"

"I can call the police detective right now, and you can tell her about the car."

"I didn't do anything! I swear!"

"Swear less. Talk more," advised Tobias. "You're fingerprints are all over that engine. We can start dialing right now."

Luke's shoulders sagged in defeat, and Tish felt a thrill of triumph.

"OK, yes, I took out the engine relay. I saw the trick on YouTube. But I had to!"

"Why?" demanded Tish.

"You saw how he was ruining my movie! And how great it went when he wasn't there. The tower scene was the lynchpin to the entire story, and he was going to ruin it. I had to do something! I figured if he didn't show up in the morning, you would shoot without him."

"That's true," admitted Tish. "I would have made Taylor direct. He did a good job on the other stuff."

"He really did, didn't he?"

"Great," said Tobias sardonically. "We all agree that Taylor has directorial talent. So you took out the engine relay. What else did you do?"

"Nothing! I took out the relay and booked it. I figured he was in for the night. I could hear him in the house yelling at Frank for shooting without him."

"Yelling at Frank?" asked Tish.

"He had him on speaker. He said Frank was a traitor. I don't even know how he got up to the tower without his car!"

Tish and Tobias exchanged glances. Luke's confusion had the ring of authenticity.

"Did you hear him say anything else to Frank?" asked Tobias.

"I heard him say that if he wanted to keep his job this time, he would keep his mouth shut. Which was odd because I didn't think they'd worked together before. Anyway, I got on the next available ferry and came back to Anacortes. I didn't hear about Skip until the next morning."

Have I learned anything I didn't already know? What am I not asking?

"Who did you hear the news from?"

"Brianna texted me," said Luke. "She's always been such a champion of my work. She wanted to know if I had anyone who had seen me in Anacortes in case the police started asking questions about who hated Skip. And since I'm not sure anyone did, I've been nervous ever since."

"Thoughtful of her," said Tobias, rubbing his chin.

"Well, she was in that police procedural show for three seasons," said Luke. "So she knows about this sort of thing."

"I'd forgotten about that," said Tish thoughtfully. "She played the macabre coroner who was always unfazed by the dead bodies."

"She won an Emmy," said Luke.

"Acting ain't real life," said Tobias drily.

"I'm very aware of that," said Tish. "The ferries have security cameras, by the way. You might not find anyone who remembered you, but there would still be evidence that you got on the ferry."

"Oh!" Luke looked instantly relieved.

"Did you run into any of the rest of the cast or crew after you left Skip's?" Tish asked.

"No, I headed straight for the ferry. Well, I saw Taylor, but he was talking to some guy, so I didn't stop to say hello. I don't think they saw me."

"Some guy?" asked Tish.

"This guy?" asked Tobias, holding out a picture on his phone. Tish took a side-long glance and saw that it was Neil McKinley.

"Yeah," said Luke, surprised.

"Thanks," Tobias said, nodding.

"It makes sense," said Tish.

Luke looked between the two of them. "It does? I thought it was weird."

"Behaviors are only weird when you can't see the entire pattern," said Tobias.

Luke's hand-scrawled out another note on the pad.

"Just follow Words from Granddad on Twitter," said Tish, eyeing the chicken scratch.

"Don't bother," said Tobias. "She never puts any of the good stuff on there."

"The internet is not ready for the good stuff," said Tish. "Luke, thanks for your time. I recommend that you not leave the state. The police detective will want to talk to you eventually."

"Oh," said Luke, looking nervous.

"It's fine. Just tell the truth."

Out on the porch of the hotel, Tish glared out at the incoming ferry on the bay.

"We didn't find out enough," said Tish. "I didn't really think he did it, but now I have to go dig up Taylor."

"Yeah, I've got the island gossips hunting for him."

"He's probably back in Seattle or something," said Tish.

"Well, we'll find out," said Tobias. "But I hear he's been crashing at a yurt near Olga for the last few days."

"He can't have," said Tish. "How is he getting around the island without Kyle to drive him?"

"Hitchhiking and probably that Neil guy from the description of the car."

"Where'd you hear that?" demanded Tish.

"George Fujiyama," said Tobias with a shrug.

"And why didn't you tell me?"

"Because you got run off the road yesterday, and I forgot. Also, I'm telling you now," said Tobias. Tish made a sour noise and shot more death stares at the hapless incoming ferry.

"Tish," said Tobias, sounding cautious.

"What?" she demanded.

"You have been grumpy since we started this business," said Tobias. "What's eating you? And don't tell me Nash or the dead guy or whatever. You've been out of sorts for a while."

I hate it when he calls me out. He's right every damn time, and that's worse than the actual problem itself.

She chewed on her answer for a long moment.

"I don't want to be doing this," she said at last.

"Well, no one wants to be in a murder investigation," he said reasonably. "But it's what we've got to contend with."

"The murder investigation is fine. I mean, it's a bummer, but it's fine. It's the movie. I don't want to do it."

"What? You love all the movies and stuff."

"I do. And I loved acting. But I think I thought that if I could do this, it would make up for failing as an actress. Only it turns out I hate it, and I wish I'd never done it. I don't care about these people enough to do the job properly, and I know I'm not giving it my best, but I can't seem to care."

"You didn't fail," said Tobias. "I've seen your IMDB page. You didn't make it big, but you didn't fail."

"It feels like failure from here," said Tish.

"And this was supposed to make you a success?"

"In Hollywood terms it would have."

"You don't live in Hollywood anymore. So why are you living on their terms?"

Uh... I don't know?

"You're running a successful business and you're making a huge difference in your community. Why don't you feel successful?"

"I wear leggings a lot."

"Uh... What now?"

"Successful people dress up and go places and have meetings. I just have lunch with Nash a lot. And I don't have expensive things and... I think I probably have too much fun to be considered successful."

"I believe you are confusing appearances and busy-work with success. It's OK to want recognition, but don't let someone tell you how to judge your achievements."

"I didn't think about it. I just did it."

"And now you're regretting it?"

"Yeah."

"Well, I think you're probably stuck with it until it's over, but the good news is you don't have to do it again, and now you know."

"And I keep telling myself that I can power through and then go back to having life just be the normal amount of crazy, but I'm mad about it."

Tobias nodded. "Ah, yes, being mad at the unchangeable. A Yearly trait. Sorry."

Tish laughed. "Thanks, Granddad."

"For what?"

"Not telling me to suck it up or change it or anything. I appreciate being allowed to just be mad."

"Anytime," he said with a shrug, but Tish reached over and hugged him.

Her phone chirped, and she looked at the screen.

"Nash says I should come over. Did he say anything else when you talked to him?"

"He was on his way to work. I don't think he had much time for chit-chat," said Tobias. "Why don't you leave me up at Eleanor's. I need to have a chat with her."

Oh, shit. Uh…

"Yeah, no problem," said Tish.

CHAPTER 21

MELT DOWN

Tish parked Tobias's beater white truck in front of the garage, leaving plenty of room for Nash's car. For some reason, the bouncy suspension and touchy brakes felt extra harsh today.

Some reason slash car wreck.

She gingerly exited and attempted to stretch without injuring anything.

How did Granddad ever crash things for a living? No wonder his back makes more noise than a box of pop rocks.

She had left Tobias at Eleanor's, and he'd entered her shop as if half the island wasn't buzzing about him stepping out on Eleanor with Brianna.

Zero guilt or, possibly, awareness.

Tish had kept her lips zipped and driven off in a hurry, but now that she was at Nash's, she had to admit that she was feeling a little nervous about her impending rendezvous.

She was slowly making her way up to the porch when the door flew open, and Claire came out.

"You're not Dad."

"No, he called and said to meet him here," said Tish.

"You aren't supposed to be here," said Claire, hands on her hips, glaring at Tish.

"Your father called," repeated Tish, trying to remain calm although her heart began to race.

Behind her, she heard Nash pull into the driveway, but she didn't know if it was better to wait for him or not.

"You're not supposed to be here," repeated Claire.

"Claire," said Tish, her voice wobbling. "I thought we were friends." Nora came out onto the porch.

"I don't want you here!" Claire yelled.

"Claire!" exclaimed Nora, sounding surprised. "You love Tish."

"She's ruining everything!"

Tish stared at Claire, tears forming in her eyes.

"That is enough!" Nash yelled, slamming the door on the SUV. "I have had it up to here with your attitude. You will not speak to Tish that way! I do not care what your mother says about her. Tish is your friend, and she is my girlfriend. You will treat her with respect."

"I don't say anything about Tish," said Nora.

"Shut up," barked Nash. "You don't belong here. You are the one who is ruining everything!"

"Excuse me?" snapped Nora.

"No!" wailed Claire. "No! You love Mom!"

"No, I damn well do not!" Nash yelled back. The father and daughter stared at each other in horror.

Shit. Shit. Shit.

The silence seemed unbearably intense.

"I'm on timeout," said Nash abruptly and walked away from all of them.

Tish glanced at Nora, who looked as wide-eyed as Tish felt, and then Claire burst into tears.

"We're going to go inside," said Nora, wrapping her arms around Claire. "You should..." she jerked her head toward Nash.

"Yeah," agreed Tish.

Tish found Nash behind the garage, staring at the swing set and play area. Nash let out a bellow of rage and punted a red rubber ball with a hard kick that sent it arcing over the swings.

Uh… Shit. Uh…

He stood with his hands on his hips, looking after the ball, and Tish tried to decide if touching him was a good idea.

Throwing a fit is usually what I do. Hm. That doesn't seem fair that I'm the only one who gets to melt down. OK, uh, what do I like when I'm having a moment?

"Do you want a hug?" she whispered.

"What?" He gave her a glare.

"I don't know what I'm supposed to do or say, and I thought maybe…"

"No!" he snapped. "I don't want a hug! I want everything to go back to the way it was. I want Claire to stop being a brat. I want my week off of parenting, And if I'm going to be divorced, I damn well want my ex-wife to *not* be at my house rearranging my furniture!"

"Yeah," agreed Tish.

"And I want to stop pretending I am fine with it! I am not fine with it! I don't want to be the adult. I don't want to have to suck anything up and be the bigger person or whatever. No. No, no, no, no! When do I get to get my way? When do I get to throw a fit?"

Now is fine. Don't say that. Say something validating.

Tish nodded.

"I count on you a lot. We all do. It's not fair that you have to be responsible all the time."

"I like being counted on," he protested.

"But no one likes being taken for granted. It feels like everyone assumes that you'll *do the right thing, take one for the team,* and be *the steady one.* But no one asked if you wanted to do that. And it extra feels like Nora's assuming that you'll suck this up, and that feels like it's partially my fault."

"It's not your fault," he said automatically.

He said that too fast. He thinks it's a little my fault.

"I mean…" Tish hesitated. "I feel like, at minimum, I've contributed, which makes it really hard for me to throw my own shit-fit and demand that you kick her ass out."

"It feels like you're mad at me for it, though!"

"I am! You're not saying anything, and I can't say anything because I'm just the girlfriend. And then I'm mad at me *and* you. And then it feels like we're mad at each other for the situation, and I hate that because I don't think either of us meant for this to happen."

Nash let out a gusty sigh, and his shoulders slumped. Tish waited.

"You have a right to be frustrated and mad,'" she added in case that hadn't been clear.

"OK, now I want a hug."

"OK, great."

Tish let out her own sigh as she wrapped her arms around his waist and burrowed her head into his shoulder. "God, this is the good shit right here."

"Tish," he whispered into her hair, "am I your drug of choice?"

"Oh, yeah," said Tish. "Totally addicted. Need a hit daily."

He chuckled. "Although, I can't say you're wrong. This is kind of the oxytocin hot spot."

"Delicious, delicious oxytocin," murmured Tish, hugging him tighter.

"You can't squeeze it out of me like orange juice," he protested.

"Opinions vary," said Tish.

"I love you," he said.

"I know."

You put up with so much weird stuff from me that it's the only explanation.

"Don't get cocky on me, kid. Just say it back like you're in a drama. You're not Han Solo."

Tish looked up at him, feeling the warm glow of an appropriately applied movie line.

"I really do, but I don't want to say it like a drama because someone always dies after it gets said."

"And we have enough problems with that already. Better say it like you're in a romantic comedy."

"Mmmm… Can't we go, like, action-thriller?"

"I think we run into the same death problem."

"No, it's only *near* death in an action movie. We'll totally triumph in the end."

"Don't we need more of a wind effect, though? I feel like if it gets said in an action movie, the helicopter is usually about to take off or something."

Tish couldn't stop the happy giggle that came out of her.

"I really do love you," she said.

"You're ruining it. That was a real-life love you."

"I'm that good of an actress. I can make even real life sound like real life."

"Better than real life," he said and leaned down to kiss her.

With the softness of the kiss and the strength of his arms around her, Tish, for one moment, felt perfectly happy. Then she heard the backdoor open.

"Dad?" called Claire's plaintive voice.

"Nope!" he bellowed without moving from his hug. "Not done yet. Back inside."

"OK," said Claire and shut the door again.

"What was that?" asked Tish, maintaining the hug.

"In my house, we're allowed to take a timeout," said Nash. "If you need a moment to collect your shit, you just declare that you need a minute, and you can go take it. It was one of the things that always drove me nuts about Nora. Once a fight started, she was in my grill non-stop until I gave up. I couldn't get a breath. And then I realized I was doing the same thing to Claire, so now we're allowed to call a timeout."

Tish cranked her head back and looked up at him. "You didn't tell me I could do that."

"Yeah, well, we usually don't need it because we don't fight."

"We haven't been fighting this week?"

He sighed, then frowned. "You know what? No. We haven't been fighting. We've been having some damn problems because life has been throwing us curve balls. And maybe we don't know how to solve them, but I don't think we've been disagreeing. In fact, if anything, we're in total agreement that this bullshit has been sucking."

Tish let out a ragged sigh. "Yes. Sucking so much. I wish I'd never taken that meeting with my agent or jumped into this project. I wanted to be able to say I won at the movie game one way or another, but now I just want it to be over with."

Nash groaned. "Tish, baby, this is not your fault, and you did not fail at the movie game."

"It feels like failure from here," said Tish, hiding her face in his chest.

"No, you aim high, and I love your ambition, but I think you underestimated this project. But we will get the murder thing solved, and then you can kick the movie business's ass."

Tish cranked her head to look up at him. "I love movies. I loved acting. I think what I underestimated was how over making movies I am."

There was no mistaking the hint of smugness in Nash's smile.

"Shut up," she said, glaring at him.

"I didn't say anything."

"You haven't said anything since I told you about the movie," said Tish. "And I appreciate the hell out of that and you."

"I have been so good," said Nash. "I have kept my mouth shut soooo hard."

Tish giggled. "Yes. Thank you."

"OK," he said, stepping back. "I now feel like I can manage not yelling at my child and maybe expressing myself in a calm and rational manner."

"OK," said Tish. "I guess I'll go…"

"Exactly nowhere. Because the first thing that we're going to establish as a ground rule is that you are not *just the girlfriend* or whatever bullshit you keep saying. I love you. We are together. This is our relationship, and you will be treated with respect, and you will be welcome in my house."

"Emmett," said Tish, her eyes filling with unexpected tears.

"Patricia," he said, his eyes twinkling.

Tish sighed. She still didn't like her name.

But, boy, do I love this man.

"Also, I called you because I totally pumped Ronny for information, and I found out that when they searched Skip's place, they found something really interesting."

CHAPTER 22

WHITTLING

Claire saw them walk in the door and promptly hid her tear-streaked face in Nora's side. Nora hugged her and kissed her head, and Tish felt a swell of jealousy. Nora was always going to come first for Claire, and that was how it was supposed to be, but Tish couldn't help wanting to be able to hug Claire, too.

"OK," said Nash. "Claire, I'm sorry I yelled at you. I shouldn't have raised my voice, and I shouldn't have used a swear word. But we need to talk about how you've been treating Tish lately."

Claire mumbled something, but it was muffled by Claire's face being buried in Nora. Nora kissed Claire's head again and murmured something that Tish couldn't catch. Claire pulled her head out and looked at both of them.

"I'm sorry, Tish," Claire muttered.

"That's OK," said Tish, feeling like a wicked stepmother and hating it.

"No, it really isn't," said Nash. "Claire-bear, what's going on?"

"Mom said she was coming back to the island," said Claire sheepishly. "I just thought... Well, last time, you guys tried to patch it up..."

Nora and Nash exchanged a look that Tish couldn't interpret.

"Daddy and I aren't getting back together," said Nora.

"But you're staying here," protested Claire.

Nora nodded. "Yeah, you know, I shouldn't have done that. I didn't mean to confuse you. I thought it was only going to be one night. You can stay with Dad, but I think I'll have to go back to our house."

"But I think we're filming tomorrow," said Tish. "Maybe. If the police let us have the tower back. They said they would let us know tonight."

"Not helping," said Nash.

"I know," said Tish tiredly. "But I still need this stupid movie to work out, and she's perfect for the damn part."

"I have an idea," said Nora, eyeing them. "I don't know if you're going to like it."

"Hit me," said Tish.

"What if you and I swap for the night?"

"What?" asked Nash with the frigid tone of disapproval.

"Claire and I can go stay with Tobias, and Tish can stay here for the night."

And… I'm not hating that. No clue what Granddad is going to think.

"Sold," said Nash and held out his hand. Nora nodded and shook to seal the deal.

"Do I get a vote?" asked Tish.

"No," said Nash.

"OK, just checking. Should we warn Granddad?"

"Mmm… later," said Nash.

"Tobias lets me use knives," said Claire, sounding pleased.

"Wait, what?" demanded Nora.

"It's for whittling," fudged Tish.

Mostly. Sort of. It's a pocket knife, and what else does a kid do but cut stuff with it? Mostly sticks, but… whatever.

"Yeah, sticks. I whittle sticks."

"Uh-huh," said Nora, looking like she knew she was being bull-shitted.

"OK, so are we all clear? Tish is our friend. Mommy and Daddy are not getting back together. And Tobias will *not* be letting you use knives," said Nash.

Claire looked up at Tish, and Tish met her eye.

I swear to God, kid, as long as you don't cut yourself or the dog, I will let you use whatever knives you want.

"Yeah, Dad," huffed Claire. "I got it."

"OK, great, because Tish and I need to go fight crime with Tobias."

"Um, actually, I just left him at Eleanor's," said Tish.

"Oh my God," gasped Nora. "Really? What happened? Did she say anything?"

"I chickened out. I just dropped him in the parking lot of her shop and high-tailed it," said Tish.

"What?" demanded Claire. "What's wrong with Eleanor?"

"Nothing," said Tish and Nora together.

"Granddad might have ticked Eleanor off, so he might have to apologize," said Tish. "That's all."

"Oh," said Claire. "Well, he'd better apologize good then, or she might take her jam out of his basement, and we don't want that."

"Uh…" said Nora, glancing at Tish and Nash. "Is that a metaphor?"

"No, she's got a bunch of jam in the storm cellar," said Tish.

"And I like jam," said Claire.

Nora made an exasperated sigh. "You know, this is why I'm happy to be off the island."

"Oh," said Tish. "That's why I kind of like it."

"Let's go get Tobias," said Nash abruptly.

"OK," said Tish with a shrug. "Nora, I guess I'll text you later?"

"Yeah, sounds good," said Nora.

Nash practically pushed her outside, and she let him because he seemed to be in a hurry.

And frankly, I'm still just confused as to what's going on.

"That went OK?" Tish said hesitantly.

"Yes, it did," he said and kissed her on the forehead.

I will take that. I don't know what it's for, but I will take that.

"If I tell you to ride with me instead of driving yourself, are you going to fight me on it?"

Tish hesitated. "We'll have to come back here at some point to get the truck," she pointed out. Nash shrugged as if shuffling cars around wasn't going to be a problem. "I mean, as long as I don't have to ride in the back."

Nash snorted. "We'll make Tobias ride back there. He'll find it funny."

"I feel like it's possible that we may be signing Granddad up for a lot of things without his permission," said Tish. "But..."

I'm tired, and I need help. Hopefully, Granddad won't be too mad.

"But I guess we can always get a new plan if he dislikes it."

She looked up at Nash, hoping for reassurance.

"Yes," he said with a sharp nod. "I've got a plan B and C for all of these things."

"Oh." Tish felt relieved. Nash was good at plans. She usually had to walk people through coming up with what to do, but he never seemed to need it. "OK. Let's go."

"That's it?" he asked suspiciously as he opened the passenger door of the SUV.

"What's it?"

That got her another kiss, this time on the lips.

I will take that, too. No clue what I'm doing. But I'm not complaining.

Her phone started ringing before they were all the way to Eleanor's, and Tish saw with trepidation that it was her grandfather.

"Hey, Granddad," said Tish, picking up.

"OK, I know you were dealing with Nash stuff, but I need you to come up back now because Eleanor is not equipped to help me chase down Taylor Blake."

"Well, running in Birkenstocks is very difficult without the right socks."

"Neither of us are running anywhere at our age. That's why we've got you and Nash. But she's narrowed in on his location, so now we need to go get him."

"Well, Nash and I are on the way to get you. We got waylaid

with talking to Nora, but he says he's been pumping Ronny for information."

"You've had such a positive influence on him! I'll cancel Kyle and redirect him and Quincy to their secondary mission."

"Oh, OK," said Tish.

"See you in a few! Bye!"

Tish looked at Nash. "Have I had a positive influence on you?" she asked.

"Well, I mean... *An* influence, certainly. But positive? Seems open to debate."

"Debate? What debate?! There is no debate. I have been the worst influence. I have worked so hard at it. I'm insulted to even have that implied."

"I would kiss you, but I'm driving."

"Thanks. I'm concerned because Kyle was our backup, and now Granddad's redirecting him to a secondary mission, but I don't know what that is. I need to get my head back in the game."

"Can't let Tobias get ahead of us," agreed Nash.

"Oh, he's always ahead of us," said Tish, rolling her eyes. "Most of the time, I'm just trying to keep up."

Nash chuckled. Tish reached out and laced her fingers through his free hand as he drove and only took her hand away again when he had to slow down to pull into the parking lot.

"Come on, come on," said Tobias, yanking open the back door of the police vehicle. "We've got to get a wiggle on before Taylor gets on the ferry."

"Burn rubber, Toretto," said Tish.

"I live my life a quarter mile at a time," said Nash, easing out onto the road at a snail's pace.

The Fast and the Furious, 2001. Vin Diesel is so underrated. Or a sell-out. I'm never sure which. Possibly both.

"You're not allowed to quote movies I haven't seen," said Tobias.

"You need to watch more movies," said Tish.

"I watch plenty of movies.

"I can't stick only to the oeuvre of John Wayne," said Tish.

I mean… maybe I could. There's a lot of material there, but I'd have to brush up.

"Cary Grant has more to work with," said Nash.

"Wittier certainly," agreed Tish. "But would they be more applicable? The point of movie lines is that they must communicate the current situation or emotion in a way that simply speaking would not. John Wayne may have more breadth."

"Mmm…." Said Tobias.

"Can she switch sides like that?" asked Nash.

"Dunno. But now I'm thinking about switching sides. Cary Grant had better writers. I will have to consider who would be the most usefully quotable movie star."

"It's hard to quantify. Do you need someone with a large film catalog or someone with an impactful career so that more people would have seen the movie and recognize the line?" mused Tish.

"Not the second one," said Nash. "Movie lines aren't intended to communicate to a broader audience. They are meant for a select group of insiders. You only need a movie that the other person would recognize, not that everyone would know."

"He's got a point," said Tobias. "OK, pull up here." He pointed to the upper parking lot. "I bet he's going to try to walk on, and if you go up to him and say the police want to talk to him, I bet he'll bust out toward me."

Tish and Nash exchanged glances.

"I'm not sure he's going to bolt," said Tish.

"I am. He's got the anxiety, and Kyle hasn't been around to keep him doped up."

Tish rolled her eyes at her grandfather's description of edibles.

"OK, well, I'll go talk to him," said Tish. "And if he runs, you and Nash can block the exits or whatever."

Nash nodded, his eyes twinkling.

Tish walked down to the ferry dock. It didn't take her long to spot Taylor. He was wearing a ball cap and sunglasses. He looked like a caricature of a movie star trying not to be spotted. The only surprising thing was that no one else seemed to have noticed.

Tish sidled up behind him.

"Avoiding the cops, Taylor?" she asked.

He spun around, panic suffusing his face.

"I…" He seemed to already be gasping for air.

"You can see the Sheriff's Department car from here," she said, pointing to Nash's vehicle.

Taylor made a panicked noise and ran for the stairs up to the parking lot. Tish groaned. She was too stiff to be going up those stupidly steep steps. Following slowly, Tish hoped Tobias and Nash were in position. She watched his running figure and squinted. His form looked very familiar.

Taylor sprinted around the corner and then bounced back and fell down on his ass like he'd run into a wall. Tish slowed her run and then walked as Nash came into view. Nash put a hand under Taylor's armpit, hoisted him to his feet, walked him firmly to the nearest bench, and plopped the movie star down. Taylor looked so startled at the manhandling that she nearly laughed.

"Hello, Taylor," said Tobias, settling down next to him on the bench with all the beaming gentility of a senior citizen who just happened to be passing by.

"I…" Taylor looked around at the three of them.

"You've been a mite hard to get ahold of," said Tobias. "But that's OK. I understand. Feeling a bit skittish about having it known that you hired that photographer to follow Skip. I admit it does look bad when there's a murder investigation going on."

"Skip was blackmailing people!"

"Yeah," agreed Tobias. "You said that in your voicemail to Tish."

Taylor blanched.

"I hired Neil to find out something about Skip. I figured if I could get something on him, I could get him to back off of me and leave the movie alone. I was tired of being under his thumb!"

"So you killed him, then?" asked Tobias conversationally.

"What? No! I was with you at dinner that night with Emma!" He looked desperately at Tish.

"Emma saw Skip after the two of you left the restaurant," said Tish. "She said you went back for your jacket."

"I did," said Taylor.

"But you didn't get on the ferry with Emma," said Tobias. "What did you do?"

"When I got my jacket, I saw a text from Neil. He said he wanted to talk. So I walked Emma down to the ferry and told her I would crash at the hotel so I wouldn't be late the next day. Then I ran back up the hill and talked to Neil. He said he was calling it a night. He showed me a picture of Luke Green messing with Skip's car. So we figured Skip was in for the night, and that was that. Neil went to his Air BnB, and I really did go to the hotel. Although, I'm not sure anyone noticed me or will remember. It's like the most low-key place ever."

"And that's why you went to Skip's house after you found out he was dead," said Tish. "You wanted to make sure there wasn't any evidence against you at his house. What'd you do? Call Neil to give you a ride from our house?"

"Yeah," said Taylor shame-facedly. "Sorry about scaring you, but I wanted to find that evidence. I had Neil drop me off a little way before East Sound and told him to go back and see what you two were up to."

"But you didn't find any of the evidence?" asked Tobias.

"No! And I don't understand it! He always brought it to every movie we did together," said Taylor. "He loved waving that damn folder around in front of other people. I found the folder, but…"

"But the folder was empty, wasn't it?" asked Nash. "There were folders with names on them, but the pages were all blank."

"He must have hidden the evidence somewhere," said Taylor. "And I'm sorry I got a DUI at seventeen and hit a dog, but I don't understand how he got the file when it's under my real name. Maybe that mattered when I was still with Disney, but it's been ten years. I just wanted Skip to leave me alone. I haven't found where he hid anything, though. It's probably back at his place in L.A. or something."

"Or," said Tish, "he was bluffing everyone."

Taylor stared up at her in shock.

"What? He was manufacturing a problem for me or possibly you and me. That tells me he didn't have enough on you to make you do what he wanted. The guy was a narcissist. I doubt he'd be interested in doing the legwork to find actual evidence."

"He was totally bluffing," said Nash. "Juvenile records are sealed."

"Oh," said Taylor, looking affronted.

"Whose names were on the folders?" asked Tish, looking between Taylor and Nash.

"I'm not sure," said Nash. "Ronny only caught a glimpse before Warshaw sent the CSI guys in. I know Taylor had one, but that was it."

"But you saw them," said Tish, turning back to Taylor. "You had a folder and Thiago, but who else?"

"Some people I didn't know," said Taylor. "But I think I saw one for Frank."

"Frank," said Tobias thoughtfully. "Hm."

It was a puzzle piece that didn't quite seem to fit anywhere.

"Um... Is that it?" asked Taylor.

"Well, eventually, you are going to have to talk to the detective," said Nash.

"Bummer, bro," said Taylor, looking defeated.

"Yeah, but not yet," said Tobias. "I think we want to talk to her first."

"Oh, great," said Taylor, looking relieved.

"Yeah, except now I'm blackmailing you," said Tish and felt Nash and Tobias giving her looks.

"What do you want?" asked Taylor, sinking in on himself.

"Well, I'm short one director, and if I get permission to film tomorrow morning, then I'm not missing my window of opportunity. That means it's on you."

"Oh," said Taylor sitting upright. "Seriously?"

"Yeah. I told the studio we'd pull through on this and I don't have time to be monkeying around while they find a new director. If we can get footage in the can, they'll see that it's more profitable to just keep going."

"I've been thinking about getting into directing and I think the story has a lot of promise," said Taylor, eagerly.

"And that's why we're going back to the original pages," said Tish. "Plus, if we can get something in the can in spite of the murder investigation you know they'll let you stay in the chair once you get back to L.A."

"Yeah," breathed Taylor and Tish could see that she'd sunk the hook. Taylor was now committed to the project.

"Great. Luke's up at the hotel if you want to go talk to him and prep up.

"Good idea," said Taylor, standing up.

"And you don't tell anyone you talked to us about any of this until we give you the say so," said Tish.

"Sure," said Taylor, with a shrug.

"OK, off you go." Tish clapped her hands at him and he looked puzzled but then went in the direction of the hotel.

"OK, that's some of my ducks all rowed up. Now, I just need Warshaw to release my location and round up Emma and the rest of the crew and then I'm in business."

"Also, maybe figure out if Frank killed Skip?" asked Tobias.

"OK, that too," said Tish.

"I can't believe he just did what you told him," said Nash,

scratching his head and watching as Taylor left.

"Yeah, but you're you," said Tish. "And you don't live in my benevolent dictatorship."

"Where do I live then?" asked Nash.

"In the kingdom next door with Princess Claire," said Tish.

"Am I supposed to be Prince Charming?" asked Nash, looking like this was a bridge too far.

Always.

"Don't be ridiculous," said Tish. "You're the handsome wood-cutter."

"Oh, OK. I can chop things."

Yes, a Prince Charming who sometimes chops things with his shirt off.

Tobias gave a gusty sigh as if he couldn't believe he'd been saddled with either of them.

"OK, well, now that we've settled that. I think it's time we called the Detective for a sit-down. Obviously, without the woodcutter in tow. Don't want to get him axed."

"No," said Nash firmly. "You need the woodcutter. I'm the one that will be arranging your sit-down."

Tish and Tobias exchanged looks.

"As long as you're not putting yourself at risk," said Tish cautiously.

"There's nothing risky about asking a Detective to interview her top suspects. We'll just also give Sam a call, so she's there in case you get arrested."

CHAPTER 23

PAMELA SPILLS THE TEA

"This doesn't feel like neutral territory," Tish whispered to Tobias. They were sitting in the outdoor patio area of the Sheriff's Department offices. It had the unloved feeling of a publicly owned space that multiple people used, but no one was responsible for. Tish was trying to figure out who was accountable for the cigarette butts in the coffee can tucked away by the gutter spout. But there was a nice picnic bench, and a sun tarp covered the rockery and cement slab.

"But we had to go along with it for Nash," Tobias whispered back. "He's been a real team player on this case, and we have to respect his police stuff."

"He really has been! I don't know what's come over him!"

"I think he's been feeling left out of the crime-solving," said Tobias. "I think most cops probably want to solve crimes. It's got to be on their list of goals when they sign up for being cops."

"I guess," said Tish.

Solving crimes has never been on my list. It's not as much fun as it looks like on the crime shows.

The door swung open, and Pamela marched out, looking as sour as last time. Nash came after her, wearing his special parent look that said Pamela was trying his patience. Sam Arlen, Tobias's local lawyer, came out afterward with a handcrafted coffee mug and a perplexed expression.

Probably not sure what she's doing here, but it might be keeping Granddad or me out of jail.

Sam was wearing her usual low-key cargo shorts, TEVAs, and

t-shirt, but the glorious red textured glaze on the mug was an island masterpiece.

"OK," Pamela said, scrutinizing them. Her bangs looked slightly better than last time. Tish thought there might have been intermediary trimming. "I have read your statement about the incident on the road, and I have spoken to all your movie people. Mr. Jones and Mr. Heron appear to have disappeared off the island. I can only assume it's because you told them to stop speaking to me."

"No, that's because they don't like you," said Tobias.

"I told Kyle he could talk to you, and he said..." Tish paused. They were all looking at her. "That he would prefer not to."

"She might be paraphrasing," said Tobias.

"Believe it or not, I got that," snapped Pamela. "I realize that you don't like me, but I have a job to do."

"We didn't get a chance to like you!" exclaimed Tish.

"You accused Tish of murder," said Tobias. "And me of being one of those yahoos who want to bring back the *good ol' days.*" He put air quotes around the phrase. "Which, trust me, as a senior citizen, I can tell you they were not that great. They just had fewer people to be annoying. And I am fine with the alphabets."

Sam did a spit take into her mug.

"Did you just call the LGBTQ+ community the alphabets?" she asked, laughing.

"Tish says it rude, but I get the letters in the wrong order every time," said Tobias grimacing. "I figure alphabets is less rude than leaving someone out."

"Meh," said Sam with a shrug. "As long as you put the *Ls* first, then I don't care."

Tobias snorted. "Yes, but you ain't my only alphabet. Quincy is a they-them now. What if they don't think I care because I leave them out? I looked up suicide rates on young people in the plus community. I ain't having that on my island."

Sam froze, and then she cleared her throat and smiled at Tobias.

"It's also OK to just say queer," said Sam, softly.

Tobias made a face. "Are you sure? It seems blanket-y."

"Stop pretending you care about gay people!" barked Pamela. "I know all about how you targeted poor Dorothy just because she's gay and got Sean put in jail!"

Tobias and Tish exchanged looks, and Tish scratched her head. "Aunt Dorothy's gay? Since when?"

Pamela's eyes went wide in horror.

"Huh," said Tobias. They were both silent, and then Tobias rubbed his chin. "Well, is she dating anyone?"

Pamela made a stuttering noise of confusion.

"Because I know a gal over in Friday Harbor that's single. Plays a mean game of pinochle. About Dorothy's age. Really likes 'em with big personalities. I mean, Dorothy was never my cup of tea, but I could see her making someone happy."

"You mean Sissy Stapleton," said Sam. "And she got back together with her girlfriend."

"Well, drat. How about you?" he asked the detective. "Are you going to ask Dorothy out?"

"I'm not gay," said Pamela.

Tobias scratched his chin again. "Are you sure?"

"This is just a very bad haircut!" Pamela yelled, pointing at her head. "I'm not gay!" Then she froze, and her eyes swiveled to Sam.

"She's not," said Sam. "We can tell the difference between butch and bad hair."

"Well, maybe I can convince Sissy to break up again," said Tobias thoughtfully.

"Tobias!" exclaimed Sam. "Not all the lesbians you know have to date each other. I mean... we all do, but we don't have to."

"Yeah," said Tish. "Besides, then Sissy *and* Dorothy would be coming to family gatherings."

"Yeah, but then I'd have someone to play pinochle with," agreed Tobias. "I mean, I love you, Tishkins, but let's face it, you're terrible at pinochle."

"What?" gasped Pamela.

"Tish," said Tobias more loudly, as if Pamela were the deaf one. "Is very bad a pinochle. Nearly caused a riot. She's that bad."

"It wasn't a riot," said Tish reassuringly. "Barely a scrum. More of a shouting match."

"But Dorothy said…" began Pamela.

"Said what? That Tish and I targeted her poor baby Sean? Uh-huh." Tobias shook his head. "That kid's a liar and an addict, and Dorothy's not doing him or herself any favors by pretending otherwise."

No wonder she didn't get my Wizard of Oz reference. She probably thought I was talking about Aunt Dorothy.

"Sean literally dropped his bag of coke in front of me," said Nash. "When he tried to assault Tobias at a memorial service."

I like how he tactfully left out Aunt Dorothy trying to throw me on the floor.

Tish smiled at Nash, and he winked at her from his position, leaning against the wall.

"What?" Pamela looked like she was taking a few too many blows to her personal narrative.

"He did," said Sam. "I was there. Well, hell, everyone on the island was there. We all saw it. Sean jumped at Tobias and then took a cane to the gut. Then Dorothy tried to tackle Tish, and Nash had to put her in a headlock. And then the band played, and we all ate Talia Granger's cake. It was the best damn party we've had in years. Reginald would have been so proud."

"I often think that," said Tobias, looking happy about Sam's assessment of Reginald's wake.

"I still don't understand when Aunt Dorothy started dating women," said Tish. "My mom didn't say anything, and I just talked to her the other day!"

"Your mom doesn't know?" wailed Pamela. "I wasn't trying to

out her! Dorothy said you didn't like her because she was gay! She's in my support group for parents of addicts!"

"No, we don't like her because she tried to make Tish pay for Sean's theft and back rent," said Tobias. "Never even occurred to me that she was gay."

"Oh, Jesus," swore Pamela.

"Better not let Aunt Dorothy hear you take the Lord's name in vain," said Tish. "I don't care how gay she is. That's not going to fly."

Pamela covered her face with her hand.

"Now look what you've done, Tish. You've made her do the facepalm emoji."

"I'm tweeting that," said Tish.

"Stop twittering me! Not everything I say needs to be reported to the online masses."

"Stop saying things that fit perfectly in a hundred and forty characters then."

"I don't even know what that means."

"Did someone in the support group cut your hair?" asked Tish. "Mom said Dorothy got her hair cut."

"Sabrina, in group, is practicing for her stylist's credentials," said Pamela with a stoic expression. "And we're trying to be supportive. Obviously, Dorothy went second."

"They do look better today," offered Tish, feeling bad.

"Thanks," said Pamela, but she sounded as if she had given up.

"OK," said Sam, taking a seat at the picnic table next to Tobias, "so we've established that Tish and Tobias don't hate the alphabets." She paused to snort-chuckle. "Yeah, sorry, I'm going to be texting that to like eight people in a minute. Can we also maybe establish that Tish didn't kill her director? Because from what I hear, the guy was a total douche-canoe, and there are plenty of people who wanted him dead."

"Yeah, yeah," said Pamela, still sounding grumpy. "Currently, I suspect Frank Brooking, the cinematographer."

"Oh," said Tish.

No! He's our suspect!

"Well, he was on the list," said Tobias cautiously. "Why do you think it was Frank?"

"Because he's the one that OK'd Thiago giving Skip the combo to the lock box up at the tower. He also sent Skip the dailies and had other email communication detailing your actions the evening of his death. And Skip's phone records indicate that he called most of the cast and crew before he left the house, but Frank Brooking was the last person he talked to. And because I'm pretty sure he's the one who ran Tish off the road."

"You got into Skip's computer?" asked Tish.

"Well, that password was *Password,* so yes, we managed it," said Pamela.

Tobias glared at Tish. It was a look that plainly said he was mad they hadn't tried the computer when they had the chance.

"Well," said Tish, clearing her throat, "what we wanted to share with you was that I received a phone call that indicated that Skip was blackmailing people."

She took out her phone and played the voicemail.

"And you don't know who left the message?" asked Pamela when it was done.

"They didn't use a number I recognized," said Tish. "And you can hear that they're disguising their voice."

Pamela nodded. "We found a number of empty folders at Skip's place with names on them. Frank was one of the ones with folders. We assume that the contents were removed. So it could be that he was blackmailing Frank and tried to make Frank help him with something up at the tower."

"Having OK'd giving Skip the combination to the equipment, you could argue that Frank knew Skip was going up there," said Tobias.

"Exactly," said Pamela.

"It's not proof," said Tish.

"No, but it's enough to press him on."

"Hm," said Tobias thoughtfully.

"So, is there anything else that you've been holding out on telling me? Because now would be the time to tell me. I need to be fully aware of circumstances before I start interrogating Frank."

I feel like something still isn't right. It wasn't Luke. It wasn't Taylor. But Frank?

"I can't think of anything," said Tobias.

"Great," said Pamela. "So you're going to be staying out of my way while I get this wrapped up."

"We will not interfere with you arresting Frank," said Tobias solemnly, and Pamela looked suspicious but pleased.

"I'm assuming this means I can shoot at the tower tomorrow, though?" asked Tish hopefully.

"Still? I might be arresting your cameraman!"

"But you might not, and I do have a second DP." She looked at the assembly of blank expressions. "Director of Photography," she added.

Pamela shook her head, but Tish shrugged. If she wasn't going to win at solving a murder, then she was damn well going to make it across the line on the stupid movie.

"Fine, yes," said Pamela, rolling her eyes. "Knock yourself out. Go make a movie."

Tish waited until they were in the truck and well away from the Sheriff's Department before speaking.

"I know I just agreed to not put a spoke in her wheel, but… we're really not interfering?"

"If she thinks it's Frank, then it one hundred percent is not," said Tobias. "Maybe he was driving that Subaru—I don't know. But we need to go back to the murder board and have another look because I'm telling you… it doesn't feel right."

CHAPTER 24

MORE MURDER BOARD

Back at the house, Tobias pulled out the board and flipped it over. Tish was surprised to see that there were more lines on the timeline.

"What are these?" asked Tish.

"I bought a multi-color pack of dry-erase markers," said Tobias.

"I can see that, thank you. What do they represent?"

"This case has two problems," said Tobias. "Everyone has a motive, and everyone has an opportunity."

"Those are pretty big problems," agreed Tish.

"Right. So we need to start eliminating the suspects, and I figured that the easiest problem to attack was opportunity. That means nailing down the whereabouts of the suspects that had the most interaction with Skip."

Why the most interaction?

"Because those are the people that could get close enough to Skip to push him over the edge," said Tish, answering her own question.

"Right. But you've collected quite the passel of folks for this movie thing and that's a lot of legwork. Also, we're too out front on this case."

"Out front?" asked Tish, although she was still trying to figure out passel.

But I will not be asking what it means. I will Google later.

"From the police detective on down, everyone on this case knows us. They can see us coming. So, I did a little outsourcing to Kyle. He's been friendly with all the cast and crew and can ask questions without sounding like he's asking questions."

"So you mean that his low-key drug dealing is coming in handy?" asked Tish.

"Yes. Using illegal substances to integrate with a culture is a common infiltration technique. Doesn't mean I'm going to approve. Don't press your luck."

Tish grinned, and she caught the twinkle in her grandfather's eye. She looked at the board again, tracking the names against the lines.

"So we're eliminating the key grip, the gaffer, and Thiago?"

"They alibi each other. They did some drinking at Olga and went back to the ferry and over to Anacortes. They were all on the ferry before Emma saw Skip on the moped."

"We already talked to Emma and Taylor," said Tish, pointing to the lines. "This is how you knew Taylor didn't get on the ferry with Emma, isn't it?"

"Yeah," said Tobias. "The island snoops have been snooping overtime on this movie, so Kyle and I put them to good use."

Tish scrutinized the board. "So I take it Frank was drinking with them but didn't get on the ferry?" she asked, pointing to the circled *F* hanging out next to the word Olga. "The key grip must have told Ellis about Skip's phone call. So where did Frank go after they left?"

"I don't know," said Tobias. "That's one of the reasons he was on the top of my suspects list."

"Maybe Pamela's right," said Tish. "Her circumstantial evidence is pretty good. It just…"

"Doesn't feel right," said Tobias. "Although… I am pretty sure he is the one who drove you off the road."

"What?"

"You were on the phone, and you mentioned that you were going to tell the detective to check Skip's phone records. Pamela said there were calls to Frank. I think Frank didn't want that to be found out."

I feel like I should be more mad about that. I'll be mad later. Right now, I'm just glad to have that explained.

"See, that just makes him look more guilty."

"I know. And believe me, that ticks me off, but I'm still not sure he killed Skip. I'm going to call George and have him ask over at the bar if they remember when Frank left. I'll tell him to text you if he finds out anything."

"He couldn't text you?" asked Tish.

"I'm going to go talk to Brianna," said Tobias.

"Granddad," said Tish hesitantly.

"She's one of the people on the set that seems to talk to everyone."

"She does," said Tish thoughtfully. "More than I thought she did. I feel like everyone's mentioned her at some point. She said she was feeling motherly. I guess she wasn't kidding."

"Bit odd since I don't think she's mentioned her daughter more than once," said Tobias. "But I guess I don't get to dictate someone else's definition of motherly."

"Particularly since you grandparent half the island," said Tish drily.

"Grandparenting is way more fun," said Tobias with a shrug. "Well-known fact."

Her phone beeped, and Tish read the text.

Hey Tish! I'm packing up over at Nash's. Can you pop in before we head over to Tobias's? I wanted to talk.

"What?" asked Tobias.

"Nora wants to talk before she comes over."

"Why is Nora coming over?"

"Uh… So… You know how I was all, I don't want Nora staying at Nash's house?"

"I thought Nash was on the same page with that."

"He is. And surprisingly, Nora was also on the same page. But I still need her for the shoot tomorrow. So… we agreed to do a swap."

196 | BETHANY MAINES

"A swap?"

"I said she could stay over here with Claire while I stayed with Nash."

"Well, Claire's welcome any time, but why I gotta get stuck with that woman?"

"Please, Granddad!"

"She's annoyingly on trend, or whatever it is you say. She's always judging things."

"Yeah. That is kind of true." He glared at her. "I know! I'm sorry! But I want to see my boyfriend, damn it!"

"And also make a movie and also solve a murder," said Tobias, with an eye roll.

"Yes! And Nora was really making an effort to not be a bitch."

"I don't like that word."

"Sorry. But she was really trying to make it work with Nash and I. I feel like I should reciprocate."

"How did I end up horse traded away in this deal, though?"

"Oh, whatever. You bartered me off to Kandace last month."

"We're still getting eggs off of that deal," said Tobias nodding. "Your plumbing skills were much appreciated. Although, speaking of which, that's all I'm cooking them for dinner."

"Plumbing?"

"Eggs!"

"Oh, right. That makes more sense. Well, that's fine."

"Uh-huh," said Tobias, sourly.

"I'm going to go pack for tonight and tidy my room. Claire can stay in there, and Nora can stay in the guest room, right?"

"Yeah, whatever," said Tobias, going back to the board.

Tish was heading out to her car when she saw Kyle pull into the drive.

"Hey! It's our official leg work guy," she said. "The police detective was really pissed about being unable to find you."

"Really?" he asked, beaming.

"Oh, yeah. You and Matt were specifically mentioned as having disappeared into the wind."

Kyle laughed. "I'm not giving it up to some fresh out of Seattle detective."

"Yeah. We found out that she's in a support group with my Aunt Dorothy, and that's why she hates Granddad and me."

"What? Seriously? That's bullshit."

Tish shrugged. "It's fine. The detectives got her sights set on Frank, my DP. Which, honestly, is going to be a bigger problem for me than Skip dying."

"I was going to ask Tobias about him," said Kyle. "From the board, it looks like he's one of our dangling threads."

"Yeah… I think Granddad's got George Fujiyama asking about him."

"You've got thoughtful face," said Kyle. "What's up?"

"Do you know Cooper? Retro Betty's kid. He and Ten and Grover are in a punk band together."

"Sure. Their sound is pretty raw, but it's not the worst thing I've ever heard."

"That is quite possibly the nicest thing anyone's ever said about their sound, but he said something the other day, and it's been bugging me. I don't suppose you have time to ask him about Brianna Meadows? I don't want to mention it to Granddad."

"Please tell me the rumors aren't true," said Kyle. "Eleanor knows I'm Team Yearly. If they break up, I will lose my jam privileges."

"Jam is life," said Tish. "But I'm not sure anything is going on in any direction with anyone. I just want to discreetly inquire where and when Cooper saw Brianna Meadows."

"Yeah, I got you," said Kyle.

"OK, I'm heading over to Nash's, so call or whatever once you know something."

"On it," said Kyle, restarting the Jeep.

I don't know if that was the right thing or if it actually is anything. But I want to know. And I don't want to bring it up to Granddad.

CHAPTER 25

MACHIAVELLIAN MALARKY

"Hey, Tish," said Nora, opening a door with a laundry basket on her hip. "Thanks for coming."

"No problem," said Tish cautiously. "Where's Nash?"

"At work, I think. I told him I'd be out of here by the time he got back, but I wanted to talk to you."

"Oh," said Tish.

I feel suspicious. Is that warranted?

"You did clear tonight with Tobias, right?" asked Nora, moving back into the living room to scoop up a pair of Claire's socks and tossing them into her laundry basket.

"Yeah. He stomped his feet, and you'll probably have to make do with whatever food was in the freezer, but he was fine with it."

Tish edged into the front room and then didn't know whether she was supposed to act like she belonged or not and then didn't know what belonging looked like.

"Oh, please. I'll be cooking," said Nora, shaking her head. "We all know his culinary skills are stuck at fried egg sandwiches."

"He's improving at those," said Tish. "He rarely gets the eggshell in them anymore. And I've convinced him to try Siracha instead of Tabasco."

"Do you ever wonder if old people have just burned out their intestines?"

"Yes," said Tish, honestly. "Half of them can't seem to eat more than a biscuit without more intestinal distress than six cows, and the other half seem to have stomachs made of iron. I'm not sure which is in store for my future, but I would really like to put off finding out as long as possible."

Nora laughed. "Yeah, I think I'm in the biscuit category. Having Claire made me re-assess what I considered spicy at the most basic level. Anyway, I know Nash and Claire got things sorted out, but I felt like we should have a chat, too."

"OK. About what?" Tish took a quick scan of the living room and kitchen. "Where's Claire?"

"She was outside doing… something? There was some sort of pine cone gathering art project plan."

"Possible fairy house construction," said Tish. "There was a contest at the library."

"Maybe? The plan seemed to involve a lot of tools. Anyway, I wanted to talk about our situation."

"OK," repeated Tish.

"Oh, for crying out loud! Stop looking like you're waiting for the other shoe to drop."

"I *am* waiting for the other shoe to drop. We're not exactly friends, and call me crazy, but I've never gotten the feeling that you like me very much."

"I don't. You're tall. It's really annoying. I'll take it from Nash because he's always a little embarrassed about it. But having you go around flaunting it at people is really annoying."

"Flaunting my tallness?"

"Yes! And blondness. You could at least compensate by being less nice."

"I'm not nice," said Tish. "Bit selfish. Arrogant. General troublemaker. Bad at pinochle."

Nora chuckled. "Oh, yeah, I heard about that. Made me laugh. Elyane is a pompous old busybody. And I don't know… maybe you're not nice to everyone, but you've been nice to Claire."

"I love Claire," Tish blurted out and then blushed. Nora smiled and headed toward the laundry room.

"Yeah, I know. But you've been nice to me too. Which… I know you're probably doing it to make sure Nash thinks you're the best thing since sliced bread, but I still appreciate it. And I know Claire gave the impression that I was talking smack about you, but I haven't been. I don't know… maybe I said something when you two first started dating, but I really have been trying to keep my mouth shut."

"Me too," said Tish.

Nora nodded. "Yeah, I got that. So, look, for the future… maybe we'll never be best friends, but can we just call each other if something's getting weird with Claire or Nash? I don't mean that I want you in the middle. But, like, Fourth of July would have been less of a three-ring circus if you'd just been on the text thread to start with."

Tish felt as if the breath she didn't know she'd been holding had been released. "Yes. That would be great."

"Great. Now, for crying out loud, tell me all about the movie! I've finally got a direct line on the movie business, and between Nash and Claire freaking out, I can't get any dirt. I'm dying!"

"I'm not sure what there is to tell. Possibly, the Director of Photography killed Skip. Not sure. The police detective thinks so, which makes Granddad and I not think so. Emma might be trying to date Taylor. But, you know, Ellis, the second DP, will probably be OK with filling in if Frank actually did it. He has child support payments. The makeup department is starting to worry me, though. They texted this morning that if we don't start shooting soon, they're going to call their union because maybe they could be getting out of their contract and on to a different job."

"I'm sorry, back up. Emma might be dating Taylor? How is that not top billing over all the murder stuff?"

"Because murder stuff is what is a little more important!"

"I guess. Who are you going to get to direct now that Skip's in the morgue?"

"Oh, Taylor. He's been wanting to direct, and Luke, the writer, is over the moon about it. I think I got some sort of double heart emoji at lunch. So maybe Taylor's dating Luke, for all I know. My only current wildcard is Brianna Meadows."

"You should get her to talk the makeup crew down. She's probably got an in with them because of her daughter."

"Yeah, one of them worked with her, I think. What's up with the daughter anyway?" asked Tish. "Brianna showed me her picture. She looked sweet, but then I said something about her, and it got weird."

"Well, she was a makeup artist, and she was on that one makeup reality show, came in second or something. So, everyone is sympathetic to Brianna because of that situation. She can probably talk them into staying."

Tish's phone beeped, and she pulled it out to check the message.

COMING TO NASH'S. NEED TO TALK ASAP.

"What?" asked Nora.

"Kyle's coming over," said Tish, rereading the text.

"Seriously? I don't understand how you get Nash to be fine with these things," complained Nora. "I had like three cocktails one time, and he gave me a lecture on responsible drinking, and you have a drug dealer coming over."

"I'm working on it," said Tish. "I'm trying to get Kyle to go to work for Matt Jones."

"An even bigger drug dealer! How is that better?"

"Matt's record got expunged. He's legit now."

"Oh, please," said Nora, rolling her eyes. "I don't see how it is at all fair that you get flexible Nash, and I got by-the-book Nash."

Because I supported him when he needed it, and he knows that my intentions are pure. Whereas you were only interested in yourself. And we're not saying that.

"No clue," said Tish. "Anyway, you were telling me about Brianna's daughter and what she does in L.A. or whatever."

"Oh, Brianna's daughter isn't L.A. Well, I mean, maybe that's where they keep her."

"What do you mean *keep her?*" asked Tish.

"Well, her remains." Nora poked at the washing machine. "How does this even work? And I don't understand what was wrong with the old one."

"You took the old one," said Tish.

Something Nash was extremely bitter about since you had just bought it together.

"Oh, that's right. Yeah, I got rid of that. It was too big, and I got two hundred dollars for it."

Granddad's right. I could commit murder.

"Her remains? You're saying—"

"Remains of what?" asked Claire, coming around the corner, armed with a hammer and a bag of what looked to Tish like pinecones that were about to become something else.

"Um," said Tish.

"Remains of a body," said Nora bluntly. "That's what they call a body after a person is dead and when they go to a funeral home." Nora looked pleased as there was finally the hum of the washer starting.

And she just put that out there. Like, bam, we're just talking about death. OK.

"Oh," said Claire. "Huh."

"What are you doing with a hammer?" demanded Nora, eyeing her daughter.

"Cute girl stuff."

Ducktales, 2017 edition. Webbigail Vanderquack being her most Webby.

Nora looked at Tish. "Why do I feel like that is complete malarkey?"

"Machiavellian malarkey?" suggested Tish, going for Scrooge McDuck-like alliteration.

"I am a reprehensible recreant," said Claire.

"Nice one," said Tish.

Taking that as her cue, Claire exited quickly.

"I'm just going to pretend I didn't see that," said Nora. "Her father can deal with the destruction that follows in her wake."

"That's what I do," agreed Tish. "Brianna's daughter is dead?"

"Yeah! Don't you remember? It was three or four years ago."

"That was about when I left L.A., and I shut down all my Hollywood channels."

"Oh. Well, she committed suicide and left a YouTube suicide note. She was a makeup artist. She claimed she'd been raped, but the police said there wasn't any evidence." Nora rolled her eyes. "Do not ever say this to Claire or Nash, but honestly, if I got raped, I wouldn't bother to report it. What's the point? It's just signing up to be interrogated and humiliated and then watching your rapist get away with it all over again."

"When I was seventeen, I would have been shocked and argued with you," said Tish.

"Now you know better?"

Tish shrugged. "Now I understand where you're coming from anyway. It is what it is."

"Anyway, I guess after being raped, she had alcohol and depression issues and never recovered. I don't think Brianna even managed to get the suicide note taken down from YouTube. It was a minor scandal at the time. In her video, she said if bitches ruin everything, then there why not ruin one more thing. It was really depressing."

"She said what?" Tish hopped off the dryer.

"Why not ruin one more thing?"

"No, before that."

"Bitches ruin everything," repeated Nora, looking concerned.

"They didn't catch the rapist?"

"I don't think she ever even said who it was publicly. Maybe Brianna knew, I don't know. But I think they were estranged at the time."

"Oh, damn," said Tish.

"What?" asked Nora, looking up. "You've gone all funny colored."

"It was Skip," said Tish. "That's who raped Brianna's daughter."

"But if it was Skip, then… Oh." Nora looked at Tish, and her eyes filled with tears. "If this is what you do, I don't want to do it anymore. I don't want to know this."

"Neither do I," said Tish, "But she's with Granddad right now."

CHAPTER 26

PAINT LINES

Tish dialed the house, but it went to the answering machine after a few rings. She was about to dial Tobias's cell phone—although she thought it would be pointless—when a text beeped through from George Fujiyama.

Bartender at Olga remembers Frank staying until closing. Says he got a beer with Brianna Meadows and then left after her.

"What are you going to do?" asked Nora, following Tish out onto the porch.

What I don't want to do.

"I'm going to see Nash," said Tish, heading for her truck.

She dialed Kyle on her way to the Sheriff's station.

"Hey, Kyle," she said, flipping on the speaker and pushing down on the gas pedal. "I need you to change direction."

"No, I need to talk to you. We've got a problem."

"I'm heading for the Sheriff's Station *because* we have a problem. What'd you find out?"

"I talked to Cooper. He says he was taking out the trash the night Skip was killed and saw Brianna Meadows come out of Skip's house and drive away."

"What time?" asked Tish.

"After Skip left on the moped. Cooper said he was thinking about calling you or Tobias, but he didn't recognize her off the head-shot on the board. It wasn't until he watched Technotronic Legend with Grover that he realized who she was."

"Did he remember what time it was?"

"He said it was close to eleven," said Kyle. "But you and Tobias were pretty sure Skip was dead by then."

"Yeah," said Tish. "I think he talked to Emma and then drove up to the mountain right afterward. I think he was dead by ten."

She did it. It feels right. But, damn it, I can't prove it.

"But... that means she doesn't have an alibi."

"No, she doesn't. Meet me at the Sheriff's Station. And try Granddad on his cell phone. He might respond to you."

"Got it," said Kyle and hung up.

Tish parked in the handicap stall and ran into the Sheriff's Department building.

"Hey," said Nash, looking up.

"Where is Pamela?" asked Tish.

"She's interviewing Frank in the office."

"Great," she said, unlatching the gated portion of the desk and walking through.

"Tish, we've talked about this. You can't walk in like you own the place. It makes people uncomfortably aware that social conventions aren't laws," said Nash.

"And the lines on the road are just paint. I don't have time for everyone else's feelings," said Tish, heading for the office.

"She's going to be pissed," said Nash with a sigh, but following her as she headed for the office.

Tish slammed open the door to the office and saw the gray-haired Frank sitting uncomfortably while Pamela leaned on the desk with her arms folded. Tish appreciated the subtly enforced message that Frank was under scrutiny. Both Frank and Pamela looked startled by her arrival.

"Frank, how many times did Skip call you that night?" demanded Tish, ignoring Pamela's glare.

"I... I didn't talk to Skip."

"He emailed you, and you responded," said Pamela. "And we know he called you. You have two phone calls in both your phone records."

"OK, I talked to him one time," admitted Frank.

"Yeah, when he was still at his house. He called you a traitor and said you had to help him in his stupid scheme to boobytrap Taylor's climbing rig."

"I wasn't going to do it," said Frank, going pale. "I told him that!"

"OK, you told him that then, but what did you say when he called back later?"

"There were two phone calls," said Pamela. "The first one lasted ten minutes."

"Yes," said Frank. "Probably. He wanted me to help him screw over Tish and Taylor. I hung up on him. I didn't talk to him again!"

"But you did," said Pamela. "The second phone call lasted two minutes. So someone must have been saying something."

"I didn't talk to him later! He must have left a message or something."

"And later, when you realized that you were the last person he called, you got nervous," said Tish.

"Um…" Frank's eyes darted nervously around the room.

"You got nervous, borrowed someone's rental car, and drove me off the road so I wouldn't ask the detective about Skip's phone records."

"No," said Frank, weakly.

"Yes," said Tish, impatiently. "How many of the crew do I have to call to figure out whose rental it was?"

Frank's shoulders sagged.

"Just admit it, and we can move on," said Tish.

"It was Irving's," said Frank quietly.

"Great. Now, back to Skip," said Tish.

Pamela blinked at her in shock.

"No! I didn't kill Skip! I didn't have anything to do with his death. And I didn't want to hurt you. I just didn't want anyone to know about the phone calls!"

"Uh-huh. Let's review. Skip called the gaffer and asked for the code to the locked storage on the mountain, and you told him to give it to Skip," said Tish, attacking an earlier point in the timeline.

"Skip was the director! There's nothing wrong with that!"

"Yeah, except no one wanted to do it because they knew he'd screw something up. Then, the crew left. When did Brianna come in?"

"I mean... I don't..."

"Before or after the crew left, Frank?" pressed Tish.

"After. Right after. We'd told everyone we were going down the bar. Lots of people were there. Brianna and I are old friends. So what?"

"OK, then what happened? Brianna asked you about Skip? You told her about his call for the lockbox info?"

"I guess? Maybe? I don't know. I'd had a few beers. We commiserated about what a jackass he was. She wanted to rehash his back catalog. He did some real dogs."

"A specific movie, maybe?" guessed Tish.

Frank's mouth opened and closed like he didn't know what to say.

Doesn't know whether or not to lie.

Tish pulled up Skip's IMDB page and looked for the correct date. "Downward Spiral or Coffee Date?"

"I don't remember," said Frank, looking obstinate.

"Coffee Date had a late release," said Tish, and Frank shrugged.

"Sure," he said.

"Downward Spiral didn't have a stateside release." Tish was naming random facts.

"I really don't remember," said Frank, dropping his eyes and shifting in his chair.

"Downward Spiral it is," said Tish. "Did you get up from the table at all?" asked Tish as she scrolled through the cast and crew credits, looking for the right name.

"I don't know. Maybe? I probably went to the bathroom or something."

Tiffany Meadows. Makeup.

"OK," said Tish, looking up. "And you are absolutely sure that you never talked to Skip that night? Because the phone records say you did."

"No! I don't care what the phone records say. I didn't talk to Skip."

"Are you sure?" asked Tish. "Because you could have talked to Skip. He would have told you he was up at the tower and wanted your help putting a squib on Taylor's climbing harness. Then you went up there and pushed him off."

"No! I didn't do that!"

"Then who talked to Skip?" asked Pamela. "Someone did."

"You were there with Brianna," said Tish. "I can ask her. I'm *sure* she'll say she saw you talk to Skip."

Frank swallowed nervously.

"When did Brianna leave?" asked Pamela.

"I guess… I guess she left before me. I came back from the bathroom, and she said she was getting up early in the morning and left."

"And you left your phone on the table while you went to the bathroom?" asked Tish.

"I don't know," said Frank. "Yeah, maybe."

"Someone talked to Skip that night," said Pamela. "If it wasn't you, then who was it? Did you leave your phone unattended?"

"Maybe. I don't remember." Frank was starting to look scared.

"Brianna asked if Skip worked on Downward Spiral," said Tish, making it a statement. "Then you went to the bathroom and left your phone on the table."

"And my keys and half a beer," said Frank, attempting to make a joke.

"Frank," said Tish, looking him square in the eye, "did you know what Skip did to her daughter?"

Frank swallowed hard.

"Answer the question, Frank," said Pamela.

"I didn't know," he said quietly. "I didn't put the dates together until after Skip was dead." He looked up beseechingly at them. "I don't know anything. I never talked to Skip."

"Someone did," said Pamela. "If it wasn't you, then it was someone who had your phone."

"I wasn't there. I don't know," said Frank stubbornly. Then he looked at Tish. "It wasn't right. What Skip did to Tiffany. It never should have been allowed. But I didn't know about it."

"Allowed?" hissed Tish angrily. "Skip should never have been able to do any of the things he did, but everyone was just going to keep on letting him do it because they didn't want to risk something happening to their own career, because it was easier, because it wasn't happening to them. Tiffany is dead. She killed herself, and that's not just on Skip. That's on everyone who enabled that low-life."

Frank sank further into his chair.

Her phone dinged with an alert from Kyle.

TOBIAS TEXTED ME BACK. HE SAYS HE'S AT THE TOWER. PULLING IN AT THE SHERIFF'S OFFICE IN A SEC.

"Shit," said Tish. "Nash, how fast can you get me up to the mountain?"

"Pretty fast if I put the sirens on. But do you want the sirens?" asked Nash, looking over her shoulder at her phone.

"Does someone want to explain what the hell is going on?" demanded Pamela.

"Brianna Meadows killed Skip," said Tish. "Her daughter committed suicide because of him. No one knew who was responsible, but the day he died, Skip used a phrase that Tiffany Meadows used in her suicide video. Brianna figured it out. She figured out that he was working on the same movie as Tiffany, Downward Spiral, and then

I think she took the phone call meant for Frank and went up to the tower. And I think she pushed him over. I think after that, she went to Skip's house to see if she could find any of the blackmail material that Skip kept threatening people with, but she left empty-handed because all the folders were empty."

Frank looked surprised.

"We'll go back and canvas at the Olga bar," said Pamela, nodding. "We'll see if we can find a witness who saw her on the phone. We fingerprinted the house, but we'll have to get hers for comparison."

"Yeah, that's great. We don't have time for that," said Tish. "She's with my grandfather up at Mt. Constitution."

Pamela flailed in anger. "You said you wouldn't interfere!"

"Yeah, with Frank," said Tish. "We just didn't think it was him. So we investigated the other suspects."

"OK, fine," snapped Pamela. "And you think Tobias is in danger? What does his text say?"

"He said he was at the tower," said Tish.

"That's not exactly a strong statement of danger."

"He texted," said Tish.

"So?"

"He doesn't text," said Nash.

"He just did!"

"He *can* text, but he chooses not to," said Nash. "The fact that he texted at all shows that he considers the situation an emergency."

"I can't mobilize based on the existence of texting," said Pamela.

"I don't think you understand," said Tish. "My grandfather is a fully certified private detective."

If Pamela says no, then I can't ask Nash. I can't ask him to jeopardize his career on my say-so. So… back-up guy it is.

"He's seventy-eight," said Pamela. "And he took a pretty woman on a sightseeing tour. No offense, but you just connected all these dots now. He probably doesn't even know. And she won't know that we know either."

"He's also ex-CIA, and no offense to you, but he's smarter than ninety-nine percent of the police force. He has literally been ahead of me on every single case. And he doesn't always tell me when he's up to something. The fact that he texted tells me he knows damn well what he's dealing with."

"That's not evidence," said Pamela. "You can't know that."

"Mainlanders," said Tish, shaking her head. Then she turned to Nash. "Kyle and I are going up there."

"I'm not OK with this plan," he said. "I said I would take you."

"I'm not a fan either, but if they're not coming, then I don't think I can wait."

"I'll come with you," he said calmly.

"I'm ordering you not to," said Pamela.

"Then I'll quit," said Nash, without missing a beat. "I'm not putting someone's life in danger because you won't listen."

"I'm listening, but how am I supposed to mobilize based on Tobias Yearly's texting habits?" Pamela looked outraged.

"We're asking you to mobilize based on the circumstantial evidence that you just heard," snapped Tish. "And I'm not asking for an entire SWAT team. I just want Nash and Ray and you to come make sure Brianna doesn't do something stupid!"

"I can go," said Ray, sticking his head into the office. "I'm off phones. If it helps any, Tobias said texting is for the conversationally impaired. Also, real men aren't afraid of the phone, and the autocorrect is a demon that Satan has sent to live in our phones."

"I forgot about the demon one," said Tish.

"He said all that?" asked Pamela with a frown.

"Thanks to Tish's *Words from Granddad* account, I can give you exact quotes and dates," said Ray.

"It's what you might call a documented pattern of behavior," said Nash.

Pamela sighed. "OK, but I need a few minutes to clear things and lay out a proper plan. We're not going off half-cocked here."

Tish looked up at Nash. "Go on," he said. "We'll be right behind you, but please don't get shot."

"I don't think she has a gun," said Tish.

"Actually," said Frank, "she does. She has the code for the storage locker up there. There's a gun in it. It's a prop gun, and it's not loaded, but if you put an actual projectile in it… it could be lethal."

CHAPTER 27

THE TOWER

Kyle's Jeep was bouncy in a different way from her grandfather's truck, and Tish found that it jogged her spine in unique but equally uncomfortable ways.

"How are we playing this?" asked Kyle as they both leaned into the corner. "Do I drive all the way up?"

"You're going to drop me off before you get to the parking loop. Then you drive up and park. Give me a few minutes to get into position. We don't know for sure that anything's going down. You'll approach—slowly—and I'll sneak up on the trails. You keep it casual. Maybe just showing up may be enough to keep anything from happening. I hope. Maybe."

"What do I do if something *is* happening?" asked Kyle nervously. "I've never had to anything like this before."

"You just back off and wait for Nash and the others," said Tish.

"OK," said Kyle seriously, as if he were trying to memorize his instructions.

"We're not out here alone, Kyle," said Tish, trying to find the thing that would get him to stop freaking out. "Nash is right behind us, and Granddad isn't incompetent. We're just going to go and make sure everything's fine."

They reached the lower part of the loop, and Kyle slowed down and idled to a stop next to the opening of one of the unplanned paths.

"I'll wait two minutes here," said Kyle, "and then I will drive and park as slowly as possible. I'll try not to get out until I know for sure that you're up there. Are you sure Nash OK'd this? He kind of doesn't like it when you do dangerous stuff."

"He said we could come and confirm that they're here," said Tish. "You should text Nash once you see the car."

"OK," said Kyle.

Yes, Nash did say that. But don't ask if he knows about me going up to the tower on foot.

"I just wish I'd actually followed through on having Nash teach me how to punch people properly," said Tish.

"Oh, punching is easy," said Kyle. "Make a fist like this." He demonstrated. "Try to hit with this part." He pointed to the front of his first two knuckles. "And try to line up this first hand bone with your arm bone. And don't roll your wrist. After that, it's just having the guts to swing."

"Kyle, that was exactly the amount of information I can absorb right now, and I sincerely appreciate it."

"OK," said Kyle, looking perplexed. "And?"

"That was it. OK, I'll meet you up there. I've got my phone on silent, but if you hear anything from anybody, let me know."

"Got it," said Kyle, nodding.

Tish got out of the car and jogged toward the trail.

And I'm really doing this.

The problem with the tower was that the top of Mt. Constitution was a bald and rocky outcropping. Approaching the building without being seen was difficult at best. Tish slithered through the underbrush and around to the side of the tower with the door. She could see Tobias and Brianna out on the balcony, but she could only hope they weren't looking her direction. She breathed a sigh of relief once she was on the back side of the tower and looking at the door. Keeping an eye on the top of the tower, Tish sprinted for the door. She stopped just inside the entrance, panting and listening. Nothing seemed to move. The inside was cool and dark compared to the bright sunshine outside.

Tish edged up the stone stairs. They were wide and well-worn, and her sneakers didn't make any noise as she moved toward the room at the top of the tower. The observation tower had a single dark chamber at the top that opened to a wide balcony area. From there, visitors could climb up to a glass enclosed viewing area that gave a 360-degree view of the San Juans. Turning the last corner on the stairs, Tish peered cautiously upward.

"Brianna," said Tobias, his voice echoing as the wind brought it down to her. "You need to think about this a little more."

"I have had years to think," said Brianna. "About all the ways I failed my daughter. I failed to protect her. I failed to listen to her. I failed to be there for her on the most basic level. She tried so hard to get my attention, and I kept saying *later*. Always later. And then she was gone. Skip tormented her. He kept threatening and using her, and I didn't see it because I wasn't there."

"Yeah," said Tobias, in his usual wry way. "It can be hard to make up for missing out on a childhood. Believe me, I know. When Scott died in that car wreck, I felt so angry and cheated. And part of that was because we had finally reached the point where I was supposed to be able to spend all my time with my family. I put everything off because I was supposed to be able to make up for it later. Only there was no later."

Tish stopped moving and felt her heart breaking a little. Tobias rarely talked about her father's death. It hadn't occurred to her that he would have regrets about his parenting.

"But you got a second chance, didn't you?" snapped Brianna. "Everyone can see the way you dote on Tish. I don't have that luxury. I will *never* get another chance, and it was his fault. Skip didn't just take my daughter. He took any possibility of a future."

Tish crept forward another step, peering into the gloom of the room at the top of the stairs. There were only thin faux arrow slits for lighting and the contrast between the inside and outside light was blinding. She could see Tobias and Brianna out on the balcony. Brianna had a gun that she was pointing at Tobias. Tobias was leaning on his cane as if guns were of no concern to him.

"Mmm, no," said Tobias. "That's not true. There are lots of chances to matter in this life. I've got lots of kids. I've got Quincy, Kyle and Amber, and even Nash once in a while. There's plenty of kids around that need an extra parent. That's what it means to be part of a community. I know it's hard when people leave our lives, but they are the stone in the pond. Their ripples keep going. So will mine when the time comes."

"No! It's not the same," said Brianna vehemently.

"It's not the same," agreed Tobias. "But that doesn't make it worthless."

"Skip took her from me. He took my legacy."

"This week alone, I've heard at least six people say how much they loved Technotronic Legend. You can matter in people's lives without having given birth to them."

"No," snarled Brianna. "That's just make-believe."

Tobias laughed. "If I have learned anything from Tish, it's that make-believe matters. The stories we tell are the things that shape our lives. That's why you need to be careful with what you choose to believe. Tell yourself the right story, and you can conquer the world. Let someone convince you that you're worthless or that the world doesn't need you, and you've bought a big whopper of a lie."

"Tobias," said Brianna, shaking her head. "You live here on this tiny island. You can keep the world at bay. And that's great for you, but it makes you naïve."

Tobias chuckled. "Big city people always think that. You think somehow we have a different brand of human on the islands. We don't. We got bad and good and all the usual in between."

"No one was going to do anything about Skip," said Brianna.

"Are you sure about that?" asked Tobias, and Brianna laughed a little hysterically.

"Yes. I promise that no man was ever going to stand up to him. Frank hated him. Taylor hated him. But no one did anything. None of them were going to stop Skip from taking advantage of every-one."

"Seems like Tish managed it the other day," said Tobias. "She wouldn't let him target Emma."

Inside, Tish froze against the wall.

"It doesn't matter," said Brianna, impatiently. "The point is that something had to be done, and I did it. Nothing was ever going to happen to him. There was never going to be any justice."

Tobias sighed and leaned more heavily on his cane. "I can't say that you're wrong, but Brianna, you didn't even try."

"I don't have to try," said Brianna. "I saw what the police did to my daughter. They laughed at her. Called her crazy until she was. I don't need to *try* for justice. Skip got what he deserved."

"Yeah," said Tobias. "But you didn't have the right to make that decision, and now that I know, I've got to do what I think is right."

"You don't even have to lie. You just have to keep your mouth shut," said Brianna impatiently.

"And what about Frank?" asked Tobias. "The police are talking to him. What if they arrest him? Am I supposed to let him go to jail? Are you going to let him go to jail for a crime you committed?"

Brianna was silent.

"Mm-hmm," said Tobias. "Seems that the distance between jus-tice and self-interest is a wee bit short."

"Oh, shut up," said Brianna, hoisting the gun higher.

"Are you going to shoot me?" asked Tobias, sounding amused. "I think that two dead bodies showing up on the tower is going to make even the police suspicious."

"I'll say it was an accident. I'm a very good actress. They'll be-lieve it."

"Not that good," said Tish, stepping out into the sunshine. "I figured it out."

Two things happened very quickly. Brianna swung the gun to-ward Tish, and Tobias flicked out his cane, snapping Brianna's arm upward. There might have been a large noise, but it was so loud that Tish ignored it. Quickly closing the distance and taking Kyle's advice, she made a fist, lined up her wrist, and punched Brianna sharply across the jaw.

Tish stood breathing heavily, looking down at Brianna's unconscious body.

"Did I just knock her out?"

"Yes," said Tobias, nodding. "Nice job."

"Did she actually shoot at me?"

"Yeah. Good thing you hit her, really. I wasn't going to be comfortable with punching a woman."

"She had a gun!"

"Did I or did I not tell you not to get shot?" demanded Nash, stepping out onto the balcony.

Tish jumped in surprise, flailed in anger and spun to face Nash who had apparently managed to sneak in after her.

"And I didn't!"

He looks hot in his bulletproof vest.

"Uh-huh. Pretty sure I also said to wait for us."

He went to the edge and waved toward the parking lot. She could see Kyle hovering at the edge of the path down to the parking lot with Ray and Pamela.

"The situation evolved," said Tish. And Tobias chuckled.

They both looked at him.

"Nothing. Sorry. I just used to say that all the time."

"Yeah, she's a chip off the old block," said Nash sourly.

Tish looked at Tobias, who smiled at her and patted her shoulder.

Yeah, maybe a little.

CHAPTER 28

CHANGES

Tish lay on the Chesterfield and stared into Coats' big brown eyes that were precisely at her eye level. He appeared to be trying to beam doggy information and desires into her brain.

"I'm dead, Coats. I died. I know I'm still talking, but my legs no longer work. I cannot even get up to let you out."

"Tish," said Claire, coming around the corner from the dining room and leaning over the high arm of the Chesterfield. She put out her arms like she was flying and balanced on her stomach, hovering over Tish. "When is Mom coming home?"

"No clue. She was networking when I left."

Claire put her head down and stared at Tish—even upside down, Claire looked skeptical.

"That's grown-up for talking."

"Yes, it is," agreed Tish. "But sometimes that's important to do. Your mom wants to be an actress, and it's really important for her to talk to as many people in the industry as possible because they are the best bet for recommending her or telling her about jobs."

"Tish?" Claire lifted her arms and feet again, and Coats snuffled directly into her armpit. Claire shrieked, and Tish laughed and pulled her down onto the couch. Claire giggled, and Coats barked and hopped excitedly, pleased with more animated humans.

"Can you let Coats out?"

"Yeah, OK." Claire got up and opened the sliding door.

"Tish, why does Mom want to be an actress when you don't want to?"

"People want different things at different times," said Tish.

"She got a role in a play in Seattle," said Claire. "She got the call last night. She was really excited about it."

"That's awesome!" exclaimed Tish.

"And she has an audition for a car commercial," said Claire.

"More awesome!"

"You don't think it's... dumb?"

Tish sat upright like someone had kicked her. "Absolutely not. I think the world needs actors. Big parts, small parts, it doesn't matter. I think your mom is brave. Auditioning is really hard, and it means a lot of rejection. She's pursuing her dreams, and I want her to be successful."

"But you don't want to do it anymore," said Claire.

Claire was outlined by the sunshine. Her gangly figure, knobby knees, and judgmental tilt to her head made beautiful angles but left her face in shadow. Arrogance warred with a blissful lack of awareness of how she looked. Usually, it was hard to remember that Claire was almost eleven, but sometimes pre-teen looked and sounded a lot like full teenager. This was one of those moments.

"Because I realized it wasn't my dream anymore. I know how to do it. I have the skills. But... I want to be here now."

"You want to be like Tobias," said Claire, and she turned a little so that Tish could see the glimmering flash of a smile.

Tish chuckled. "Yeah. I want to be like Granddad when I grow up."

"Me too," said Claire. "Only I want to cook better."

Tish laughed harder. "Yeah, we all want that."

"But I think being a pilot would be fun."

"Well, OK, but I would prefer that you not crash as much as he did," said Tish.

"Well, yeah," said Claire. "Obviously. I'm going to go throw the ball for Coats." She wandered out of the house, leaving the door open, and Tish sighed and melted back into the couch cushions. She could hear the sounds of puttering in the kitchen. It didn't sound like Tobias.

But if I'm too tired to go close the screen door, then I'm too tired to go investigate who's in the kitchen.

Nash wandered in, carrying a plate with a sandwich on it, and eyed her skeptically.

"You've died, and these are the remains," he said.

"Yes. Meanwhile, your child left the door open. Can you go close the screen before Granddad yells about flies?"

Nash did as instructed but had barely shut the screen when the kitchen door banged open.

"Any Yearly's home?" yelled Kyle.

"In here, Kyle," Tish yelled back.

"Hey!" Kyle came in carrying what looked like a cinder block and plunked it down on the bricks in front of the fireplace.

"What is that?"

"A cinderblock. Tobias said he wanted one."

Sure. Because... Who knows?

"I wanted to say thanks, by the way," said Kyle, dropping into the wingback chair that Nash had been about to sit in. Nash shook his head and went to sit next to Tish.

"For what?"

"I had like an hour-long talk with Matt Jones yesterday," said Kyle. "We've never exactly seen eye-to-eye, but now that we're no longer in competition, he's suddenly much nicer. And we had a whole conversation about how to integrate our business models. Like, if I work for him, I can't be dealing, but at the same time, I don't want to let my customers down. But if I bring my customers on board with his new model and I can guarantee them pricing, then the whole idea about me delivering via watercraft becomes viable."

"Holy crap," said Nash, around a mouthful of sandwich. "Also, la la la, I'm not hearing this. But please, for my sake, yes, go legal."

Kyle laughed.

"So, are you guys actually going to do it?" asked Nash, now that the legal disclaimers were out of the way.

"I think so?" said Kyle. "We're both interested anyway. But it definitely means that I'll be living in Anacortes for a while longer. I know Amber isn't going to be stoked about that, but I'm going to see if she can move in with me. She doesn't have to work here. She can waitress in Anacortes, too."

"Uh."

Shit. Granddad will not be pleased if his favorites go wandering off the island.

"Anyway," said Kyle cheerfully, "it's still in talks. Nothing is serious yet. But I appreciate you putting in the word with Matt."

"No problem," said Tish.

"Can I make a sandwich too?"

"Sure."

"How'd the filming go?" asked Kyle as he moseyed toward the kitchen.

"Good," said Tish. "You know, except for our Director of Photography and Brianna getting arrested. Pamela wouldn't let me even bail Frank out for the day."

"He ran you off the road!" exclaimed Nash.

"He's an excellent DP," said Tish sadly. "I wish he hadn't done that. But I think Ellis did a good job."

"Bummer," called Kyle from the kitchen. "Tobias is outside. I'm going to go talk to him."

"We ran out of entertainment value," said Tish.

"Apparently," said Nash, settling back to finish his sandwich.

Outside, Claire and Coats ran by. It was unclear who was chasing whom, but there was a large stick involved.

"Two more weeks, and then I ship this entire circus off the island," said Tish.

"Looking forward to it," said Nash.

"Me too."

The silence was comfortable, and Tish tilted over and rested her head on his shoulder.

"I think I want to take the Detective's exam," said Nash.

"Oh, dang it!" said Tish, struggling upright.

Nash looked surprised.

"Granddad is going to be smug. He said you wanted to solve mysteries."

"Well, you two look like you're having fun with it," said Nash with a grin.

"I'm not sure that's the fun part. I think he just likes causing trouble."

"Mm-hmm. And you don't enjoy that at all?"

"That is…"

Possibly accurate.

"Not the point. The point is that you're going to do a thing! That's exciting! Is there studying? What do we do?"

"Study. Sign up for the test next time it becomes available."

"That sounds anticlimactic."

"Um, well, the stressful part is that it would change up some things at work, and I'd probably have to be in Anacortes and Friday Harbor some days. But…" He shrugged. "I can't worry about that until after I take the test."

"What happens if you don't pass the test?" asked Tish. Her heart started beating faster.

"It's like I just watched you start to freak out. Nothing happens. I get depressed. Study some more and retake it."

"Oh."

"Yes. So there's no panicking."

"Did we really inspire you to be a detective?" asked Tish.

"Well, you did. Tobias inspires me to never be in a plane crash."

Tish laughed. "How did I inspire you?" She stared at him, puzzled.

"This is probably going to sound dumb to you, but when Claire was born, it was like I went into emergency mode. I kept things efficient and made sure I met every expectation, but I didn't have the bandwidth to do new things. It made Nora angry, but her being mad just made me dig into my hidey-hole more. I needed to be Mr. Reliable, and the only way I knew how to do that was to keep things predictable and safe. And after a while, that became my default mode."

Tish took a deep breath. "That isn't dumb. That is survival."

"Yeah, well, then I met you, and you've always got something new to challenge you."

Tish considered that. She did usually, and Nash always seemed annoyed by it. That's why she had thought it would be OK to pull back. She had been planning to rest on her laurels and focus on the event business for a while. She didn't have a next mountain to climb, and she had been thinking that was OK. Was it not OK? Everyone seemed to have something new to pursue except her. Tish squashed the nervous feeling in her stomach. She was in a good place. She had a stable relationship. She and Granddad were in a nice rhythm. She could afford to coast for a little bit.

"And you attack every new thing like you're going to kick its ass and personally pin its name to the Wall of Defeat."

"And sometimes I fall flat on my face! If you hadn't blessed me with your drywall skills, I probably still wouldn't be done with my remodel at Reginald's!"

Nash laughed. "You would have goat-traded your way into drywall somehow."

"Oh. Well. Yes, that probably would have worked. But you see my point? Not everything I do goes perfectly. Octothorpe this movie as an example."

"Octothorpe?"

"Granddad says that's the real name of the hashtag."

Nash chuckled. "I will be Googling that. But my point is not that everything goes well. My point is that you dive in. And I have been thinking I could do more diving myself. Also, if I'm a detective, next time one of you finds a dead body, it won't be such a pain in the ass."

"We can investigate together!" Tish clapped her hands excitedly. "I really do need to get that punch card from Mitch."

"Please don't," said Nash. "I don't actually want you to find more dead bodies."

"Well, me neither. But this case wasn't so bad. We solved it, and I didn't even almost die this time."

"Yes," agreed Nash. "But let's not push our luck. We don't really want anyone to die."

"Of course not," agreed Tish with a happy sigh and snuggled back onto his shoulder.

But with our luck, someone is totally going to die.

THE END

LOVED IT?

Please consider leaving a rating on Amazon, Goodreads, or Bookbub. Reviews help authors gain advertising opportunities and new readers. Your positive reviews make a difference!

WANT MORE?

For a free e-book visit:
www.**bethanymaines**.com

WANT MORE ADVENTURES FROM BETHANY MAINES?

TRY THE DEVERAUX LEGACY SERIES

The Deveraux Family: wealthy, glamorous, powerful… and in a lot of trouble. Senator Eleanor Deveraux lost her children in a plane crash, but she has a second chance to get her family right with her four grandchildren – Evan, Jackson, Aiden and Dominique. But second chances are hard to seize when politics, mercenaries, and the dark legacy of the Deveraux family keep getting in the way.

TAKE A SNEAK PEEK AT BOOK 1

THE SECOND SHOT

MAXWELL AMES

I have better uses for my mouth.

The words were etched in his brain.

Maxwell Ames looked across the room at Dominique Deveraux and felt himself physically flinch at a memory-driven whip of embarrassment.

An eighteen-year-old Dominique had arrived at college with an ice queen reputation and a pair of legs that had fueled half the hot dreams on campus. But it hadn't been the legs that had gotten to Max—it had been her lips. Max had taken one look at Dominique and decided he wanted, no, *needed* to know what those lips felt like on his body. And he'd declared, drunkenly, to an entire frat party that he would melt the ice queen. He hadn't doubted for a minute that he could do it. He was a senior. He was a nationally ranked college wrestler—his body showed his effort—and he rarely had to do more than lift a finger to get panties to hit his floor. Perhaps it had been the liquor that had made him stupid, but whatever the reason, he'd simply walked over and told her what he wanted her to do to him. He recognized his mistake the second he heard the words come out of his mouth. Her horrified expression only confirmed how badly he'd misjudged. Then she'd gone from shocked to furious, but instead of slapping him, she'd pulled herself up to her full height, looked him in the eye, and declared loud enough for the rest of the room to hear: *I have better uses for my mouth.* And then he'd stood there and let her pour the entire contents of her red solo cup down his front.

And now, six years later, his father had dragged Max into the

Galbraith Tennis and Social Club and directly into revisiting one of his top ten stupidest moments.

"Dad," said Max, turning to look at his father.

"She donates two-k a year," said his father, staring across the party hall at a woman in beige everything. "She's worth like eighty million. Would it kill her to scrounge a little more change out of the couch cushions for needy kids?"

"Dad," said Max again.

"Yeah, what?" asked Grant Ames, finally making eye contact.

"You didn't say this was a Deveraux party."

"Uh, yeah?" said Grant, looking away again—probably scanning the crowd for more targets. "Oh, that's right. You went to school with them, didn't you? Dominique and Aiden? They're probably around somewhere if you want to dig them up. Eleanor usually commands appearances from the family at these little shindigs."

Eleanor Deveraux was running for congress. Again. Or still. Whichever. These *little shindigs* were fundraising events masquerading as cocktail parties. Max didn't know why she bothered. Her nearest competitor was a bitter Republican that sounded crazy even to his constituents. But his father, always on the hustle, spared no thought about why the party existed—he simply enjoyed that it did. And of course, it hadn't occurred to Grant to mention to Max who was hosting.

After the frat party incident, Max hadn't even had the courage to apologize to Dominique. His only consolation was that during all their other encounters she had treated everyone in the room with an equal amount of cool disdain—he hadn't been singled out. Generally, she hadn't even acknowledged him, let alone what had happened.

"You said we wouldn't be here long," said Max, looking back at Dominique. Her golden blonde hair was longer than the last time he'd seen her, laying in soft waves against her pale skin. Those lips that had made him lose his judgement were painted a wine red that emphasized their size. Her conservative pencil skirt and long-sleeve, high-necked blouse should have taken her allure down a notch, but as far as he could see, she was even more gorgeous than she had been in college.

Max had been with plenty of beautiful women—hell, his last girlfriend had been a model-slash-actress. Dominique shouldn't have been able to make the impact she did. But here it was, six years later, and Dominique still hit him like a Mack truck to the libido even when the only skin he could see was her knees.

"We won't be long, I promise," said Grant, scoping the room, oblivious to the direction of Max's gaze. "I need to make the rounds. Say hi to a few people and then we'll be off for burgers."

It was a lie. Max didn't know why he'd thought his first visit to his father's in over a year might warrant special treatment—particularly, since his entire childhood held evidence to the contrary. He wondered if there was a point in adulthood when a parent's failings stopped mattering so much.

Dominique nodded along as the guy next to her talked. He was a lean, good looking twenty-something with black hair and a designer suit. Max watched in surprise as Dominique burst out laughing at whatever he'd said—Dominique had never been very demonstrative in public. Her laugh made the guy grin, but, still talking, he leaned over and snagged something off her plate. Dominique smacked at his hand, but the man leaned further away, dragging the morsel with him, and popped it into his mouth. She flicked at his ear, miming patently faked annoyance. In equally mock penance, her companion lowered his head and held out his plate and Dominique made a show of selecting something in recompense. The only person he could remember bringing out that sparkle of playfulness in her had been her brother, Aiden. It seemed that the ice queen had been melted after all.

Still chewing his stolen goods, Dominique's companion looked up and scanned the room, homing in on the location of the other Deveraux family members. Max followed the man's gaze to the matriarch, Dominque's stately and poised grandmother, Eleanor, holding court by the bar at the far end of the long, narrow room. Then he shifted to Dominique's red-headed investment manager cousin, Evan, amongst a bevy of Wall Street bros in the middle of the room. And last, Dominique's brother, the equally blonde Aiden, hovering by the buffet table in front of a wide expanse of floor-to-ceiling windows.

All of the Deveraux children had lived with their grandmother after a plane crash had left them orphans sometime during their early teens. Max remembered thinking how nice that had sounded when his father had missed every single one of his college meets and was late for graduation. He supposed it hadn't really been pleasant for the Deveraux cousins, but at least they'd had each other and Eleanor.

Max realized, too late, that the scan was continuing on to the new arrivals in the room, which, in this case, were Max and his father. Max found himself awkwardly making eye contact with the guy and knew that he'd been busted staring at Dominique. He broke eye contact and turned to follow his father.

Max pretended to be absorbed in his father's conversation with a white-collared, black-shirted Jesuit priest. After a few minutes of discussing the endowments and scholarship funds, Max's eyes glazed over and he looked around the room, desperate for anything to take his mind off his desire to blurt out a question about pedophiles. How did anyone take priests seriously anymore? He found himself fidgeting with one of the tiny decorative pumpkins placed on the bar-height tables and biting his tongue.

With Halloween and the election around the corner, the party was decorated in a patriotic harvest theme. The red leaves and orange gourds seemed attractive, but Max thought the hay bales by the buffet table seemed a bit too folksy for the Deveraux, not to mention the tennis club locale. He suspected that the entire reason for their existence was to support the stars-and-stripes-bandana-wearing scarecrow. After all, a politician couldn't fundraise without at least a nod to the flag.

He snuck another glance at Dominique and realized that her boyfriend was scanning again. Same pattern—Deverauxes first, then new arrivals, then the rest of the room. There was something professional in the appraising stare, and Max felt the weight of it resting thoughtfully on him. Max checked his watch and angled so he could watch Dominique and her guy. She chatted in an easy, unaffected way, but at a minute fifteen, her boyfriend made another scan. Then again a minute later. It was definitely a more than a casual glance. Max tried to get a better look at the guy. What was he? Boyfriend, bodyguard, security? The suit was expensive, but he was drinking water as he watched the crowd.

Dominique reached out and put her hand on his arm, tugging impatiently, demanding attention. The guy laughed and complied, turning toward her with an affectionate smile. He was definitely not the hired help. For some reason, that burned. In the intervening six years, Max had put Dominique out of his head. Mostly. Sort of. Max would never have admitted it out loud, ever, under any circumstances, including a court of law, but Dominique had always been one of his go-to fantasies. He was perfectly sure that she hadn't thought about him once in that time. So why did he feel jealous of this guy?

Max turned back to his father and tried to focus on the conversation. Dominique was none of his business. What did he care if she dated someone with an over-active sense of security? None. Of. His. Business.

Grant moved on and Max followed him dutifully, the same way he had when he was twelve. He was a prop to his father's socializing. He met a dozen people and forgot their names instantly. Finally, he turned away from a blocky woman in a Chanel jacket and found his father about to introduce him to Dominique and her date.

"Max, I don't know if you've met Jackson, but you went to school with Dominique. Max is staying with me for a few weeks while—Hey, Frank! Frank! Be right back. I've been trying to get five minutes with that guy all month." Grant buzzed off and left Max staring uncomfortably at Dominique and her date.

"So, Max," said Jackson, his expression derisive, "do you need Dominique to get you another drink? We could send the catering staff out for some beer and solo cups."

Max glanced at Dominique, who was visibly restraining a laugh.

"No," said Max, trying not to feel like an ass—any hope that she'd forgotten him or the incident slipping away. "I think once was enough." Did she really have to tell everyone?

Dominique actually did giggle this time and her boyfriend looked amused by her laughter, but his attention was pulled away.

"Nika, what is Aiden doing?" asked Jackson, looking past Max.

"Um," she squinted toward the door, "exactly what you told him not to do?"

Jackson sighed. "OK, I'll be right back." He ducked around Dominique, his jacket swinging open. For a second, Max clearly saw the strap on a shoulder holster and outline of a gun. Max looked back at Dominque, but she seemed not to notice. She was watching her brother attempting to sneak out of the room and biting into her bottom lip with a frown. She transferred her gaze back to Max and smiled, but it was the same old cold smile.

"I'm glad you can laugh about that uh… incident," he said, deciding to man up and do what he should have done six years ago. He glanced down at the floor and realized that she was only conservative from the ankle up. Her heels were stacked, strapped, and had a black satin bow at each ankle that begged to be untied. "I really apologize for that," he said, tearing his eyes off her feet.

She looked startled and suspicious.

"I was a total asshole," he added.

"Um." She frowned, then smiled—a real smile this time. "Well, apology accepted."

It was his turn to feel surprised. He hadn't expected her to simply believe that he was sorry. "And I wouldn't say total. I'd go ninety-eight percent."

"Ninety-eight percent?"

"Well, I'll give you a one percent discount for being young, dumb and in college."

"Yes," he agreed fervently.

"And another one percent for standing there for the entire cup of beer."

"I knew I'd earned it," he said. She glanced over his shoulder, still following the action across the room.

"Your boyfriend's a little intense," he said.

"My boyfriend? You mean Jacks?"

He wanted to comment on the intimate shortening of their names. Jacks seemed weird, but he liked Nika. On the other hand, it really was none of his damn business.

"Does he always carry a gun?" he asked instead.

"Oh, you know…" she said, trailing off and not answering the question. Max decided that meant the answer was yes. "Grandma has gotten some… Well, they're death threats, really, in the last few weeks. She's chairing that Senate Committee Hearing on Absolex. And nothing brings out the crazies like Big Pharma."

"I don't understand," he said. "I thought that was about government fraud?"

"Absolex falsified research and then sold their drug Zanilex to the VA as a solution to treat complex PTSD. Suicide rates sky-rocketed. Turns out that, in fact, it makes the symptoms of PTSD worse, particularly the paranoia and depression. Or at least that's what Grandma intends to prove. She's going to haul the CEO out on the carpet next week. But ever since the hearings started, she's been getting hate mail."

Max looked around the party. "Where is the Secret Service?"

"None of the threats have been active. It's all kind of vague. And she's not a party leader or anything. So, no Secret Service."

Max frowned. If he had been Eleanor, he would have been putting his foot down and demanding an investigation. He also wouldn't be hosting a party and looking as relaxed as she did.

"Besides," continued Dominique, "we have Jackson. Although, even he couldn't get her to cancel this stupid party. She claimed that we all just didn't want to go."

He raised an eyebrow and she looked guilty.

"That may be partially true. Anyway, Jacks said if she was going to insist on having the party, we should at least be smart about it. He gave us all rules and hired additional security. Of course, Aiden is not following the rules. I would accuse him of being willful, but it's more likely that he's just not taking the threats seriously."

Max nodded. His memory of Dominique's older brother was a sunny personality to whom nothing serious was allowed to adhere and who never seemed to get mad about anything.

"I expect Jacks will tell him about a secret stash of bourbon under the bar and rope him back in."

"Sounds like Jackson knows what he's doing then," said Max, turning to look at the two men who were now making their way back toward them. Aiden stopped to adjust the bandana on the scarecrow with a disapproving shake of his head.

"He does," agreed Dominique, looking up at him with a flash of a smile, "but Jackson isn't—"

Whatever she had been about to say was drowned out by the sound of a car engine and then a thunderous crash as a car exploded through the windows, slammed through the buffet table, plowed across the room, and buried its nose in the far wall.

FIND OUT WHAT HAPPENS NEXT IN...

THE SECOND SHOT

OR TRY THE STAND-ALONE MYSTERY

Eye Contact

Sometimes the hardest move is making eye contact.

Lexi Byrne, UW grad student, brilliant researcher, and high-functioning autistic is working on cutting edge research into bionic eye technology. But Lexi's normal, safe, science-based life takes an abrupt left turn after her prototype is stolen. Lexi must fight her own limitations and lean on the strengths of her friends to stop a misogynistic, greedy thief and recover her work.

CHAPTER 1

ALEXIS BYRNE: UNIVERSITY OF WASHINGTON

"Alexis Byrne, the only reason you're working on that fucking bionic eyeball is so you don't have to see people!"

Lexi tried not to re-run the argument with Shea again, but the words played on a loop in her head. Shea had been angry and crying, but that didn't mean she was wrong. The best part of their friendship had been that Shea was usually right about people. And since Lexi was almost never right about people, she was used to relying on Shea's judgment. But now Shea wouldn't talk to her. How was Lexi supposed to analyze the data points of her own personality flaws if she had no one to analyze with?

Lexi pulled the stack of quizzes out of Professor Snyder's mailbox. He'd put a post-it note on top.

FORGOT I HAD THESE. NEED THEM BY TOMORROW. THX.

Lexi hated end-of-quarter grading. Everyone who had been slacking pulled their head out of their beer and suddenly wanted extra credit. And Snyder suddenly realized that he needed to at least appear to be doing his job. Which meant that Lexi had to do his job. She shifted the quizzes to one arm, slinging her bag over her shoulder, and managed to pick up her cup in the same movement. She tried to cover the Starbucks logo with her hand. There was some kind of coffee protest on campus again. She couldn't tell if it was the Conservative Christians for Christ yelling about holiday cups or the Fair-Trade Alliance yelling about the unethical treatment of coffee growers, but either way, she was tired of getting yelled at. Particularly since she didn't actually drink coffee. She took her caffeine in the form of tea and currently had the baristas at her local Starbucks trained to make her a variety of delicious tea-based concoctions. She refused to go to a new coffee shop just because someone didn't like the Starbucks cups.

Lexi sipped her tea and pondered her argument with Shea again. What did Shea know anyway? Lexi saw people. She saw all sorts of people. And besides, it was not a bionic eyeball. It was a bio-synthetic optic implant with a mechanical neural interface. So… Shea was totally wrong. She hoped. Maybe not.

The University of Washington was a conglomeration of Ivy League-esque brick and seventies horror concrete spread across a sprawling campus that was so large it was quite possible to never visit some parts during an entire college career. In May, the student body usually hunched into the collars of their North Face jackets as they hurried between rain drifts, but today was pleasant, with only a nagging cold breeze to make people remember that it was still spring. As a result, the protestors, panhandlers, and potheads with bongos were out in full force.

Lexi crossed the University of Washington main quad and toward Johnson Hall, managing to avoid the coffee police, partially due to keeping her nose buried in the stack of quizzes. By the time she reached Johnson, she had the first five graded—mentally, at least. She was going to have to cruise through them as fast as possible. After school, she was booked solid ferrying her ten-year-old nanny charge, Olivia, from ballet to her mandatory volunteer time at the Children's Museum.

Once inside Johnson, she dodged a slow walker and avoided a chatting cluster of undergrads without looking up, but was forced to slow to a crawl as a male duo in front of her hogged the space with a multitude of bags and an ambling conversation.

"2001," said the first one, a redhead lugging a guitar bag. "Has to be."

Lexi attempted to go around to the left, but the guitar bag was accidentally kicked out wide and stymied her attempt to pass just as a class let out, and a stream of students crowded the hall going the other direction. Annoyed, Lexi stepped back behind them and went back to the quizzes.

"Horrible movie," said the other guy. He had black, spiky hair, a motorcycle jacket, and a helmet under one arm. "At least an hour too long and mono-focused on the male view of history."

"You've been taking too much Gender Studies," said annoying guitar bag.

"It's interesting, unlike *2001 Space Odyssey,*" said soon-to-be helmet-haired guy.

"What about the unparalleled scientific realism?"

Lexi pulled her head out of the quizzes. She liked sci-fi but spent a lot of time ignoring scientific inaccuracies. To date, she had skipped *2001 Space Odyssey* on the basis that it looked like the seventies had barfed up a space movie, but scientific realism sounded promising. She waited to see what the response would be.

"What about the snooze fest of a narrative arc?" asked the motorcyclist.

"What are you talking about? It literally ran the gamut of human history!"

"In the most boring way possible."

"Aren't you people supposed to love the existentialist narrative?" asked the redhead.

Lexi felt a smattering of discomfort. Even she knew that the phrase *you people* should not be used in conversation. Then she felt smug that she'd spotted that. She waited to see what motorcycle guy would think about being a *you person.*

"Nah," he said. "I want to sell out. Give me some aliens and laser beams any day."

Behind the two men, Lexi nodded in agreement. She also preferred aliens and laser beams over existentialist narrative. Whatever an existentialist narrative was.

"Seriously?" demanded the redhead. "Where is the drama in that? That moment when what's-his-face, the astronaut guy, takes that breath right before he goes out into space without air... it's small, but it's huge."

"His lungs would have shredded," said Lexi, and then realized that she'd spoken out loud.

Both guys turned toward her, and Lexi felt her own lungs pop. Proto-helmet-hair was, in fact, Carter Zheng.

Carter Zheng of the chest like a chiseled Greek sculpture. Carter Zheng of the mocha-colored eyes. Carter Zheng of the sexiest paper on Technology and Ethics she had ever read.

Carter Zheng that she might have stalked a tiny bit.

She realized they were waiting for her to defend her previous statement.

"The air in his lungs would have expanded in the vacuum of space," she said. She could feel a blush start to burn on her cheeks.

"Then... pop! Like a balloon?" asked Carter with a grin.

"Right," said Lexi. "Excuse me." She pushed between them and picked up speed, ducking into the doorway for the lab and quickly swiping her card to be let in. She shut the door behind her and leaned against it with a sigh of relief.

"Hey," said her lab partner, Bentley, coming around the corner. She let out a startled squeak and dropped all of Snyder's quizzes on the floor. "You OK?" asked Bentley as she knelt down to retrieve the papers.

She looked up at string-bean Bentley with his tangled mass of brown curls and beak of a nose. How was she supposed to respond to that question in a meaningful way?

"I just talked to Carter Zheng," she said.

"I don't know him. Is he in Materials Science?"

"He's the... He's really good-looking," finished Lexi lamely.

"Oh. Did you talk a lot?" Bentley sounded like he was reaching for the appropriate conversational rejoinder. Which he probably was. This was why she needed Shea.

"I pointed out a scientific inaccuracy in *2001 Space Odyssey*," said Lexi.

"Which one?" Bentley looked more interested.

"A guy takes a lungful of air before going into space?"

"Nice!" exclaimed Bentley. "What did... Carter?" Bentley stretched to remember the name, "think?"

"I don't know. I ran in here."

"Right," said Bentley, nodding. "Still, high-five for human interaction!"

They didn't actually high-five. Bentley was still working on his germ phobias. Bentley had a lot of phobias: stop signs, ants, and rubber bands, to name a few. He was also thirty and still hadn't finished his dissertation. Lexi guessed it was because of an undiagnosed completion phobia. At twenty-three, Lexi was one of the younger people in the program, a year away from completing her doctoral thesis, and considered a rising star. She knew people were confused by her friendship with Bentley, who was considered something of a vestigial nub, but Lexi liked him. He was never offended by unintentional brutal honesty, he never mansplained, he never hit on her, and he made good muffins. Unfortunately, he frequently made them in the lab toaster oven, a lab rules violation, but they were still tasty muffins.

"Hey," said Bentley, returning to his workstation. "I ran into Snyder this morning."

"With your car?" asked Lexi, still feeling annoyed about the quizzes.

"I ride the bus," said Bentley.

"Uh, right. I forgot," said Lexi, and then decided it wasn't worth explaining her comment to Bentley. "You saw Snyder?"

"I walked into him as he was coming out of here. He said he was looking for you."

"He probably wanted to give me all these quizzes," said Lexi, slapping the pile down on her desk.

"Don't know," said Bentley. "I didn't ask. You know, he kind of makes me hyperventilate."

"You shouldn't let him stress you out," said Lexi. "He's not even your advisor."

"He's sarcastic at me," said Bentley.

"You can't tell sarcasm half the time anyway," said Lexi, practically.

"I know," said Bentley. "That's why he stresses me out. I don't know how you can always tell. It's a great talent."

Shea said Lexi liked Bentley because he made her feel socially competent. Lexi denied it, but sometimes when Bentley congratulated her on baseline human behaviors, she had to admit that Shea was at least partially correct. Which made her wonder what else Shea was right about.

FIND OUT WHAT HAPPENS NEXT IN...
EYE CONTACT

ABOUT THE AUTHOR

Bethany Maines is the award-winning author of action adventure and fantasy tales that focus on women who know when to apply lipstick and when to apply a foot to someone's hind end. When she's not traveling to exotic lands, or kicking some serious butt with her black belt in karate, she can be found chasing after her daughter, or glued to the computer working on her next novel.

ALSO BY BETHANY MAINES

CARRIE MAE MYSTERIES
Bulletproof Mascara
Compact With The Devil
High-Caliber Concealer
Glossed Cause

SAN JUAN ISLANDS MYSTERIES
An Unseen Current
Against the Undertow
An Unfamiliar Sea
An Unfinished Storm

SHARK SANTOYO CRIME SERIES
Shark's Instinct
Shark's Bite
Shark's Hunt
Shark's Fin
Peregrine's Flight
Shark's Blood

THE DEVERAUX LEGACY
The Second Shot
A PNWA Literary ContesttAward Winner
The Cinderella Secret
The Hardest Hit
The Fallen Man

THE SUPERNATURALS
Wild Waters
A Little Red **(3 Colors #1)**
A Deeper Blue **(3 Colors #2)**
A Brighter Yellow **(3 Colors #3)**
Maverick
Hudson **(Rejects #1)**
Killian **(Rejects #2)**
Alekos **(Rejects #3)**

GALACTIC DREAMS
When Stars Take Flight **Vol. 1**
The Seventh Swan **Vol. 2**
A Book Excellence Award Winner
The Beast of Arsu **Vol. 3**